Lantern Lane

Small Town Librarian and Her

Big City Millionaire

by

Jean Cullen

Clocktower Books
Exciting Reading for Avid Readers on the Web Since 1996
P. O. Box 600973
Grantville Station 92160
San Diego, California 92160-0973

E-Mail Contact: Editor/Publisher
editorial@clocktowerbooks.com

Look for other exciting fiction and nonfiction at the website of Clocktower Books: www.clocktowerbooks.com/. For more information, see the back of this book.

Lantern Lane
A Romantic Novel by
Jean Cullen

Dedication

This novel is dedicated to librarians everywhere across the United States, from the largest city to the smallest town or village. The men and women of this honorable profession do as much as teachers do in assuring the continuity of civilization and culture. Where else, in neighborhoods across the land, will you find Shakespeare, Homer, Ovid, Virgil, Dante, Jefferson, Lincoln, Washington, and all the great minds of history under one roof together? The library is truly mankind's greatest invention, and a light to the world.

Special mention goes to the librarians of U.S. military posts around the world. When I was stationed far from home during the Cold War, the U.S. Army library system in West Germany offered me a wonderful refuge—I could close my eyes and pretend for a half hour or so that I was really thousands of miles away in my home town. This gift meant the world to me at the time. Troops stationed overseas will understand. Thank you, librarians.

Contents

SUMMER 15

FALL 47

WINTER 95

SPRING 219

Free Public Library
Emery Township

~ Stop By ~

Friendly Librarian On Duty
To Fulfill Your Every Need

Introduction

They lived happily ever after. But the real story is how Richard and Marian got there, by those jolts and twists of life, and that includes a bit of a suspenseful mystery story. Their fate was written in the stars, to mangle Shakespeare a tad. Here is their romantic, sentimental tale in all its glories and surprises, including some sad moments with tears shed, some wistful glances exchanged, some laughs here or there, and a quantum of misunderstandings soon enough corrected. In a world where so much goes wrong—Rick and Marian were meant to be. That's the wonder of it. But the story is what we want to really know, so here it is.

There was, not long ago, a tired traveler—a handsome, sharp-eyed man in his early 30s, wearing a finely-tailored business suit and driving a nice gray imported car. He made millions of dollars wheeling and dealing in New York City, and usually was just eager to return home to his 5,000 square foot exclusively gated house in West Hartford for a beer, a sandwich, and a dip in his large, elegantly interior-lit swimming pool surrounded by mosaics and marbles. He'd been through a nasty divorce, and was single again. For a while, he surrounded himself with hot and cold running beautiful women. Soon enough, he'd tired of their glamor, beauty, status, money, sensuality—their seeking, like hard, sterling currency. That mode of companionship had become merely what he called elevator music. You had everything except a deep sense of satisfaction. People in that mode seemed perfect and modular—they could plug or unplug from relationships with all the sincerity of snap-on toys. He longed for deeper waters. Lately, he tended to swim alone.

About once or twice every week for several years, he passed

through the small town of Emery (not the board or nail file, but actually in backwoods, small town New England, and founded in the 1600s). This one particular, fateful day, chance led him to stop for gasoline, pizza, and some air-conditioned library atmosphere.

The traveler's name was Richard Moyer.

He had to look on a sign to see what the name of the little township was, but after today, he would never forget that name. There, in Emery, in the heart of rural Connecticut, he was to meet a beautiful young woman named Marian. And yes, she was a librarian. Marian sometimes jokes that they should have been electricians, for the spark that passed between them the moment they first met.

Or lightning rods, he may reply—because that is how they are, always together. They think alike and finish each other's sentences.

Or lightning bods, she may joke. They get along really well, those two. Having a sparky sense of humor is the medicine for most maladies.

Getting there was a different matter all together, as we learn from their story. It was a tough time for each of them, with many tense moments.

Theirs was a relatively slow burn—though the initial spark was instantaneous—so this was a process that took some time to zap them both, amid all the jolting (sometimes awful) situations that life throws at us all.

Marian and Rick did not know each other until a fateful summer day. Each had experienced a unique personal tragedy, but they had the bounce it took to get up, dust themselves off, and look for a strong new start. This is their story.

Like a place of refuge, the Main Public Library of Emery Township lay on a quiet street near the main highway where cars and trucks whizzed through the town's outskirts in minutes. Few ever stopped for gas or lunch, much less to check out a book—or a librarian, as the rather silly sign outside seemed to imply.

Season after season, the long, low building maintained its stark, simple lines against the woodsy New England landscape. By day, its west-looking windows looked dark when the morning sun was in the east. Toward evening and closing time, its windows took on a lantern-like glow, first as the late sun slanted into the book-lined halls, then as the inner lamps glowed with a yellow, homey light amid all of history's stored learning.

This was, as our traveler was soon to think of it, a magical place. The library building was elegant in its plain, Old New England style. Set into its white exterior walls were church-like windows: rectangles of sea green and mellow amber glass with rounded tops. The sidewalk by the quiet street was lined with small plots of grass and set with elm and oak trees. The sidewalk surface was still lined with old-fashioned gray pavers. Every forty feet was a slender metal, ornamental pole with an ornate, Victorian-looking iron lantern on top. The lanterns, like little wrought iron cages, trapped a wondrous soft-yellowish electric light that cast its luster across the surrounding surfaces of sidewalk stones, white walls, and window glass. A modest portal, set between two dark wooden pillars and topped with a Pantheon-like decorative lintel, waited between twin coach lanterns for the interested reader to push the doors open and enter this book world. The legend above the door, in a modest Times New Roman lettering, read: 'Emery Public Library' with the words 'Welcome Everyone.' A similar script, in wrought iron, graced a black metal fence that enclosed the parking lot nearby.

Yes, here, in the small New England town of Emery as in myriad similar small places across the land, Plato and Socrates rubbed shoulders with Shakespeare and Jefferson, Homer and Virgil came out to chat with Dante and Emily Dickinson, and F. Scott Fitzgerald raised a glowing toast to Mrs. Mouse and Mrs. Rabbit in their Beatrix Potter garden hole houses.

With utmost fidelity, the librarians worked at their tasks, usually bent over in dutiful concentration. As Chief Librarian Linda Damien liked to say, "We are members of the world's oldest profession since the invention of writing, unless you count scribes." The librarians worked in their quiet, sacred realm under Mrs. Damien's guidance. Here was a woman pushing a cart loaded with books. There was an elderly man cautioning a table of grammar school children to keep the whispering down.

And over there was a startlingly attractive young, dark-haired woman writing something at the Help Desk, wearing a modest blue dress over which flowed a twirling mass of rich, dark, glossy hair surrounding a pale, pretty face. Her name was Marian and she really was a Librarian, just like in song and in legend, except here she was, a young woman with a life—full of joy and tragedy, and right now in limbo. The quietly adorable but remote Marian Charles had made a journey in her young life (28) from being the girl next door to being a happily married young wife to being a war widow. That, and more. Like a sleeping beauty, she was going through the motions every day, living life in a kind of suspended animation. Every day, she still had at least one teary moment, quietly and alone while in her usual positions—standing at the Check Desk or the Help Desk, or sitting on a foot stool with a stack of return books on her lap to be filed away. No stranger could guess why she wore a black ribbon, some days on her wrist, and other days like a pretty, drooping bow over her heart. Marian was not even remotely thinking there could be a charming prince to wake her from the slow amber drip of the hours and days in her shattered life.

Marian had studied English and Library Science in college, and was the Emery Township Free Public Library's chief story teller. She was the number one entertainer for miles around if you happened to be in Kindergarten or First Grade. Everyone looked forward to story hour with Mrs. Charles—or, as she knew she must eventually think of herself again, under her maiden name as Miss McLaughlin. Beautiful, sad-eyed Marian McLaughlin was from a small town in Oklahoma, but after marrying a handsome, brave young New Englander named Thomas Charles, a soldier stationed at nearby Fort Sill at that time, had followed him gladly, transplanted to his even smaller, far older town in the tiny state of Connecticut.

Like Sleeping Beauty, Mrs. Charles or Miss McLaughlin lived in a kind of library slumber amid all the great names of history. She had wanted to give herself to her husband and their children, but all that had been taken from her. What she still had was the degree in Library Science and the desire to give some little thing more to the world. She had thought about teaching, but had felt she was not enough of a control freak to closely manage several dozen children all day long. She had thought about nursing, but did not relish all those fluids in pans, syringes, and test tubes, not to mention dirty sheets and sad outcomes. So her heart (or, as they say in the South, *mah hort*) had led her to the marvels of the library universe, and she had never looked back.

In the stories she told to children (she could handle an hour of story time), she and the children together dreamed about an inquisitive, handsome, courageous prince. He would come into the tower, did not take no for an answer, was not scared of evil fairie godmothers, and would find his sleeping beauty in the tower. If he could wake her, she would be all his. She would give her heart and soul to him, her smile and the dazzle in her eyes, and all her beauty, and make him a very happy man indeed. In the story, of course, it took a hundred years for such a man to bumble along.

Marian was about to find out that her man, should she decide to wake up, drove a Jaguar and wore sharply tailored Fifth Avenue suits. He had been alone for some time, and though he was a busy millionaire, he was kind of looking for just such a princess. It would not be giving away too much, and spoiling the story, if we said his name is Richard.

Richard Moyer, 32, had the key to the tower, only he didn't know it yet. But give it a little time, and a few coincidences, and one huge, major act of fate that nobody would ever be able to explain. Okay, a hint: the moment they first met, it was as if the sun got brighter—those caramel-green eyes could get no wilder, like an animal being hunted; the forest got deeper, the primordial tale was very powerful--as their eyes met and their future was sealed forever. But there were still all those steps to be taken up the winding tower with its unpredictable twists and turns. One or two real ogres lived in there, who were miserable and mean, and did not want a charming prince and a beautiful princess to be happy together.

Folks who are curious about how this all happened—so many things went wrong that it was not at all certain they would actually live happily after—such curious people (like you, dear reader) would have to continue reading here, which means hanging around Emery Township and lingering in its wonderful, dusky library; or learning about the dark, awful thing that nearly happened by the lake, and so much more.

Aside from the break room, the cloak room, the offices, and of course the Stacks where all sorts of shadowy books slumber awaiting their call to shelf life, the two most important public spots are the Check Desk and the Help Desk. At the Check Desk, you could check books in or out. At the moment, all the staff were women, although men also worked here—just not at the moment. At the Help Desk was a veritable cockpit of resources. Above the Help Desk was a sign that read: Reference and Help—Cheerful Librarian Available to Answer All Your Questions & Fulfill All Your Needs.

Or something like that. Despite the comments, nobody ever had time to take the sign down and replace it with something a little less intriguing, so it stayed there with a nice fringe of old library dust across the top. Once a month, the custodian and guard, Mr. Perez, might run a rag over the rim so it would not drizzle dust on the library folks standing under it. At Emery, the librarians and staff took turns serving at the Help Desk, among them Marian Charles, at 28 the youngest of the permanent employees.

The library was and is an island, a refuge, ever present. In winter, when the trees around its flat roofs were barren, you could see the ancient brick grammar school looming behind it. Sometimes it lay blanketed in a frosty layer of ice and snow.

In spring, its lawns were so green, and its trees so shocked full of newly born leaves, that it was hard to imagine how that same dutiful woman with dark hair could remain indoors and continue scribbling in such concentration—but the records must be kept, the accounts must be tallied, and the rolls must be called. Children must be entertained, and classic fairie tales must be told again and again as they had been for ages.

In summer, when humidity and heat rolled over the parched landscape in a haze, the interior was a shadowy, air conditioned warren smelling of paper, floor wax, and crayons.

In fall—Rick Moyer's favorite time of year—the library was a passing lantern in the evenings when he made his long journey home from the concrete canyons and business arenas of the Big City. He never had any reason to stop there, but he wondered vaguely—if just for a passing moment, what it was like inside; and he knew, in his heart—because everyone remembers such a library from their childhood. It is a lantern passed by road traffic, a glowing refuge on rainy afternoons, a steady beacon or light house as darkness falls and the street lights wink on, as the universe passes by and stars wheel overhead.

Part One

Summer

One humid, sticky August afternoon, our traveler—Rick Moyer, 32—was coming home early from a successful business trip to Manhattan. He needed gas for his car, and maybe a bite to eat, and it just happened that his stomach growled loudly as he neared Emery. He also spotted a big blue sign among the full tree crowns:

Food Gas Lodging 1 Mile.

He'd been through here more times than he could count, if he even cared to do so, but today was his first time in Emery.

"Yeah," Rick said out loud to the three empty seats around him in the air conditioned car, "It was a successful day. I think I might just treat myself to a little lunch."

He told the car, which listened attentively and did not interrupt: "If you have to have guzzle your gallon of gas, I might as well have a soda or some coffee for myself. And a sandwich, or a slice of pizza."

Rick was a tall, handsome man with tousled light brown hair, twinkling blue party eyes, and a winning athlete's self-assured facial expression. If he had a cocky grin, it was primarily about putting others at ease. Despite a rough divorce in recent years, and related difficulties, he was quite relaxed with himself and his car, as he was with most people who swirled through his life.

He spotted the *Food Gas Lodging* sign—now just 100 feet and a quick, spur of the moment stop ahead—through a mass of glowing green leaves. Another sign read: *Welcome to Emery Township, Connecticut—Pop. 5,000. Stop By.*

The thruway was an ancient concrete turnpike built a century ago with many quaint bridges over it. That had been during the early days when automobiles became popular enough to demand smoothly paved roads. Each town along the route had won its own contract with the state to build a local bridge, and the towns had competed with each other for originality of design. Each bridge was a different and unique masterpiece of Art Deco design.

Here, the thruway continued without interruption as a slightly sunken road. The exit took Rick along an upper, local frontage road that ran on either side of the thruway. He came to the gas station, pulled in on a concrete apron under some advertising signs swinging in a light wind, and turned off the engine.

No matter about the shave. He was always self-conscious about that, but hey, he was done with his day's work in the City, and he could kick out the jams. In another few hours, in fact, he'd be home in his jammies, speaking of jams, holding a beer, and catching the latest UConn basketball game.

Before stepping from the car—from force of habit—he looked in the rear-view mirror and ran a fine-fingered but strong hand over his jaw. He sighed. One of the crabbies of his life (not a curse, so much; just a pain in the wazoo) was that he was one of those two-shaves a day guys. He'd made three meetings in Manhattan today, nailed down a million dollar deal, missed lunch, and forgot to run a shaver over his tanned features. Now he had a growing beard shadow, growing like dusk around his easy-mannered mouth, and the shaver was back home where he'd forgotten it by the entrance to the garage. He'd also forgotten to fill the tank before leaving home base this morning.

And it was a hot, humid day to boot. One good thing about making endless meetings in skyscrapers was that you forgot Manhattan was hot enough to melt gum on sidewalks. He was always happy to cross over the Connecticut state line into peaceful, green New England. Usually, however, he simply drove on through to home base in Hartford. Today was an exception, since the car needed servicing.

When Rick stepped from the car, that wave of New England heat struck him like a baseball bat. A thermometer in the service station window read 102F, and the humidity had to be close to 100%.

"Afternoon,' said a brash but friendly middle-aged man in technician's overalls. He had graying, slicked back hair, along with a Roman nose and blunt features. "Need your oil checked?"

Rick's first impulse was to look for a catch—like, what is it going to cost me?

"I'm the owner," the man said. "Name's Tony. I'd shake your hand, but I've got grease all over me and that's a mighty fine suit you are wearing." Tony wiped his hands with a rag as he spoke, like a man who never wasted a moment or a motion.

"I'd appreciate that," Rick said. Tony acted like the Caesar of his little domain here on the macadam road above the thruway.

Location, location, location, Rick thought. Tony gave comforting evidence of a well-off middle class of business owners in the area.

"Hot one." Rick loosened his merlot tie. Already, his white linen shirt was soaked with sweat. He started taking off his jacket.

Tony popped the hood. "Brutal day." His olive-skinned Italian features glistened with sweat. "Can't wait to get home and pop a cold one."

"Yep, I hear ya." Rick carefully laid his expensive jacket across the back seat. He went through the motions of paying and pumping.

"You're a little low here," Tony said, showing him the exposed oil dip stick. "You'll make it home, no problem; but I wonder if you have an oil leak. Sometimes a pebble kicks up, nicks the oil pan, and there you go—a slow leak. You don't notice it, and sometime soon your engine coughs its last feeble breath."

"Usually at the worst moment," Rick said, "like in a snow storm, or a hurricane or whatever."

"Yep. I can check that really quick for you."

Rick sighed. "Cars."

"Yeah," Tony said businesslike irony, "can't live with them, and can't live without them. Hey, I'll put her up on the lift and have you checked out in no time; tire pressure, coolant, the works. You might want to go get yourself a cold soda or something." He pointed to a lounge in his station, with two rows of worn black plastic seats and several vending machines in it. "It's air conditioned in there."

"Thanks," Rick said. "I might do that. Actually, I'd rather stretch my legs a bit."

"Suit yourself."

"Been cooped up in a skyscraper all day."

"Manhattan, huh?"

"Yeah." He'd been reviewing contracts, as usual, signing documents approved by accountants and lawyers. His father's firm specialized in salvaging deleveraged firms that had gone over the edge and crashed in negative amortization valleys. Moyer brokered the assets, paid off the departing stock holders, and (usually, ideally) seamlessly sold a newly reconstituted package to new owners, often in mergers, pocketing ten or twenty percent on a good day. He did not tell Tony any of this; it would take too much jaw motion when he really just wanted to plant his lips on an icy cola or a beer and sit back by the pool at home, maybe with a takeout pastrami sandwich or small pizza for one, picked up along the way into West Hartford.

"You from Connecticut?" Tony made conversation. A little of it was curiosity, as Rick could read in the older man's eyes.

"Yes. Hartford."

"The big city." Tony meant it ironically, and they both laughed. Tony amended: "Don't feel bad. Here we are--Emery, population 5,000 during rush hour, half that by supper time."

"Looks like a nice little town."

A young man drove Rick's car into the garage, with one dirty boot and greasy overall leg hanging out the partially open door. That must be Johnny—maybe a nephew, a son, or a local trade school apprentice.

"Most of us that live here wouldn't trade life here for anything else," Tony said. He looked a bit distastefully down on the noisy swarm of headlights and taillights in the sunken thruway carrying traffic between major cities.

Rick's eyes tracked Tony's gaze, and gave a lingering look around. The constant zooming of cars and trucks on the ancient, four-lane turnpike was distracting. Other than that, you could hear birds and crickets chirping in lush undergrowth that fell down reddish stone outcroppings into the valley.

It felt good to have his feet on firm ground. A breeze blew up from down on his left, below the upper thruway that housed Tony's station and other roadside businesses.

"That's a nice breeze here," Rick said.

"You noticed," Tony said appreciatively. "The air is always kind of fresh in our little town. Comes in from that valley down there." He pointed north, over the heavy, rusty cable guard rail that was tangled with tall grass, flowers, and weed. He pointed over miles of tree crowns, toward nestled rooftops far out, surrounding a shimmering lake. "That's Emery. The town, as opposed to the thruway business district up here."

Nearby was an overpass on top of the thruway. Red taillights headed east and northward into New England in the two right lanes, and some cars already had their headlights on coming west toward New York City. The overpass carried a two-lane local street with traffic lights at either end of the bridge, where the frontage roads crossed the bridge road. The bridge road became a quaint little country lane on the other side of the freeway by a library, school, and roadside businesses. On this side, the bridge road crossed the frontage road at a traffic signal not far from Tony's garage; the bridge road became a two-lane blacktop road heading downward, between weedy embankments, into Emery Township proper.

"Beats the City by a mile. I was just in Manhattan two hours ago," Rick said, as he bounced on the balls of his feet in his tasseled loafers. He had his hands in his pockets. "It was stifling hot there."

"I'll bet," Tony said. "Always nice to get back to the green stuff here in New England." He slowly lowered the hood shut with a wincing expression as if he felt a sudden pain.

"Something wrong?" Rick asked.

"Naw. Real gas station owners never slam hoods or trunks shut, unlike most people. We are acutely aware we might dislodge something, jiggle something loose, and next thing you know it's a repair job or a law suit or who knows what."

"You see it all, I bet," Rick said with a grin. Unspoken between them was the fact that each had a stake in a business. Tony owned his own, probably not as lucrative as Moyer LX Holdings Inc., but Rick was still somewhere between an employee and a partner at the whim of his father. Aside from the divorce just two years ago, the constant pressure and the traveling to New York, Boston, Chicago, and L.A. among other destinations was the other big bane in his life. That, and an empty apartment that had been meant for sharing with Cindy, with whom he could have had at least one child by now if she had not turned out to have a different plan in life, involving lawyers, alimony, and the freedom to cavort. Cindy had not gone through a war, as Rick had, and there had been too much distance between them on account of the changes he'd gone through in the Middle East, including the deaths of two comrades; while she simply remained a spoiled party girl—high maintenance, as guys said among each other about women like Cindy.

Rick sighed. At times he thought of renting a room or two in his large town home to a responsible, younger business man or woman, or maybe a college professor—someone he could talk to sometimes, even if it meant bickering over laundry, refrigerators, and parking spaces.

"Been a long day?" Tony said, regarding Rick's shifting moods with evident empathy. The way that drama worked, unspoken, and shifting like clouds on a windy day, was that Tony was obviously older and settled in life, while Rick sort of carried this attitude on his sleeve, that he might be doing well in business, but he was truthfully starting life over. But of course he would not tell that to a stranger; yet this small town businessman seemed shrewd enough to read Rick the same way Rick could read a cagey board of directors official, or a partisan lawyer in a corporate lawsuit, or an acquiring or divesting investor with some kind of axe to grind.

"All the days are long," Rick said.

"Yeah." Tony turned his attention back to the open motor, signaling he did not want to pry any further. Must be the beard shadow, Rick thought. His mother had always told him he should shave so he wouldn't look like a pondering professor or a troubled artist. Mom was a fond, doting mother, who took a backseat to her captain of industry husband, Rick's stern but guardedly affectionate father.

The tank was full. Rick hung up the hose and screwed on the gas cap. "You might as well give it the works. The car is overdue for a checkup anyway."

"All right," Tony said. "I'll have Johnny check the water, the tires, and the whole shebang. It can never hurt, especially when you have to drive in this kind of heat. Stresses a car right out."

"The last thing I would want is a stressed out car," Rick said. "Is there a restaurant nearby?"

"You mean like food? Something more than a vending machine?"

"I know you pride yourself on your cellophane wrapped cookies and wafers, but yes, lunch, like maybe a nice Italian sub or something."

Tony nodded. As he stood wiping his hands, and then his face, with a blue rag, he pointed with his chin. "Other side of the turnpike, across the street, those shops there?"

Rick followed the chin motion, and saw a row of store windows across the busy thruway with its constant stream of zipping and zooming cars and trucks. On the quieter frontage road there, he read signs: dry cleaning, a bar, a barber, a pizzeria, and a sewing machine repair place. Beyond that was a large white stucco building with a parking lot—the Emery Free Public Library. Beyond that were a very old brick grammar school with gargoyles in the second story eaves. The main entrances to the adjoining library and school lay on the quiet little side street that descended into rich tree crowns from the bridge overpass.

Rick walked two hundred feet to the big intersection with overhead traffic light. He crossed the north frontage road, walked a few hundred feet over the hundred-year-old overpass bridge, and crossed the south frontage road at the opposite traffic light. Rick found himself walking at a leisurely but determined pace. A few huffing and chuffing vehicles passed on the local roads above the teeming freeway. It felt good, despite the heat, to be putting his legs through walking motions. He patted his left rear pocket to reassure himself of the sturdy wallet that always rode on his gluteus. He was a tall, muscular man with pinched rear end. A long-ago female admirer had once told him that he had a gluteus minimus rather than a maximus. He had a complete set of exercise equipment at home, which could see more use if he had time; but he actually considered joining a private gym or even the YMCA just to get out and meet more people outside of his constant work. As he walked along the curb, the sidewalk had a sizzling summer quality, almost greasy from much use—imagine all the dropped ice cream cones, spilled sodas, dogs doing what dogs do, and so on. The pizzeria inside smelled of baked crust, steamy tomato sauce with basil and other spices, and meatballs or sausage.

The air conditioning in the pizzeria was broken. The doors stood open to let in that little valley breeze. The pizza maker and his family were big, heavy persons who sat waiting for business. They sat with their tongues protruding and their eyes bugging, as if the effort of making yet one more pie would be their last. They looked upon Rick with suffering. Then the mother rose on thick legs and sighed. "Would you like a couple of slices and a soda, mister?"

"Smells divine in here," Rick said. It did, indeed—the crust, the cheese, the pepperoni, the sauce, were all to die for. "How about your lunch special?"

The papa rose, like a bear lumbering from his cave. "I'll have to make a fresh pie," he said in a voice as thick as his fingers and his bulging arms. "I'll have a nice fresh new pie just for you, mister," he said as if he had never had a more wonderful customer than Rick. Meanwhile, a dozen wise ass kids on bicycles whizzed past, and a few stopped in the store to bang their quarters on the hot, steamy counter glass as they stared rudely around waiting for service, and cast yearning eyes upon the empty pizza trays inside.

"We're making a couple of fresh pies," mama said loudly, as if she were ready to swat them.

The boys made acquiescent, if guilty, faces and indicated by squirming and other body language that they would wait.

Rick found the air stifling, the store too small, and the smell of pastas intoxicating. He ordered a medium cola to tide him over while he waited to eat. The drink was served promptly by a demure high school girl, probably a nephew or daughter of the family. The waxy cup was full of ice cubes and dark liquid full of happily jumping bubbles. It came with a plastic lid and a straw to travel. Rick took a long, shuddering, delighted drink that slaked the worst of his thirst. "I'll take a walk to the library for a few minutes," he told mama.

A wide, dark-haired woman, she said as she worked behind the counter: "It's air conditioned in there. You'll love it. You'll have icicles hanging from your nose."

He touched himself on the nose. "Thanks, just what I need."

"We'll have your lunch ready in fifteen minutes," papa said as he spun a ball of dough in the air. It turned into a whirling disk in a matter of seconds.

The walk to the library, which took about two minutes, was about to change Rick's life—although he did not know it yet by a long shot.

Leaving the pizzeria, he sauntered along the cracked, uneven sidewalk with its stray grass, occasional discarded candy wrapper, and ancient stain of oil or whatever. It was a pleasant town here, Rick thought, if you had time to slow down and enjoy things. It was that kind of place where you could stop and watch the trees grow, as the saying went. As solitary as his life was, in a huge, empty gated community house meant for a family with kids--the more the merrier--he was afraid a place like this would drive him crazy. He relished the constant distraction of travel, of business, of meeting strangers, and the challenge of finding his way around in strange cities. He hoped in the coming years to expand the family business into Canada, particularly Montreal and Quebec City, and then into the European Union—especially the Greater London area, and a few odd capitals here and there like Brussels, Luxembourg, and maybe Prague. He would leave Rome, Paris, and Berlin among his vacation and fun spots. In recent years, he'd tended to date female airline attendants (formerly known as stewardesses)--not immersed in business, but usually anchored someplace in some small town hideaway to get away from their life-bending travel schedules. He'd made friends, but not the kind you took on vacation with you, or traveled far to spend a few days with. That delight was reserved for his few remaining close college friends, all guys who were by now married and stuck in the fast lane between family and careers.

The Emery Township Free Public Library was a plain building of weathered stucco that had once been white but now had a kind of amber, ice tea patina. Its lines were simple and severe, in a style that had seemed modern half a century ago or more. Now it looked more like a shipwreck that had weathered many seasons of heat and rain, of storms and snows. At the moment, its plate glass windows had a stunned, baked look. On the inside, the glass had all sorts of children's projects taped to it in decorative arcs. The current theme was the approach of Labor Day at the end of August.

Outside on the lawn was a wooden sign, comparable to that on the church lawn across High Street. The library's sign read: Welcome to the Emery Township Free Public Library. Stop In Anytime You Feel Like It. Our Friendly Librarians Will Care For All Your Information and Reading Needs.

How funny, Rick thought. Is that the town motto? *Stop By.*

Entering the main library building by its side door on the frontage road, Rick stepped into an atmosphere of books and ink. His body shivered thanks as a chill swirled around him. The dry, dehumidified air had a faintly rancid, vinegar scent. He closed his eyes for a second, and let all sorts of taupe and mauve balls of light rush toward him inside his brain. Inside the building, as in any of its tens of thousands of sister institutions large and small across vast America, was a hushed, dignified peace. These heavy walls and massive wooden doors shut out all the stray highway noise and other mortal distractions from the secular world. Rick was a lover of books, libraries, and bookstores. This was a sacred place to him, full of a kind of ephemeral green forest energy, a light filled with whispers and charm. Among its fragrances was a faint blossom of mixed perfumes, like an anthology of fading flowers.

The instant he opened his eyes, he saw her: a singularly attractive young woman, among the several older, or married looking women working at various library tasks. The older ones looked matronly, fussy, pleasant but reserved (like books already spoken for). She was just coming down the front hall, pushing a light cart from one office to another. She hardly stopped as their eyes found and arrested each other; she slowed way down, as if he were stopping her just by the force of his surprised and helpless look.

As he spotted this striking young woman, who made his breath catch for a second, and his heart skip a beat, she saw him also. An atomically charged look full of mystery and desire crossed between them for a fraction of a second, like lightning and thunder in a summer storm. She carried herself with a kind of eternal, patient dignity and grace, but her eyes sent a different message. Like the faint, enigmatic smile that played knowingly around her lips, her eyes radiated something positively wild to Rick. It was actually almost scary. He felt as if he had just glimpsed a mythical forest grove filled with nymphs and satyrs, or an outdoor picnic of knights and damsels in some legendary feudal manor far from everyday life. There would come a day when she would surprise him, and tell him what had been going on with her that very day. Scary was the word. And breathtakingly beautiful.

Rick felt a strange something haunted, bleak, painful—something that stabbed into his soul like a knife. It was a look of loss and grieving, which met the barely healing scars of his own losses and wounds deep in the heart.

He noticed a black ribbon on her dress. Instantly, he loved the little imperfections that made her heart-stoppingly real: a little silk-coated button half undone to one side of her modest blouse—that one button in a row of five over her left breast, as if she had innocently been in a hurry and forgotten to finish push it through its eyelet, but left it carelessly sticking sideways, half in and out. He saw a streak of dark, sky-blue ink along one tea-colored hand from some little mishap with a pen, probably while busy with children and a dozen other things all at once. He noticed a cute, almost school girlish unevenness about her skirt, as if she had risen too quickly from kneeling to file a book in its shelf, and had not yet found time to smooth her clothes down with a quick, busy brush of both palms. She was not perfect, but that in itself was her supreme perfection, just as she was, human and real. The long, delicate fingers of her capable hands rested on the handle to push the cart, which just now slowed to a crawl like time and the universe itself. Everything about her was so nice—so very nice—but nicest, and most deeply piercing, was how she looked straight at him and into him. Her eyes widened—expressionlessly, he thought—was she annoyed? shocked? pained? Something emotional passed through her gaze, and her mouth opened slightly. She had such a captivating face. He might have described it as attractive or even beautiful, but her face perfectly matched his tastes, in a way he had never imagined in any woman. Another man might pass by without noticing more than her pleasant, well proportioned features. A woman might have thought of her as handsome, or pretty, or felt jealous, or whatever.

In that wonderful but incredibly awkward moment, they stopped and looked at each other in the library's front hallway. He felt like a schoolboy, and awkwardly stammered: "This is a really nice library." He almost said *a little* town or a *little* library, but he didn't want to offend her. More pragmatically, he realized, he might have said it was a surprisingly large library for such a small town scattered and hidden among millions of New England forest trees, but he imagined they were a township and serviced even smaller hamlets and villages in the area.

She seemed flustered as well, which lent her soft voice a faint, delicate, just barely perceptible lisp as she echoed the advertising billboard on the library's front lawn: "Stop by anytime you like."

With that, she pushed her cart away and, with just a hint of a smile, turned her back to him. Something in how she held her shoulders and moved her hips told him she was acutely aware that his eyes and gaping expression followed her as her figure down the hall.

He stared for a few long seconds after her as she walked away, pushing a little cart with a few books, papers, pens, and inking stamps on it.

He would relive that moment many times, and it would bring him back, time and again, to stop for a breath of air and peace in the little township of Emery along the busy highways of his constantly working hours.

This is a really nice library.

Stop by anytime you like.

These were the only words they would speak to each other for a long time to come. Neither would ever forget the moment, as it turned out. But like roads to small towns anywhere—especially for a busy and successful man racing between major cities—the one that wanted to bring them together took its winding time and way.

For just that instant, with its massive voltage that passed, even as she walked away, they seemed to communicate from the one's heart to the other's heart. He knew she meant the library (*Stop by*) —and it was maybe just the library's advertising slogan—but it almost seemed as if she meant for him to stop by and see her again; that she might be available.

She was slender, modestly dressed, and quiet. Her hair was combed in whatever manner it wanted to fall, in thick black waves, from under which peered the most vivid, caramel-greenish eyes Rick had ever seen. As his eyes focused, so did hers, and he felt an electric jolt go through his entire being. She was moderately tall, not near Rick's six feet; maybe five-seven. She looked crisp but comfortable in a summery blouse above a modest, calf-length white cotton skirt. The blouse was cream-colored, with tasteful images of ripe fruit and green leaves attached to crisp browning twigs. It was closed in the center, but had a vertical row of small, cream-textured buttons over the left breast, almost a Chinese touch. Her long, slender tanned arms were bare except for one delicate black bow tied from a single, tattered ribbon; in addition to a fun white wristwatch with black face and jazzy pointers on her other wrist. She had tanned skin and sharply pretty features. He instantly thought: college girl, classy, but not sorority, not spoiled, not high maintenance—just untouchable but wanting to be released from the prison of her reserve. It never occurred to him at that moment that she might be married, or something yet more complicated and dark. She seemed imprisoned on the other side of a barrier neither could cross, and he had not idea what that might be. All these thoughts crossed his mind in a blur, in seconds. They stopped, stared at each other in a shock of recognition—soul mates? And then each quickly turned away, as if blinded by the sun, stung by the fire, of what just happened in that blinding instant. For a long, paralyzed, infinitely pleasant moment, Rick seemed to continue floating in a kind of timeless nectar. He did not just see her. He inhaled her. As she walked away, he breathed her essence and felt spring flowers in the heart of summer.

Maybe, Rick thought later on his way home, it was just the moment. Sure, that had to be it. It was the heat, and his appetite (for pizza, not for librarians), or a combination of a whole lot of things. Of all the women in the world, why did this one, at a random encounter lasting only seconds, shoot through him like a bolt of lightning?

For a moment, it seemed as if she meant to say something. But what could she say? They did not know each other. He was not whispering or chewing gum or running around, and therefore not in need of chiding or shooshing. He was a grown man, for heaven's sake. Here he was, feeling like a boy who was in trouble. Those days were long behind him, in other libraries and schools and movie theaters elsewhere in New England or around the world.

For a moment, the woman stared at him with her mouth opening. Just as quickly, she looked just as he felt. She touched her hair, her collar, and a little black ribbon on her left wrist, as if checking to see that everything was properly tidy and in place. Her eyes acquired a furtive, pained look as she quickly looked down at the cart, and a flush visibly rose to her cheeks.

The one odd, striking thing about her was a fine little black bow, worn amid fine golden peach down on one tea-colored forearm with a tattered, dangling ribbon hanging down toward the hand. It did not look as if it were meant to be sexy, or an ornament, as much as a statement or a symbol—but of what? Its black hue matched that faint air of grieving or gravity that surrounded her.

She was, Rick had long to consider the afterglow of that first impression, the most beautiful woman he had ever seen. As a man, he instantly noticed how fine and shapely was her figure in those attractive but modest clothes. He loved the rich black hair that seemed to hang over her long, pale neck in curls yet also rose up in a cloud of tight curls. Her features were regular, finely apportioned, and somehow a contradictory mix of proper and exotic. It was a mystery. That was it. She was filled with mystery, like a summer afternoon's forest grove. Seeing her was like looking through a stained glass window.

For an instant, a smile played about her rouged lips. She had a sensuous, full mouth to match the hidden intrigue in her gorgeous dark-blue eyes. The covert wildness of her look did not so much shoot outward to him—it lured him toward him. And yet she seemed so distant, so proper, so taken, so owned. Her dazzling look turned almost to sadness as she turned and walked away. He stared after her sharply shapely figure as she pushed her cart before her, losing nothing in grace, and gaining naught in pretense. She was real, and he had to remember to close his mouth. He wetted his lips and mouth with a hurried sip at the forgotten soda and straw in his hand.

In the next instant, an older woman who resembled a disapproving chicken with dyed melon-colored hair and a pink-sticked mouth interrupted his stunned reverie by saying: "Is there something I can help you with, sir?"

As his eyes followed her yet another moment, she glanced over her shoulder for an instant. Her almond gaze sought Rick's eyes yet one more moment, filled with longing and questioning. As Rick savored her departing figure, a fatherly looking patron in a maroon vest, with white hair and a red face, approached from a side aisle. The man held a book, and his body language suggested he was about to ask the Goddess a question. She in turn switched her attention to Mr. Book and opened a mouth of a color inside as pink as bubble gum. She had a shy, sweet sort of smile--probably permanently minty, Rick imagined, wishing he could breathe it in more closely with his eyes closed. It was a reserved, polite smile, crisp and chicle-white, and eager to please. In turning her head suddenly, and tearing her gaze away from Rick's, her cheek made a stunned motion as if a hand had struck her out of her reverie. Actually, Mr. Book was very demure and polite, and handed the book to the Goddess with both hands like an offering.

"Sir?" Mrs. Chicken said insistently to Rick, as he stood frozen in place. The chicken lady stood behind the Reference Desk doing something with a book and a telephone and, Rick almost suspected, a hammer with his name on it.

"I'm sorry," Rick said. "I am suffering from heat stroke. Seeing visions, you know, that sort of thing. But I will be fine in a second. Just let me breathe in the air conditioning another moment or two."

The chicken sniffed. "The heat will do that to a person." She was not entirely unfriendly amid her severe sort of chalky restraint. "You'll have to step out of the main thoroughfare then, and let people get by."

Rick looked around and saw nobody—at least nobody seemed blocked. Mothers flowed past with children in tow, children ran in silently tiptoeing packs, and everything seemed normal.

"I was just leaving," Rick said. He was still bathed in the aura of the Goddess, and did not really notice Mrs. Chicken much. He turned on rubbery legs toward the door. As he exited, he looked back and saw that the woman who had just turned his life upside down had her back to him—a slender, shapely back covered in peaches and green leaves—and was conversing with Mr. Book about some esoteric library business.

Rick had spent no more than five minutes in the library, but had cooled off while being turned on. Now the summer heat struck him like Mrs. Chicken's imaginary hammer, and he thought about his pizza. He did not expect to ever see the unknown and unknowable woman again. After all, he had just been in Manhattan, with millions of attractive women flowing around him, fragrant as rose water. So many of those were available for the moment—a drink, a date, coffee, a dance or a walk along the Central Park paths during their lunch break—that he thought little about them. He kept himself buried in work, trying to please Dad, hoping to be worthy of the Moyer inheritance after his early years of constantly doing things his own way. It had always been with a vague feeling that his parents were somehow disappointed—Mom still pretty in a manicured, aging way behind her glass of lush in the shade of their sprawling West Hartford home; Dad a whipcord, red-faced, gray-haired Saturnian god of finance behind his desk. Dad seemed captain of a ship only he was qualified to run, and had to watch every moment so mortals like Rick would not run it aground. Until the shipwreck with Cindy a few years ago—to carry forward the nautical theme, since Dad had been a Navy officer long ago—Rick had been brashly self-confident and reckless. A stint in the army, followed by a disastrous brief marriage with a New York City socialite, had smacked him up on the reefs of his own youthful myopia. He was a man in a life jacket, adrift amid debris, grateful to be alive, and treading water frantically while hoping to find yet a new, saving shore. He could only hope that shore would not have a row of cannibals waiting for him. It was all metaphor, and grimly fun. Rick had once dallied with the idea of being a Liberal Arts professor one day, but Moyer LX Holdings was the road life had chosen for him, no matter how he might have protested it in his youthful exuberances. These thoughts flashed through Rick's ragged thoughts with the speed and brevity of passing light in a black vacuum somewhere far from Earth; far from a humid, crawlingly stifling late summer day in Connecticut.

Across the thruway, Tony stood looking up under the car, which was still on the lift. Rick did not worry about the money of a possible service need. He had plenty of money. He hoped his time would not be taken, or he'd have to rent a car to get home rather than be stuck here all evening. But as it turned out, the pizza and salad were delicious, the soda was quenching, and Tony had the car waiting for him with only a small tab due for two cans of premium motor oil. It was a station, and a town, and a pizzeria worth stopping by in again some day.

Before he crossed the frontage road north over the overpass bridge, Rick stopped as he waited for the little white man to appear on the crossing sign. As he did so, he looked back over his shoulder. Was that a pale, narrow, gorgeous face in the window amid the arch of green children's cards? Was that a shock of black hair, and a glow of greenish eyes from some primeval forest? Or was he imagining things? The window looked blank, the little white man went *tweet-tweet*, and Rick headed back to Tony's garage.

2

Just two or three days later, Marian Charles experienced the shock—it took her breath away—of again seeing that handsome, confident-looking man in the suit. She sat on a stool, kind of awkwardly, placing books from a stack on her lap onto their slots in the shelves before her. Then she saw him. Oh god.

She'd never expected to see him after that exchange of cascading, emotional stares, and had nearly forgotten him amid all that weighed her mind and soul down—but here he was again. Though he pretended to be casual and perhaps looking for a book, his eyes roamed about, seeking her, and lighted up when he spotted her in the opposite end of the library's main hall, sitting on a foot stool. What was it about him? The world was full of handsome, charming men, and he was certainly in their forefront. His face had such character, and there was depth to his eyes. His look was piercing, and full of understanding, and yet his eyes twinkled with mischief. His lips seemed forever poised for saying something bitingly, cleverly funny. She needed a good laugh for sure. She needed to roll on the floor and roar with laughter while holding her ribs. Fat chance that would ever happen. And there was Lawrence of Arabia, or Eighth Avenue, or whatever his handle was.

Marian was not ready for this. She was still a taken woman, or so part of her mind weakly protested, while her heart cried out for escape and freedom. She had just filed away some silly novel, and dallied over it for a bemused moment, about a young desert princess imprisoned by a cruel monarch long ago and far away. The maiden was rescued by a dashing, handsome young adventurer, disguised in a flowing white garment that blew in the wind, hiding most of his body and face except for his beautiful blue eyes, as he rode across the desert sands on a beautiful stallion to steal her. She jumped from a tower, landed in the saddle with him, and off they rode together before anyone in the towers could raise an alarm.

Seeing the stranger's glance raking hungrily across her as she sat on her stool, Marian felt an involuntary smile cross her face, which she instantly suppressed. She looked down and pretended to be busy, though this Apollo had stolen her attention for sure. How long had he been staring? At this very same moment, surprised at how rattled she felt, she had an accident, a fumble, and all the books on her lap went flying in different directions.

She'd been sitting on the nearest handy footstool, filing Young Adult books from D to F, when she became conscious of a change in atmosphere around her. That was this handsome, mysterious man with whom she had exchanged just a few awkward words in the hallway days or weeks ago—she couldn't remember—and here he was again. Could a newcomer have moved to Emery Township? Or was he just passing through like most people, who barely stopped for gas or coffee before zooming on to more exciting places in the great big world beyond Emery Township?

The realization that she was being stared at dawned on her over a period of some seconds, because she was so focused on all the things going on in her mind, between work and home and her troubles. The library wasn't making her rich by any means, but it was a steady job with books, which she loved, and with children, which she enjoyed equally well. At 28, she had expected to have at least one child by now. It had been her life's dream, but it—well, it had not worked out the way it was supposed to. Here she was, a young war widow, still haunted by a complete lost life, unable to shake the easy smile and deliciously dominating eyes of her lost Tommy. This stranger would be about Thomas Charles' age. *Stop it, Marian,* she told herself. She touched the delicate, black silk bow on her arm. Her friends all told her it was time to move on, and her mind agreed, while her heart was still like a honey bee trapped on a dusty window sill, bumbling and buzzing from corner to corner, longing for the sunshine outside, and waiting for someone to lift the window.

Working at the library helped her keep busy and forget. Her mother had been a librarian, as had her maternal grandmother, so it was a time-honored profession in her family. Sometimes, when her life crept up on her as she worked, she felt her lip quiver. *Why me?* her inner voice would ask. Marian wanted to be strong, and she kept that inner voice from whining or self-pity. Her troubles were difficult, but fixable. Her mother had consoled her over long-distance by phone: "Time will heal, baby. Time always heals."

"I know, mama," she could picture herself saying, as if she were home again, maybe at the kitchen window holding a cup of hot tea and looking wistfully out at the green Shawnee trees and the garden flowers in colorful bloom. "Just why does it have to be so hard?" She'd have to put the tea down while she held the phone to her other ear, and steadied herself against the kitchen counter. But she could not go home again, not ever; it would be like losing the beautiful dreams that had taken her away into the wide world.

As she pictured herself, in those conversations that almost seemed as if they'd happened to someone else, she'd sneak her wrist up to her eyes. She'd prop a pile of D to F titles under her other elbow, and quickly wipe a tear away when she thought nobody was looking. She did not want the children to think that Mrs. Charles was a cry baby. And she certainly did not want any pity from the other women who worked here. Everyone had their troubles, and it was just fair and decent to keep them to one's self. With her wrist still damp with a tear, she might press it against the silver roses brooch she wore over her left breast like a military decoration. It was the last and dearest gift Thomas Charles had given her that last, fateful weekend after his orders for duty in the Middle East had arrived.

Everyone had a problem of their own—whether in Oklahoma, or California where she'd been briefly stationed with her husband of a few weeks before he shipped out, or here in his little Connecticut hometown which was now her home. *For better or for worse, in sickness or in health, until death do us part,* she had promised. All too soon, the contract had been fulfilled, while the spiritual ink was still moist. In a way, the most cruel words—as yet unspoken—could be something like *It's over, and you are free to go.* Was that it? After all that hope and joy, this was the slam of the door, the turning off of lights, the bumpy road leading to the edge of cold, murky water?

Yes, Marian had driven her car to the edge of Emery Lake one evening recently when the pain became unbearable, when she was beyond tears, alone in the universe, and at the end of the line. She had driven to the chilly waters of oblivion, ready to drive in and just close her eyes as silvery bubbles rose all about, but she kept seeing sunlight in the high library rotunda, and doves flying in circles amid a shaft of sunlight slanting in through an oculus like the open eye high up in the ancient Pantheon dome in Rome where she had once been on vacation with her family as a teenager. Something inside Marian said *No!* at that moment. Nobody was around. It was dusk, and people were in their glowing little houses after a hard day's work, having supper together at family tables and talking or bickering or praying or silent in the way that people lived with each other. She, on the other hand, had nobody. She could not go home again to her parents and siblings out west, and she did not feel totally at home here with Tommy's parents and brothers. Tommy was not strictly from Emery but from another township twenty minutes away in another world, and Emery was hers to keep if she wanted it. She and Tommy had picked it out together, and in a way it was a continuity Tommy would wish for her. She sat in the growing dusk, with her hands on the wheel and the motor running, looking into the water that would take her under before anyone ever spotted the shimmering car roof way down and figured out who she had been, what she had done, and why. The memory of that beautiful strange man in the library was just one of many fleeting thoughts that passed through her mind, but it was significant. His warm, fragile, hungry gaze pleaded with her in memory, telling her that life would bring her someone or something more. She'd hoped maybe the ghost of Tommy would sit beside her and hold her hand as she drove into the cold lake, but how crazy was that? Tommy was not on board for this stunt. They had done just about anything else together, but he was not going to approve of this. So she put the car in gear, backed in a large U-turn on the seasonally abandoned, gravelly boat beach where people launched their little sailboats on happy summer days, and drove back up the road a block or so, to her empty little house, which she and Tommy had bought together.

She had never expected to see the stranger again, and he would have no idea that his spirit—his beautiful eyes, his warm thoughts— had been with her in the car at that bleak, wrenching moment.

Somewhere, distantly, Marian heard the sound of women laughing uproariously. It was a brief, rowdy laugh but was cut instantly short by some circumstance she did not fathom. Must be quite a joke being told back in the break room. Two older women and three high school aides were working at the moment, all female and capable of sharing a feminine laugh—but about what?

As Marian sat on the footstool, with the pile of books on her lap, she sensed a change in the air. It had an electric feel to it. She was not having one of those teary moments just then. She was happily humming to herself and thinking about the story hour ahead. She was a big hit with the First Graders, who were old enough to follow a story, and innocent and full of wonder, so that it was a joy to see their faces light up and their eyes grow big. At the moment, there were children of various ages sitting at tables over their homework, but the noise level was at a minimum and Marian was contentedly lost in her thoughts.

She hardly paid attention to the steady coming and going of customers at the Help Desk and the Check Desk. The two older female librarians on duty had similar businesslike though cheery voices—sort of like bland book covers, Marian thought.

Then she heard an unmistakable change in pitch as Mrs. Rose Otto addressed a man, whose voice had a certain quality that seemed to make Mrs. Otto's voice rise in pitch. Mrs. Otto was a thin, blonde (okay, rinse) woman of 50 with large lenses sheathed in pink plastic, and a narrow, thick mouth of dark rose lipstick. Marian was not overly fond of Mrs. Otto, who seemed she could be a bit of a back stabber at times. Luckily, the staff of twelve (mostly part timers) worked for the nicest mother hen in the world, Mrs. Linda Damien, who took no sides and always looked after the well-being of her employees as Chief Librarian.

Marian glanced toward the Help Desk and—as her hands jerked in shock and her body froze—all the books on her lap flew apart with a loud rattle of covers and a fluster of papers. The man standing before Rose Otto at the Check Desk was that same Mr. Suck My Lungs Dry who had caught her attention a few weeks earlier. She had forgotten all about him, yet not forgotten him, which made no more sense than the rest of her life right at the moment. She sat feeling like a fool, surrounded by scattered children's books, and her bare knees pressed awkwardly together just past the edge of her sensible skirt. Unfortunately, Mr. Evacuate All The Air From My Lungs heard the flying, spinning books, and glanced at her. Or was he already glancing toward Marian? Marian felt a hot flush rise up her cheeks as she pressed her knees modestly together and reached all around to gather the dozen or more books that had gone UFO.

Rose Otto had this talent for looking a bit like a coyote talking to a road runner (in the cartoons), especially when she spoke disapprovingly to a man. Mrs. Otto seemed to be of the opinion that libraries were for children, and adults who ventured in were suspect—especially men.

Mr. Respiratory Arrest seemed to take all this in stride. His body language toward Rose Otto was casual, hands in pockets of his expensive suit that flowed along his long, lean physique like bottled, imported $9 a bottle water, or $199 a bottle champagne.

Marian sneaked glances at him as she leaned this way and that to retrieve books. Two little First Graders in parochial school uniforms rushed to help her, a boy with mussy blond hair and a little dark-skinned girl with a pink bow in her hair. A third boy came up behind and put his hand on her shoulder. "Are you okay, Mrs. Charles? Do you need help?"

"No," Marian said, "Yes." She laughed. "Let's all help Mrs. Charles pick up these books, okay? Thank you, sweetheart. All of you, thanks." Together, they made a fresh stack of books on her lap. The little girl even filed away one book for her, which she studiously (frowning behind horn-rimmed glasses) placed among the E's. "Are you guys ready for story time?"

"Yes!" they all said, and stood by, waiting for instructions.

Secretly, she was thinking: *thanks for rescuing me*. She was glad to be able to hide among them. When she next glanced up, it was just in time to see Mr. Anoxia striding toward the main lobby where he disappeared seconds later. Gracefully, he did not look over his shoulder at her. She almost wished he would, but was relieved he didn't. She released a long, pent-up breath. She must look like a total ditz, she thought. *Oh, I don't care.* Needing a drink of water, she rose and walked toward the desk areas. She smoothed down her pink sweater, gray skirt, and white blouse as she did so. Rose Otto gave her a smug, satisfied look. Rose's hazel eyes had a smoldering look as if to say I showed him a thing or two, though it was obvious he had flustered her. Whoever he was, he seemed to have a gift for shaking up women just by being in the same room. Was that a swipe across Rose's brow to flick away a few beads of sweat, or just to push back that forehead lock of assisted hair?

As she entered the break room, Marian found the two adult assistant librarians sitting at the table amid piles of books, papers, lunch wrappers, and other bric-a-brac of real life. One was Terie Gill, a dark skinned Afro American woman with glossy hair and a beautiful smile usually wreathed in a special husky rose lipstick. Terie had large, beautiful eyes, almost almond-shaped, white as snow with glistening dark irises. Terie was only a year older than Marian, at 29, and married with two children, the lucky so and so. The other assistant librarian was Lillian or Lillie Donovan, a down to earth, chunky blonde in her late 30s, who favored denim dresses and sturdy work shoes. Lillie was a mother of four, including a teenage girl from her early, premarital adventures in life. The two women were still giggling at the joke that had made them cascade with laughter minutes earlier.

Marian bent over the wall fountain and let a long, cool trickle of refreshing water fill her thirsty mouth. She rose and turned to go back into the children's hall. Lillie and Terie convulsed with barely stifled laughter. Marian was puzzled.

"Did you see that guy?" Terie asked Marian.

"Mr. Adonis?" Lillie said.

"Did you hear what he said?" Terie said.

Marian, blushing again, shook her head. This wasn't about her, was it? She'd felt like a dodo while that man was looking at her with a certain probing, intense stare, and a knowing, dark grin. Did the entire world know that he had noticed her, as he had the previous time? What was it about her that, every time he saw her, a look came over his face as though he was standing on a curb looking across the street, watching his car being towed away, and he was afraid to cross the street because the meter maid was still writing his ticket?

Lillie pulled Marian close and said in a giggly whisper: "He walked in and went right up to Rose Otto, who started giving him the third degree. So he looks at her with those icy, dagger eyes and that saucy, wise ass mouth, and asks her—" Lillie doubled over with laughter, unable to continue.

Terie stopped choking long enough to finish Lillie's thought: "—he looks her in the eye, and says he wants to read about dinosaurs. Rose looks at him like she just woke up from a long sleep in her bird's nest, and he looks at her like, you old dinosaur, just try messing with me, I'm here to mess right back at you."

Relieved, Marian shared their laugh. Her man was a joker. Wait a second, what was this her man thing? "So did she find him a book about dinosaurs?"

Terie said: "Rose said she would order one from Central, since we don't have any adult ones that aren't checked out."

"I did have two children's books about dinosaurs," Marian remembered. "But he wouldn't be interested in something so basic." Nor in the klutz filing them on the stool, she thought.

"He said he'd be back in a few days," Lillie said.

Marian took a deep breath, smoothed down her clothes again though they did not need it, and returned to her duties. She resisted an urge to grin behind Rose's back, as Rose sat obliviously on her high stool, hunched over the check-in and check-out machinery that must give her a sense of omnipotent power.

"He looks like a guy with money," Lillie said.

"And good taste in suits," Terie said. "He drove off in a nice shiny new Jaguar."

"Probably has the same expensive taste in women," Lillie said.

Marian nodded. *What was I thinking?* Of course he would have half a dozen fashion models wrapped around him at some club, like long-stemmed roses. She sighed while washing her hands at the sink. "Story hour," she announced matter of factly.

Terie pointed to a gaggle of kids hovering around the door to the Fireplace Room across the hall. "Your fans are waiting."

Mr. Hypoxia seemed to drop in about once or twice a week as time went by. Marian would pretend to be busy, and he would find excuses to sidle by. She still wore her gold wedding band, which was however quite thin and might be mistaken for something less serious. The black ribbon on her arm was not readily understandable, she thought; no, she hoped. He'd cough politely and she'd look up from her work. He'd say something inane like "Excuse me," and she would say "Of course." She was very self-conscious about this habit of hers, which was that her tongue got all tied up when she was flustered or nervous, and her voice took on a very faint lisp. Also, she had these like Army issue black plastic glasses with slight astigmatism correction in otherwise nearly neutral lenses, which she sometimes wore for reading, like now; but they made her look like a gadzook, she thought; and getting pretty ones would mean she might as well also take off the mourning ribbon. She wasn't ready for any of that yet, lost amid the scattered puzzle pieces of her violently interrupted dream.

September had come, and with it that heart-wrenching change in the weather and in the New England soul that she'd gotten used to in this little town she'd started thinking of as home—her new life, so rudely interrupted by an Improvised Explosive Device on a dusty road in Afghanistan, now nearly two years ago. If Marian felt trapped in limbo, she had made peace with one thing. She was never moving back to Oklahoma or to California, which would be like giving up on the freedom she had made for herself. She could not move back to Shawnee—it would be like throwing away the future that she had so much fallen in love with. People were nice here, and the kids loved her. Emery was a wonderful little town in a valley, with a lake, and a small town pace while a million Apollos and Aphrodites flew by on the thruway with their suits and business deals. Tom Charles' folks were blue collar, the high-end moneyed tradesman kind—air conditioning and plumbing, to be exact, with his own store front and six trucks; but they hoped for something white collar for their son. Marian's folks had made their money in furniture and drapery sales, so she had grown up humbly in middle class comfort. They could afford an occasional summer vacation in Europe or Canada. Her dreams had matched Tommy's. He was really Thomas Charles Jr., but everyone called him Tommy to avoid confusion with his dad, and the name had stuck. Tommy had planned to return to college and get an engineering degree after the Army, using his G.I. Bill. He and Marian had planned it all out so nicely. Now, she slowly and reluctantly admitted, she must start over. What better place to do that in than right here in the valley? She'd met a few of Tommy's old high school friends—they were all married, and they'd double dated a bit, but everyone here worked hard and kept busy, so she spent a lot of time alone. So, as she sorted books and helped the after-school kids, she wondered if she might not have to really move away to someplace with more people and more night life. She had not been out with a man in years, and the thought repulsed her. Mr. Anoxia was gorgeous—a dream—but he did nothing for her beyond being eye candy. It was like seeing a template for what a man should be, if her time ever came again. What would a man like that want with a small town librarian? Probably nothing. The thought was laughable.

Marian's days passed by like a slow dream. The school year was in full swing after Labor Day, and the kids kept her busy. The library glowed with its warm interior lights like a lantern along the thruway. The days got shorter, and the trees began to change colors. The frost line started in Canada and, with a different cadence each year depending on the weather pattern that fall, would move south in a broad band extending from the Atlantic coast to the Prairie states and beyond. Every day, the weather reports followed the frost line as it moved south, a hundred miles or more a day. As it advanced, the green leaves in a trillion gorgeous oak or elm or other deciduous tree crowns got nipped at the stem and died. The leaves turned brown and dried out, falling along the empty country roads and lonely hillsides. Evening came a little earlier each day. Indian Summer, with its few days or weeks of late, wan sunshine like the left-overs of a great summer meal, came and went. It was a rhythm baked into the very hills, having gone on since Colonial times and before. For two or three weeks in October, the world was ablaze with sunshine in yellow or russet leaves, the color of autumn apples and pears. With the chill weather came winds, sometimes drizzly or sometimes just dry and mysterious, that ruffled the zillions of leaves lying piles. The leaves would lift like talking mouths and make an urgent rustling noise in some language nobody could understand, but you felt it in your bones. You might not speak the language of the leaves, but you understood that there was something as autumn in your soul as the brown. Pumpkin stands began to appear along the roadsides. Teachers and librarians began having the kids put up orange-colored Hallow E'en decorations including all sorts of hideous jack-o-lantern pumpkin designs, witches riding on broomsticks, and a few science fiction robots or fantasy princes and princesses sprinkled in. It was lonely and comforting, crazy and peaceful, all at the same time. Marian wrote letters in the evenings, in her kitchen with the window facing a street, at whose end were the dock lanterns of Emery Lake. She wrote home to her parents and sisters, telling them that she felt at home here. Sometimes she visited with Tommy's parents, who would do anything for her, though she made a point not to be dependent. So, a little distance grew, and she let it. They were digesting a lifetime of new grief, and preferred to live in the past rather than endure the present she must deal with. Time went by. Soon it would be time for the time change—fall back, spring forward—all in its seasonal rhythms.

Though she was always busy at work, she sometimes looked up in the middle of something, looked through the reflections in the windows of the interior, and saw the fleeting red taillights and white headlights outside on the sunken turnpike and the surface streets. So many people, so many hearts—was there ever a soul who might stop by and bring her a flower or ask her to dinner? *What am I thinking,* she'd ask herself, and sigh over her work.

When she looked up again just now, when she had summoned her courage and gathered her wits, Mr. Oxygen Deprivation had left. She set her books aside and rose. Smoothing her skirt down, she walked toward the Check Desk. She needed to stretch her legs a bit. In the library's timelessly soft light, Rose Otto stood busily womaning the checkout. As a little dark-skinned boy brought a stack of kid books for her to check out for him, Rose said in a sidelong way: "What is it, Marian?"

"I just came to look at something."

"Oh?" Rose went through the practiced motions, which included running freshly checked out books over the laser scanner to desensitize them so they would not trip an alarm in the exit, and bring the security officer Mr. Perez running with his walkie-talkie and pepper spray.

"There, I found it." Marian's long, red-lacquered finger nailed tibbety-tapped on the keyboard nearby, and a plain, antique green screen brought up clunky old bar-game text.

"The Grecian god," Rose Otto said with the utmost dry irony.

"Do you mind?" Marian said sharply.

"I don't mind," Rose said with a hint of humor—was it cold, or did she actually have a heart ticking somewhere behind that frilly, pinched exterior?

His name was Richard Moyer, and he lived in West Hartford. His address was 351-14 Wanderley Street, which might mean a complex of condos or town homes at Number 341 on a street by that name. *Okay, Marian, she asked herself, what are you doing?*

Rose said: "If I were thirty years young, I'd do the same."

"I am not doing anything," Marian said sharply.

Rose snapped up a stack of books and stepped away with them under her arm, turning her thin figure in its beige dress, frilly blouse, and sensible shoes back toward Marian. The look on Rose's face was enigmatic. There had been some horrible abuse in her past, Marian vaguely knew without caring to ever pry, which left Rose kind of like the walking wounded, as an older generation used to say.

Marian lingered one more minute, before Rose turned back to service another client—one of the elderly, who lived in assisted living homes around the area. The library was one of their major outings every day, bless them, along with a trip to some restaurant for senior portions followed—on a daring day, when medications permitted—by a parfait topped with forbidden whipped cream. Or was that whipped dream?

Marian web-searched Mr. Impossible Stud, and came up with Wanderley Street—in a fashionable section of pricey West Hartford, which was almost exactly halfway between Boston and the City, with Interstate 84 running through it, along with old U.S. Route 44. Busy area. Interstate 91 ran through the nearby state capital of Hartford on a north-south axis from New Haven on the Long Island shore through Hartford, Springfield, and north through New Hampshire and Vermont to the French-Canadian border. If he was from West Hartford, at such an address, racing around in a Jaguar in a thousand dollar Madison Avenue suit, he was hardly a slouch.

More than I ever needed to know, Marian thought as she walked away, avoiding any further looks or comments from the X-Ray eyed Rose Otto. The mysterious and unreachable demigod had a name and an address, she now knew. He was Richard, but was he a Rick or a Dick? She almost burst out laughing as she doubled over and choked into one fist. She scolded herself, grinning inwardly: *Terrible, Marian, you need your mind washed out with hot soap and water. You go, girl.*

What a strange adventure without words or pictures this was, Marian thought, as she went about her day's work including preparations for story hour in the Fireplace Room. In her heart, she knew he was interested in her. Or maybe she was having a day dream at best, or was crazy at worst. Whatever, it was fun to think it, and she carried a mysterious little glowing smile with her for the rest of the day. The kids picked up on it, and they all had an especially inspirational time as she read them *Sleeping Beauty*, dated 1812 and collected by the Brothers Grimm from among all the old European tales of love and wonder that they could find.

The children all clapped—especially the little girls, whereas the little boys made bemused faces and looked half-hearted. The boys wanted a story about knights and horses battling with swords in far-off lands. Marian picked a story she had read to other children. It had been told in many ways over many years, under various names. This book had it as *Sleeping Beauty*, but its older German name was

The Thorn Rose. It had been told for centuries before that under other names to other children who were now long grown up and gone the way of all roses and flowers in all ages.

In the story, a king and queen wanted very much to have a child, because they had none. When their wish came true, they invited a bunch of guests to a christening feast, including the kingdom's most important faerie goddesses. Since the king only had twelve gold plates for the table of honor, they only invited twelve fairies.

The thirteenth faerie queen, who was jealous and angry about being excluded, spoke a terrible curse. She predicted that the young princess would one day prick her finger on a sharp needle and die. When the king heard about this, he ordered all spinning wheels in the kingdom to be burned, along with their needles. Like many people without a dictionary, however, the king did not realize that in various languages, a needle may mean some pointed, dangerous object other than a spinning or sewing needle—like, oh let's say, a rosy thorn.

One day, when she had just become a beautiful young woman, the princess found a strange little door to a tower in the family castle. Out of curiosity, she opened the door and ventured into a dusty passage where nobody had gone for ages. She walked up a circular stone staircase until, under the tower roof, she found a room in which an aged woman was spinning thread at her wheel. "What are you doing there?" she asked the withered faerie goddess.

"I am spinning some golden thread for a beautiful dress," said the Thirteenth Fairie. "Would you like to take a try at the wheel?"

"Oh yes," said the princess, and touched the spinning wheel. So the two sat together, and had fun spinning beautiful thread.

Now the princess noticed an open window, from which she could see the rolling green hills and blue skies of the entire kingdom. Down below, amid rustling forests and tree crowns, nestled the roofs of a hamlet, surrounding the shores of a blue lake.

Growing around the window were thick rose bushes, heavily laden with gorgeous dusky-red roses that filled the air with a rich, nectar-like fragrance that brought honey bees from all around. "Oh how beautiful your roses are!" said the princess.

"Go on over," said the Thirteenth Fairie, "take a close look, and smell them."

The princess went over, leaned out the window, and took a deep breath. "Oh, they smell divine," she said as the sweet, rosy fragrance surrounded her.

"Why don't you pick one?" said the faerie, with a wicked grin.
"Can I?"

"But of course, child." The fairie queen clapped her withered hands together, and laughed shrilly.

So the princess reached out to snap off a particularly large, wide open rose the color of a desert sunset. As she did so, she felt a sharp pain, and realized that a big, hard thorn stuck from her pale finger. The last thing she saw was a full drop of blood falling slowly from her soft skin. Almost immediately, she fell down dead. The Thirteenth Fairie cackled gleefully and disappeared.

What nobody knew, however, was that the other fairies, knowing about the curse and unable to undo it, instead were able to change it so the princess would not die, but fall into a deep sleep without feelings or dreams.

In this manner, the beautiful princess lay lifeless, like a war widow or a small town librarian living alone in a little home by a lake, while everyone around her went about life as if nothing had happened. They all adored the beautiful princess, and wished she could come back to life. They cared for her, and kept her neat and pretty, but nobody could wake her from her sad sleep.

One day, years later, when the world she had known was long gone, and new people lived in the realm, a handsome prince happened by, and wandered up the stairs in the tower. Seeing the beautiful young woman, he at first thought she was the statue of an ancient and untouchable goddess.

He noticed a large thorn sticking from her finger, surrounded by a still wet drop of blood the color of a dusky rose. He thought to himself: She has lain here for ages, but she cannot be dead, because her blood is still fresh. Her skin looks as if she is still breathing. Maybe she is not dead, but asleep. Before he could think about it, he pulled the thorn from her finger.

The princess opened her eyes, and looked deeply into his.

The prince, captivated by her gaze, felt as if the ground moved underneath him.

The princess sat up from her long sleep. She stretched and yawned, turning this way and that, while the prince stared at her.

His heart was captive, and his life was now hers.

The princess was happy to smell the fresh air once again, and to see birds wheeling about in the blue sky outside the tower. She saw sunlight shimmering on the lake, and among the trees still lay the scattered rooftops of the little town. People went about their daily lives as ever, and the princess was happy she could join them now, and maybe, just maybe, have a new life of her own. Was that asking too much? Hadn't she slept long enough now?

Most importantly, though, the Little Thorn Rose princess realized that she owed her life to the strange, handsome prince, so she turned and put her arms around him. He had eyes only for her, because he came from a place where he had plenty of troubles of his own, which weighed down his heart. The princess, looking deeply into his eyes, realized her dear prince carried a burden. With a command of her soul, she wished his burden to be lifted from him. At the same time, she also lifted away all the sadness of her long sleep and her losses.

"You are the man I want to marry," she said to him.

If Ovid or Homer were writing this saga, he might add a typical little vignette aside: In the deep, dark, greenly fragrant forest of a feudal manor, a heavy war horse gallops, and on it sits a bearded hunter wielding a bow and arrow. Alongside run the hunting dogs of his estate, while a distant post horn sounds—a deer has been sighted. The hard hammering of the hooves, and the baying of the hounds, and the distant blowing of a horn, cannot hide the frantic thrashing of the hunted deer that runs for her life. At last, she comes to a rocky ledge among the trees and can go no further. For an instant, the hunter and the hunted stand face to face. Each is frozen in surprise, and neither can move. In that instant, they are one another's captives, before the deer breaks and escapes to her freedom, and the hunter lets her go in his greatest act of love.

To the Little Thorn Rose in the tower, the prince said: "I have fallen utterly and wildly in love with you. Will you make me the happiest man on earth? Do you consent to marry me?"

"I do," she said. So they held each other, and kissed each other, and could never be separated again. They lived happily ever after.

Marian closed the book and looked glowingly over her audience of Kindergarten and First Grade children in the Fireplace Room.

The boys overcame their reserve, and had strangely glowing faces, as if waking from a dream, while the girls held their palms to their cheeks and looked at each other with delight. All the children clapped and cheered, even the boys with all their manly reserve.

Marian joined them in smiling and clapping because it had gone really well today, and everyone lived happily for at least as long as it took them to run jostling and yelling out the door to their waiting parents. Then, Marian once again stood alone in an empty, trashed room where there was not even a fire in the place.

Mr. Adolfo Perez, the sixty-something guard and custodian, came by jingling his keys. He looked at her with a kindly, knowing look and said in slightly accented English: "Time to close up and go home, Miss Marian."

"Oh yes," Marian said. Time to close up. Time to go home.

Everyone had their troubles, she reflected as she cleaned up the disaster and locked up the Fireplace Room. Mr. Perez' wife of many years had been very ill for a long time, and hardly recognized him or their four children.

Mr. Perez pointed to his eyes and said something in a very gentle voice, as if afraid to step beyond his bounds.

"Pardon me?" Marian said pleasantly.

"You have sad eyes," he said. "You are a very young woman, with your whole life in front of you. Cheer up."

"Thank you," she said with a gush of relief and gratitude, as he pressed on with his late-afternoon locking up rounds. *Chocolate*, she thought. She would make herself a hot chocolate and sit by the window looking down the street toward the lake.

The good thing about grieving, she reflected, was—for her, anyway—that you could eat anything you wanted and never gain weight. People told her she was too thin. If she ever gained a few pounds, maybe that would mean she was finally done with it. She was, well almost, ready.

Part Two

Fall

ick had at last noticed the wedding band, and felt a bit at his own sophomoric behavior. *What was I thinking?* A painful divorce and other misadventures behind him in the recent past, he treasured this new little secret he carried with him. Ever since  that day in late summer, when he'd stopped for gas at Tony's station along the parkway, and had that burst of sunshine eye-contact with the beautiful, kind of somber young librarian, he'd felt like a changed man inside.

When he had noticed the gold band, he moderated his approach. The library had become a sort of sanctuary in itself, a promise about a new future for him. He had always loved reading, bookstores, and libraries, but now, with his busy schedule, keeping up was like physical exercise. He had now decided to read a classic novel every month for the good of his soul. He'd started with a shorter one, *The Great Gatsby* by F. Scott Fitzgerald, and planned to tackle *Moby Dick* by Herman Melville and other ambitious reading projects in the months to come. Although he could never have her, he thanked the beautiful, dark-haired young librarian from his heart—and hoped to meet a woman like her one day soon, and make that woman—whoever, wherever she might be--the focus and center of his life.

Ever since he'd finished his tour in the Army, soon to be a decade ago, he'd kept up with his fitness and diet discipline—but without the rigorous urgency of basic training. It was important for him to make a good impression, so he kept weight off and his muscles toned. It made him feel better—more energy, quicker thinking. There was nobody in his life, aside from casual dates and flings. The nasty turn with Cindy had been like a car wreck, leaving his emotions cratered. It would be a long time before he stuck his neck out again and made a commitment. He was used to having beautiful women wrap themselves around him with gestures, words, and alluring looks—and because it came easily, he thought nothing of it. There must be someone very special for him to open his heart once again.

But the language of books and libraries he understood. It was fun to stop in Emery, get gas, eat a slice of pizza at Papa's, and stop in the library to savor the atmosphere of books. The library had a timeless quality that he found refreshing. You could step into its unique air—a mix of paper, binding glue, fading fragrances, and faintly machine-oily dust—and lose yourself.

Many days, he did not have time to stop by, but he might take the exit and drive slowly along the frontage road. He'd cruise by the library, which glowed in the early dusk like a row of lanterns. He'd see the tireless librarians bent over their tasks, as if time flowed at a different pace inside there. He almost envied them their leisurely tempo—though he was sure they worked hard. He wondered if these women ever looked up and saw the cars flowing past on the sunken highway and the surface roads outside, and wonder about the many people flying in their cars among the cities.

He'd think about the beautiful young librarian with the sad eyes, and wonder what sort of man she was married to. Could he be such a man, and could he find such a woman? Sometimes, discouraged, he would just drive by rather than stop in on the pretense of wanting a book or making a copy on their dime copier.

* * * *

One day, Rick Moyer was on his way back from another business trip to Manhattan. This time, he'd taken with him one of the older sales staff, Geoff Beaton. There was a change happening in the family firm. Dad was making faint noises about retiring. Rick, as the only son, and only child, would of course inherit everything. Sometimes he thought about leaving, to make his own fortune, on his own terms, rather than as heir to a multi-generational financial firm that had its own traditions and rules, which were as much out of Dad's control as they were out of Rick's.

Geoff Beaton was 55, a retired U.S. Navy commander, and a successful sales strategist. Rick's dad had brought Geoff on board recently, with the hope that Geoff would start taking Rick's place at the New York City meetings. There was a vague promise in this that Rick would thus be promoted to become his father's shadow and protégé for five or ten years before taking over the firm.

Rick's great-grandfather, Richard Moyer Sr., had founded Moyer LX Holdings in the early 1900s. Rick's father had inherited the shop decades ago after his own tour as a Navy commander during the Gulf War years. The firm grossed over $100 million recently in gross annual sales, and stood to double that in another two years with successful mergers and acquisitions. Rick Senior was giving himself another ten years at the helm, which meant his son had a decade in which to acquire the same Yale educated, U.S. Army disciplined combination of skills, talents, and dedication.

Rick had gotten off to a shakier start in life, dropping in and out of college, screwing up ROTC and ending up enlisting as a private in the Army. The service, he liked to think, had forced him to get his act together and start appreciating the opportunity his old man had waiting for his only son. The only daughter, Lindy, Rick's sister, two years Rick's senior, had finished with a nursing degree at a small liberal arts college, married into minor money, and was happily situated in life with two nice kids and a decent husband— but Lindy was not at all corporate material. She was a bit estranged, living in Chicago and involved in an entirely new life there. Rick could not blame her. Dad and the Moyers were a hard act to follow.

Like Lindy, Rick had never thought of himself as corporate either, until his casual air and excellent manner with people proved to be a winning combination. It was enough of a formula, however unorthodox, that made Rick Senior make proud and happy noises about his son, and looked like a good fit for the future of Moyer LX Holdings.

Geoff Beaton was a big man given to fancy but tasteful clothing. He and Rick Jr kept up a nice banter on the way home. "You think that was a good meeting?" Geoff asked the younger man.

Rick felt comfortable with Geoff, and good about their day on Fifth Avenue. They had sat at a conference table in a dusky meeting room, high above the city, with third-party consulting executives from a devolving firm (Schmidt ZZ Konix, Inc.) which had already let most of its own executives go and was on the ropes. "It is usually a rescue operation," Rick said while Geoff drove. In the rarified, luxurious air of Geoff's expensive Lincoln Navigator SUV, a light heater fan was barely audible. The atmosphere smelled of leather, accounting printouts, and expensive clothing. "If anything, we can suck up their bottom line and double it in a year with our resources."

Geoff nodded. "They are pretty skinny." He meant that the

caretakers of Schmidt were desperate to place the assets with a strong acquiring firm and pay off the board members and stock holders with a suitable closing dividend and other compensation.

"It's a buyer's market," Rick agreed. "Say, do you travel this way much?"

Geoff shrugged. "Once in a while. I was working in Boston for some years after retiring, so I spent more time in Montreal than in the Big Apple."

"Good stuff," Rick said. "My favorite city. Montreal. A touch of Europe."

Geoff, who stuffed a long-sleeved, pin-striped shirt quite well, and ornamented himself with gold cufflinks and gold rings, nodded. "I'm from New Orleans myself, so I appreciate the French touches. No beignets though."

"But the croissants are superb." Rick loosened his tie and kicked back, putting one stockinged foot up on the dashboard. Geoff, by contrast, kept his jacket on and his tie firmly knotted. Must be the old Navy officer in him, Rick guessed. Having grown up with a West Point dad, against whom he'd rebelled almost as much as he loved him, he knew the type. "How long have you been married?" he asked Geoff casually.

"About forty."

"Days?"

"Try years, son."

"Try humor, Geoff."

"Touché. Oh, you'll keep me on my toes all right."

"Love sparring with you, dude."

"Let me win once in a while."

"You manage to hold your own."

Rick thought they got along all right, if one counted their manly head to head as friendship. He'd seen guys loosen up after beating the stuffing out of each other on a karate or judo mat. It took that to get guys to put the antlers away and come out shaking hands.

"Forty years," Rick said. "I can't imagine."

"You still have time. You're young enough."

Rick felt like changing the subject suddenly, since the conversation was veering in the direction of his failed marriage and successful divorce. Make that semi-successful, since Cindy had cleaned out the Moyers for a healthy piece of change. Rick's own parents had been married for as far back as he could remember, without divorce or separation—just years of bickering. Rick kept a comfortable distance from his nattering parents, but saw Dad most days at work and Mom at least three or four times a week. Mom was happy as long as he got along well with dad, showed up for work every day, and joined them for one of her pot roast dinners at least once a week, usually on Friday evenings to celebrate another solid week at the company. And she drank a bit too much, usually Chablis, sometimes scotch. Dad didn't drink, and wouldn't kiss her when she had liquor on her breath—which meant they had pretty much virginal lips.

"What about yourself?" Geoff asked without hesitation.

"Um," Rick started to say, and bit his tongue. Geoff wasn't letting him change the subject gracefully. Moyer policy was to make its few executives as close as family. It was still a smaller, closely held corporation, and not big enough for a lot of Byzantine shenanigans or back stabbing. Rick's only discomfort zone with Geoff was not so much the older man's twenty years on him, nor his education—Rick was Yale, while Geoff was Annapolis—but that certain steady state, gyro-compass personality while Rick Jr tended to be a little bit all over the map with his personal life.

Geoff laughed out loud. "I'm sorry I asked." He sobered immediately. "I know you had a run of bad luck there a few years back."

Rick did not flinch. He was done with it, finally. "I made a mistake. Yup. I must have been a real yoyo in a past life, and I had to pay my dues for it."

"No kids," Geoff said. It was a question.

"No kids," Rick said. It was his only real regret. "I don't mind the divorce and the ugliness. I was asking for trouble when I chased around the only daughter of a man who made his millions as a California fitness guru, and her mother was the horoscope queen of the carotene tan salon set." Indeed, his five year Odyssey with Cynthia Miller-Stone had been a wild ride. He was glad his father had not yet invested him in the company at that point, or she and her Mongolian horde of lawyers would have gone after every nickel. "I just regret the lost time."

"You mean kids and all?"

"Yep. Well, no at all. It's not like I lost time paying on a mortgage. But you cannot buy back lost time." It choked him up, to be honest. If he'd married sensibly and properly, he could be the father of—why do I torture myself? he asked himself. It was a calculation he did every so often. He'd married Cindy eight years ago. They could have children in grammar school. As it was, they'd not seen each other since the final shouting and slamming of doors at their Westchester mansion two years ago, and Rick was determined never again to make a mistake like that. It was burned into his brain and into his soul. His mother made sympathetic clucking noises, but her eyes radiated that mom-guilt which said I told you so. Dad tended to more clubby—get over it, champ, just don't screw up your life again because my heart cannot take the wild ride, okay? The old man had actually said that to him one day as they sat on adjacent exercise bicycles at the Fitness Club. Rick had not flinched at that either. Fair is fair, he thought.

"What do you like in a woman?" Geoff asked to make conversation. He was a big, almost fat, comfortable, chummy, self-confident sort of man. He'd overseen, led, and officered thousands of men and women as a staff chief on one of the largest logistics commands in San Diego, and it appeared—this was one of the things Rick liked about him—he'd seen everything, and just about nothing rattled Geoff.

"What do I like?" Rick sat back and thought about that. Nothing solid passed through his thoughts. Except, maybe, an image of the library in Emery, which was a few miles away at the moment and closing in fast. He felt a ball of anticipation in the pit of his stomach—an excited, dangerous, happy, scary, like I could be crazy and lose control again, but she is probably married and unreachable kind of tension.

"You can be honest," Geoff said.

"You go first."

"I've got mine at home. You've met her."

"You're still happy after all these years?"

"A happy dinosaur," Geoff said.

Rick remembered how he had moderately tormented that upchuck librarian in Emery. "Did you know that modern chickens are actually tiny dinosaurs, Geoff?"

"I have read something to that effect. Or maybe I saw it on TV." Big gorgeous trees flew past. Traffic was moderate on the turnpike at this time of day. The evening rush hour had not yet set in. They were an hour from home base. "I like entertaining myself with a little light information about evolution, nuclear physics, and organic chemistry."

"Ha ha."

"Sure is beautiful countryside out here," Geoff said.

"When you retired, Geoff, did you ever think about moving to a small town like this?"

"Like what?"

"Oh, just for example, take this one coming up. It's called Emery. I have been stopping there for gas and pizza every time I go through here lately."

Geoff shrugged. "I figure a man retires when he doesn't have much fire left in him. I retired from the Navy young, but I expect I'll have another twenty year career going before I cash in my chips and drag my weary patoot here to what did you call this dive?"

"Emery."

"Like the little nail files."

"Yes. Emery—well, I did some research, to be honest, over in the library a few weeks ago—it's a mineral called corundum or aluminum oxide, mixed up with other substances and crushed up so it becomes an abrasive. It's also called black sand."

"You do good research, professor."

"I like to inform myself. Anyway, centuries ago they found a hillside full of emery around here and started mining it. That's how the town came to be. It's been around for a long time. Someone made a fortune from it long ago. I think the mine is paved over with a parking lot and a strip mall downtown these days."

"Sounds like you are forming an emotional bond with this place."

"Yeah." Rick felt a bit embarrassed to admit he seemed so taken with this place. "I stopped here for gas one day a few months ago. It's really quite scenic. There is a valley, with a town at the far end, and a lake shimmering in the distance."

"You're scaring me," Geoff said as his heavy gold cufflinks clicked against the steering wheel. "We need gas."

"Perfect timing. I'll show you the layout."

"You're the boss." Geoff said that out loud, strategically, at least once a day to remind himself and Rick as well about the fact of who signed whose pay check.

"So why are you scared?"

"Because you make it sound like that vague dream I have been mooning with Kathy about all these years. My wife. We've been stationed all around the world, and now live in New England. We always talk about some imaginary, as yet to be named place we want to buy a little cottage in, have a garden, walk to the corner store for coffee and donuts while the crickets chirp. That kind of thing. I'm not ready yet."

"I'm not either," Rick said. "But I'm done with the wild oats."

Geoff said significantly, no doubt referring to the disaster with the former Mrs. Richard Moyer, "Your oats have been taken to the oat dump."

"My oat farm has been cleaned out thoroughly," Rick said.

"The goats got your oats."

"My wild oats got in boats and sailed away," Rick said ruefully.

"Treasure the pain, for it is learning," said Geoff as Rick pointed to Tony's gas station and Geoff pulled the heavy SUV in toward the pumps.

"Oh I do. It's the most expensive tuition I'll ever pay. And I don't mean only the alimony I paid."

"Past tense?"

"She remarried last month. I am a free man."

"Lucky stiff," Geoff said admiringly. "You got away with your life. And your oats."

"No more oats," Rick said. "Please."

Geoff stepped out, and started filling the tank. Tony walked by, wearing gray and white striped overalls, and waved. "You're getting to be a townie here," Geoff remarked.

Rick stepped up close, doing a little dance to stretch his legs. Compulsively, his eyes turned to the buildings across the street. He came through here at least once a week, and always he slowed down, stopped for gas, or even had a slice of pizza at Papa's cramped little restaurant.

Geoff had sharp eyes, and didn't miss much. "That sure is a lovely valley down there," he said to Rick, aiming his chin at the sprawl of bluish-green tree crowns that flowed like a river from the heights, and the highway, down between the thighs of some ancient hills, ending in a jumble of roofs and that lake which shimmered bluish-yellow in the late light. "You ever been down there?"

Rick shook his head. "Not yet."

"Sounds like you plan to."

"In good time. I'm in no rush." She was married and wearing a ring; that had taken the wind out of his sails. Actually, it made him admire her all the more from afar—the ideal woman, if there was such a thing. *I am a fool as always,* he counseled himself inwardly.

"Sometimes," Geoff said wisely, "It's best just to look from a distance."

Rick pulled his eyes away, which had focused on the windows

across the street, thinking he might catch a glimpse of that wild cloud of dark hair or those greenish-caramel eyes. He was not about to share this secret with Geoff or anyone else. It was something so scary, so delicate, so special, that he felt he must keep it close to his heart as a private secret.

"Yes," Rick said, "sometimes it's best to look but not touch. I hooked up with old Cynthia Miller-Stone-Moyer and what a nightmare that turned out to be."

"You can't go through life being afraid to get burned," Geoff said as he finished tanking and hung the nozzle back on its pump rack. "A wise man wears oven mitts, but is not afraid to bake."

"Burned is learned," Rick said. "Other than that, I'm not afraid of much of anything." He meant it. He scared himself sometimes by his audacity. It was how you made millions, or stepped in deep doo-doo.

"That's the spirit." Geoff screwed the gas cap of his SUV back down.

Rick took a deep breath and stared down into the valley.

Geoff followed suit, with a lock of white hair blowing in the fresh lake breeze that always seemed to waft up from down there.

"You hungry?" Rick asked, almost hopefully. He welcomed any excuse to prolong his visits here.

Geoff pulled up a heavy shirt cuff and looked at his watch. "It's getting late, and Kathy will probably want me to take her out for dinner. I think it's Chinese night. I'm getting good with those chopsticks."

As they pulled back out into traffic to head deeper into New England, Rick sat in the passenger seat and stared hard at the pizzeria, and at the passing library building. It was just about time for the start of the school year, and the windows had been cleared of their green Fourth of July cards. They looked blank as a fresh slate for a new start, a new school year, new little people starting another leg in their journey through life. What would it be like to be that little again? It was something you got to experience only once. With adult life, there were some chances to start over. Not many, but they were there. Not always. He had known one or two fellow soldiers who had not made it home alive, or who had come back minus a leg or a piece of their future. He'd been lucky, and simply returned with some hard memories that made him wake up screaming or choking in the middle of his sleep every few months. He stared at the library, and the grammar school beyond it, and the bus stop with its puddles of wan yellowish light in the first shades of dusk.

Nobody in sight there—just reflections of traffic outside. In a matter of days, the windows would become papered over with orangey sorts of Hallow E'en decorations--as the days grew shorter, leaves all around grew brown, and that fragrant, lightly smoky autumn air would linger among these quiet streets and buildings. As the SUV pulled into traffic, Rick felt a powerful longing to come back here and walk around alone, exploring, and maybe check out a book—it didn't matter about what. Dinosaurs, chickens, who cared.

In its unchanging, timeless manner, the old building was a lantern in the growing dusk. He could make out the forms of one or two women—no idea who—bending over at their tasks, presumably amid the heads of children doing homework as they waited to be picked up by their parents after school. He felt a certain yearning to be part of that culture, but he had no idea how. He was a stranger to Emery and its lives. It occurred to him that he could certainly buy some property here—but his life was in Greater Hartford. His parents, his work, his clubs, his friends, his connections... He was a city fellow, and these were country folks.

"We'll be home in less than half an hour," Geoff said.

They each slipped into a reverie of personal thoughts.

What kind of woman? Geoff had asked.

A perfect, untouchable, distant one, Rick thought. One you can adore from a distance, like the sun, without getting burned. He wondered what she'd been thinking when she'd noticed him. He'd spotted her half a dozen times now. She always looked so thoroughly shocked and rattled. Is there so obviously a rain cloud over my head? he asked himself. He, who possessed confidence, money, poise, even a touch of boyish arrogance—could she see through him and know what a lousy choice he had made, and how Cindy had cleaned his clock from A to Z? He'd flirted with a married woman, and felt like a fool, but it was okay. It was good.

She was perfect, Miss or Mrs. Kiddie Book in that forbidding fortress of a building, with that terrifying T-Rex woman with the fake hair do and the yellow teeth. She represented a type. She stood for a different breed of woman he'd newly discovered. She might be unavailable and spoken for, but she held a lantern for his life. He had a feeling now for the type of woman he wanted to have dinner and go to bed with every night for the rest of his life. It was someone very much like Miss Bookstool.

It was good. There had to be laws. There had to be terror. The world could not be in free fall. Surely Miss Kiddie Books was the most perfect of women, dwelling in some exalted sphere of perfection. A guy like Rick could only look in the bakery window and see the cookies, smell the cookies, but not eat them. He wondered what kind of man would be so lucky to have a goddess like Miss Kiddie Books fall in love with him.

"You got a good one," Rick told Geoff as night fell and the traffic flowed around them. "Kathy," he explained.

Geoff seemed to read his mind. "It isn't always easy, but it's the best ride a man can have. We don't do so well on our own. Once you get rid of the wild oats and you get that through your skull, you really grow up and make someone a decent husband. They tame us."

Rick sighed. What to say? "I guess I am about as ready as I will ever be."

"Who is she?"

"What?"

"Mr. Moyer, I thought you were going to fall out of the window back there, staring at that library building. Unless you are a fanatic about dog-eared books and old glue pots or whatever."

"Married woman," Rick said. "I had a passing crush before I saw the ring."

Geoff said nothing more. Probably figured anything further he said would fall into dangerous territory with his future boss. He said lightly: "There is a book for you somewhere, trust me. You just have to be patient."

Rick knew he was going to stop in that library yet again. Instinct told him that, somehow, the book of his life was in that building; or at least the path to the book went through there. *I want to go back and check out that book. I have no idea what it is. Maybe it's a love story. Or maybe it's a whole load of more grief. Or a horror novel. Who knows?*

Geoff said: "I met Kathy when I was at Annapolis. They keep you pretty busy there, and I had no time for wild oats or any other kind of grains or cereals. They also set you up with these teas and coffees and what not. Teach you how to hold finger foods, and how to wear a sword, and all that guffaw blah blah. I saw Kathy and fell in love. You'd think it was love at first sight. Ha. That's only in love stories. I had to chase her around half the world, fight my way through lion-infested jungles, hop over crocodiles in rivers, to get her to even talk with me. She graduated from Bryn Mawr and was just visiting a girlfriend in Maryland when she came to this tea thingie. Later she admitted she was in love with me but knew well enough to make my life hell so I'd appreciate her when she finally said 'I might'. I know your old man and I have compared notes, and he went through pretty much the same thing. That's how we used to do it in the old days. I don't know how you do it today, but I wish you luck."

"Thanks a lot."

Their road switched them onto Interstate 91.

Soon they drove into the suburbs of the Hartford.

Geoff jabbed him in the ribs. "Want to stop for a beer on the way home?"

"I could use one." Right at the moment, the thought of a cold, foamy brew in a dark, throbbing tavern full of relaxed people seemed like the best thing on earth. He wondered what sort of strategy to use to visit the library in Emery again. He'd better forget about that and start looking for a librarian in West Hartford. Or a cute lady bar tender without a scheme or an agenda. He grinned to himself as a whole imaginary saga came into being. He'd disguise himself with one of those black mustache-eyeglasses-fake nose things. He'd wear rumpled suits and pass himself off as a college professor who'd been out of work for several years. Then again— that was all too much work—what he wanted was a cold beer in a dark and anonymous tavern, and then a movie and another beer before bed. What a life. In the old days, he'd always managed to find a woman on the spur of the moment. He was good looking, wealthy, and had a certain air of piracy about him. That was the old days. He could still go out and latch up with a beautiful woman this evening—that was never a problem—but his heart wasn't in it.

That guy was here again," Lillie said as she and Marian did their bus-boy routine, pushing a cart around the library near closing time, sliding piles of books off the tables where school kids had sat while waiting for their rides home.

"Huh?" Marian said as she leaned over a table to pull a bunch of books into the cart. Lillie, as usual, wore her blue denim overall dress, dark blue hose, and Birkenstock type shoes. With her pale skin, handsomely cute face, and blonde ponytail, she seemed never to age.

"You know—Apollo, the sun god."

Marian felt a ball of fire in her gut. How silly. She didn't even know the guy's name. And she was not anywhere ready to respond to those feelings. The idea revolted her deep down.

Lillie said: "He gives me butterflies. There I was, checking him out—"

Marian laughed. "You were checking him out, Lillie?"

Lillie made her *Oh Please* face. "I mean I was checking his friggin' book out, Miss Wise Pie. I'm a married woman with four kids."

"I wouldn't blame you if you checked him out. He is quite handsome."

Lillie was still guffawing. "I swear. Missy, you are the one who should be checking him out." Seeing Marian's face, she instantly switched to a dramatically droopy face. She seemed ready to hug Marian. "I know, honey. But you cannot live like a nun forever."

"I am not living like a nun." Marian wasn't arguing, but she felt just a bit defensive. She liked Lillie, who was a steady kind of soul. It was nice to have friends in a time like this. "I am just—" she couldn't find the words. She was not going to cry. She felt cool, calm, and possessed.

"You want a bit of advice?" Lillie said making her *Severe Friend* face.

Marian laughed. "Sure, long as it's free."

They carted more books together. They kept glancing at the wall clock.

"You are still young. Keep your options open. You don't have to marry the first guy you see. It's a long, difficult path requiring patience. But what if a nice looking guy with money asks you out to a movie or dinner. Are you going to lock yourself up at home forever?"

Marian's faint lisp--barely detectible by all except her self-conscious self--came back. "I know," she said softly. "I've been thinking the same thing myself. I just don't want to rush things."

"You should not rush things," Lillie said patronizingly, as if speaking to a little sister. "You're doing just fine."

Mrs. Linda Damien, the Chief Librarian, had finished locking all the doors, and was walking the grounds with Mr. Adolfo Perez, the school security guard. He worked for a private contractor, not the city, but he'd been here so long he might as well be a city employee. He came to the library every day to make sure they got the library and the school buttoned up for the night. His patrol partner, Mr. Wilson, actually did the school with Mr. Wisniewski, the janitor there; the only one you saw here was Mr. Perez. Little Emery had systems that worked, pretty much, and everyone knew the rules. It was a nice place to live. Then again, Lillie was right; it was a nunnery for her. How much longer could she be in free-fall like this?

She had almost done a terrible thing, a year ago, when news came, and she started absorbing the fact that Tommy would never be coming to see her again. They had been married not quite two years. On almost their anniversary, the Government flew her to Washington, D. C. along with her parents and Tommy's parents and family members. The burial had been at Arlington National Cemetery. Marian had sat like a grieving, shattered statue on a little folding chair, all in a row with other mourners on folding chairs, she wearing a black dress with a veil over her face. She had held a bouquet of flowers that someone had placed on her lap. Her black-gloved fingers were so numb that she could not hold the flowers. Tommy's mother had sat on her left, and Mama had sat on her right. It had been a rainy day, as if tears were falling from the sky, and the flags had been draped in leather sheaths, including his regimental colors and the honor guard at Arlington. There had been a long ride in a cold black limousine, until they reached the grave site. Rain had rattled steadily on the cloth pavilion top above them, and the air smelled of wet grass and fresh soil. The grave lay open, and Tommy lay in his coffin nearby. Marian had broken down again, and needed help getting to her chair. Strong, kind young men in uniform had held her elbows and her waist as they guided her to the folding chair.

It all happened like honey flowing downhill in a sunny dream. She had been unable to hold down any food, and her head was light as an open tower with clouds blowing through it.

A volley of shots rang out over the hills.

She heard a man's voice shout curt orders, followed somewhere near enough to hear, too far to see, by the snap of shoes and rifle sling buckles.

A bugler played the most slow, soulful rendition of Taps she could ever imagine. She held it together, looking dignified and brave, or so people told her in the hours and days that followed. She had been to other funerals like this, and hers was the only one where there were not at least one or two little children climbing around and fidgeting and wondering why their daddy was not here. They had not had time to get a family started. It was a terrible thing to think, but she thought it would be somehow easier, keep her occupied, if they had one or two children. She would grieve for the loss in their lives, but they would carry on together—oh whatever, she had no idea, during the months that followed, what she thought or felt. It was all such a big gaping hole of time and emotions. She remembered the grief on Tommy's parents' and siblings' faces, and the shock on their little kids' features. She clung to her own mother after comforting Tommy's mother and father as best she could. She remembered sitting on a park bench somewhere in D.C., later that weekend, with her father, as they held each other and cried. He held her because he know how much his little girl was broken up, and she held him because she knew he'd been so proud to give her away, and he was actually somehow irrationally blaming himself that now she was going through this. She flew back Northeast and stayed in Emery, Tommy's home town, but she honestly did not know how much longer she could endure it. The little town was wonderful, perfect like Tommy had been—despite all of his little human flaws, and who anywhere was perfect—but in a strange way Lillie was right without knowing exactly how. It was time to let go. It was now months, and it would soon be years, after the funeral, after the rain, after the military band and the throwing of wet soil on the coffin. She was glad she had not gone that way. Just a few months ago, she had nearly driven into the lake and ended it all, but she was past that now. It had been a long-delayed low point.

"My advice is free," Lillie said as she pushed the cart through the hall. "Guys who look like that are pure trouble."

"Do you even know his name?" Marian teased lightly. She was at ease with herself now, and ready to put her life back together.

"I checked him out, remember?" Lillie saw Marian's teasing eyes and made her *Now Really Must You* face. "Him, and his book, my dear. His name is Richard Moyer, and I would not trust him farther than I could throw him. Which is about one foot if he took his shoes off and jumped when I said throw."

They sorted books into carrels together by destination sections— History, Fiction, Reference, and so on. It was a quiet, cozy time that Marian liked because the library was quiet and secure, and the people who created chaos (sometimes wonderful chaos, sometimes just hormonal, pubescent kids) were home giving their parents the run-around.

It was a time she loved because, as Terie Gill had observed during a philosophical moment once, here we are, surrounded by the wisdom of the ages. Here we are, with Socrates and Plato, Homer and Dante, Lincoln and Einstein, and yet we are no wiser. If we could absorb all those thoughts in these books, would we have more answers, or just more questions? Marian had thought at the time (coffee in the break room) that it made a person all the more determined to take good care of the library and see it on its journey across generations.

"Richard Moyer," Marian said as she worked. She didn't let on she had already checked him out (so to speak). "Richard Moyer. That has sort of a ring to it, huh?"

Lillie had a twinkle in her eye. "Sounds like money, huh? Or movie star? I don't know what Mr. Moyer does for a living, but those shoes alone are worth about what I earn in a week. I wish you would just find yourself a nice, quiet, steady man. You are a very attractive woman, you are still young, in good health, no kids or obligations, and you can start over."

"I feel sort of damaged, Lillie."

"I know, hon. I know, sweetheart. But you are a strong person. I watched you recover yourself the past two years. I remember what a good person you were before this happened. You were such a good wife, hon. You will be again some day."

"I'm going to start blowing again."

Lillie put one muscular arm around her. "Aw, sweetie. I didn't mean--"

Marian bit her lip to stop it from quivering. She was unable to speak, and slapped herself lightly on the chest with one palm. "I'm—going—to—get—through—this…"

Lillie patted her on the back.

"Is something wrong in there?" Rose Otto said severely from the doorway.

"Why don't you go eat cars in the parking lot," Lillie told Rose. "Get lost."

She hugged Marian, turning her back protectively toward Rose, who quickly withdrew from the doorway. Lillie patted Marian on the back. She said to Marian: "You are going to find yourself a nice man. Not some rotten New York playboy. I am not going to see you ruin your life with some horrible sociopath."

Marian pushed Lillie lightly, fondly, but firmly back. "I am going to get through this," she repeated in a firmer voice. She raised both hands, grasped her rich ball of black curls, and combed it sensuously with her fingers. "I am going to find my life back again."

"You go girl," Lillie said respectfully. "That light in your eyes is almost scary."

"You're right, Lillie. That guy is probably the world's biggest ding dong."

"All right," Lillie said with a big sigh. "Let's finish up and get out of here. I got to go tell Rose I'm sorry I rattled her chain, but she gets her sniffy little nose into everyone's business."

"It's been another long day," Marian agreed. It would be good to crawl into bed tonight, pull the covers over her head, and hope the night would pass without any horrible dreams. She puttered about the usual routine of putting a few last things away, checking a door or a drawer, making sure everything was ready for tomorrow. Already, Mr. Perez, the police officer, was back with Linda Damien.

Two years ago, she had died—virtually, and almost for real. Now she felt the first hint of a totally new feeling—to leave town. To start over. She was going to take this terrible loneliness, wrap herself in its protective shield as if it were a battle flag, and go far away. Maybe to a big city, or a foreign place, she had no idea just now. She must make a completely new start with as little baggage as possible. It would mean leaving her in-laws, Tommy's parents, whom she had come to love as much as her own. But they would have to understand, and she would always be within reach if they needed her. At least, it would have to be that way. She had no idea how she was going to do this, or how any of it would happen. But the time was drawing near for her to make a move. It just had to be the right thing, whatever that meant, and it was not going to mean depending on a man. She might feel she needed a man in her life, but Tommy was still so much there with her.

She thought about it, for the millionth time, after Mr. Perez had walked her and the other women to their cars in the parking lot, and she was alone on the road to the little house she now owned. She had paid off the mortgage with the insurance money from Tommy's military benefits.

It was not a long drive down Emery Lane into the valley. She drove through the town's darkened, sleepy little center, where all the businesses were closed. Shop windows glowed dimly with interior night lighting. A State Police car slowly prowled through on the main road, which was a state road. The troopers inside, wearing gray uniforms and gray Stetsons, looked at her carefully, then cautiously waved as they passed on their way. They made several patrol sweeps of the town each night, but focused their attention on the thruway. The town had its own constabulary, consisting of half a dozen men and women volunteers as it was in many small Connecticut towns, and towns all across the country. Fire, emergency, and constabulary tended to be unpaid citizens doing a civic duty for the common good. Also, the summer barbecues and autumn-spring potlucks were worth socializing over by the lake.

She could picture Mr. Moyer: tall, dark, handsome, smiling— funny thing—her stomach churned as she turned off the engine, grabbed her purse and keys, and ran up the driveway under the security flood lights. Funny thing. This man, what was his name, he had about the same hair color, height, and boyishly handsome looks as Tommy had. It was unbearable. She quickly let herself in. She locked the door loudly, rattling, with hands so shaky she dropped her key ring twice before getting the lock secured. She made it to the bathroom, just in time to throw up violently and repeatedly. It was eating her alive, this grief. She loved this little house, with its two bedrooms and its flower bed. It was to have been their dream house. Tommy had even repaired the wooden slat fence all around their eighth-acre, mostly lawn property, for the day when they had little children who must not come to harm. He would have made a good dad. All gone now.

All at once, a great calmness came over her. She felt quiet in her heart. Something told her she was really starting to be done, and ready to move on. She would not give up this house. She would make a new life here. Emery was a good place to live. She would simply have to come to grips with her ghosts. There was that old saying: no matter where I go, there I am. She could run away, and her ghosts would travel with her. Better to stand her ground right here. With that new resolve, she felt refreshed and renewed. She remembered her moment of stark depression and her drive to the lake. *Whoever or whatever you are, Mr. Moyer, you saved my life. You will never know that, because you are an unattainable god. But I thank you anyway.*

She brushed her teeth, looking at herself in the mirror. She was not crying. Her eyes had dark circles around them, and her hair was a mess, as usual requiring a long thoughtful combing. She was not sobbing this time.

What must Moyer have thought when he looked into her eyes that crazy moment back in July or August? She had just tried to kill herself, and she must have seemed like a wild woman from some primeval forest. Maybe he liked wild women. Was he really coming back once or twice a week to stare at her, say silly things like "Excuse me," and stumble over her as she sat on a stool sorting books? On purpose, of course? Or was she imagining things?

If she sold this place, then the fence Tommy had mended would become security for some other young family, maybe with a little girl and a little boy and a happily bounding dog. A ball would roll across the grass. A woman would come running from the kitchen to see to her children and her man. That man would pull up in his truck every afternoon, dirty and tired from work, and be with his family. Those were all the things that had not been meant to be. She understood now. It was almost as if Tommy were in the room with her, patting her back and telling her it was time to let go. Most of all, he was saying to her that it was okay. It is okay, he was saying. It is okay, she thought as she rinsed her mouth, inhaled the clean minty fragrance of toothpaste and sink water. "It is okay," she said out loud as she strode into the kitchen and poured herself a glass of Sonoma Merlot from its bottle in a kitchen cabinet. The wine felt warm and commanding, like bottled sunshine the color of blood. Its bouquet rose into her brain like a quenching fog. She had not felt Tommy's presence in the car that night at the lake. However, she had felt Richard Moyer's presence. Maybe they'd both been there in the spirit, preventing her from going through with her dark and final impulse. That too was over now and would never again happen. "It is okay, Tommy. Thanks. I get it. It is okay to move on now."

For the first time in years, she took off her wedding band and laid it on the white, embroidered doily that stretched across the dresser in the bedroom. She laid it beside Tommy's wedding band, which had been couriered to her from the battlefield in Afghanistan by helicopter. The ramrod colonel in Army dress blue, covered with decorations and awards, who had handed it to her at the gravesite in Arlington with a stiff bow, told her the Tommy's ring had been salvaged from his body by a comrade; had been flown by chopper to a command post; taken by a French army nurse to the U.S. Embassy in Kabul; had been courier-pouched to the State Department in Washington, D.C.; had been driven by a four star general's personal aide, a brigadier general, to the mortuary command at Arlington; and had been personally placed in this colonel's hand by the command sergeant major of that institution. "Just so you know we all loved him, and this entire nation loves you, Ma'am," the colonel had said, stood straight up at attention, and saluted her while she held the ring in one small hand and showered tears all over it in the rain.

Now it was time to say goodbye at last. She could almost hear Mama telling her from far away in Shawnee: You have done your duty, Marian. You have been a good soldier's wife. Your heart died on that battlefield, just as if that IED blew you apart and left you bleeding helplessly in the dust. Tommy was taken away, but life is giving you a second chance. Your duty now is to take that opportunity and who knows—maybe you can start a new family now and serve them.

She slept a deep, sound, dreamless sleep that night after just one glass of wine. She woke up the next morning early, feeling more rested than she had in years.

A light rain made the early morning streets shimmer as she rushed to her car for the drive up the hill, which was barely two miles. The days were getting shorter, and the nights longer. The weather grew rainier and stormier. By November, it was growing grayer and darker as well. As usual, one hoped for a white Christmas in Connecticut, like in that old Bing Crosby movie from nearly a century ago. Either way, there was usually a cold spell, followed by a short warm snap called the January thaw. This would last just a few days, with temperatures as high as the 50s. Then, as

February began, winter would set in with a fury and last until early April. These were the long, gray, dreary months when Connecticut was not an ideal place, and many people nowadays went on vacation in Florida or out west. Most people did not have such luxuries, and simply toughed it out as local people had been doing for centuries.

5

One rainy day in November, Rick Moyer was driving through Emery and could not resist the urge to stop for a slice of pizza. He always saved his gas stop or his pizza stop for this little town. It was getting to be a habit. Besides, it was conveniently halfway between the New York State border and Hartford.

This had been a good day, business-wise. He had earned something like a million dollars in stock options in the past few hours, not to mention a retainer check for $50,000 from another firm's grateful board of directors. He was getting better and better at the negotiations that rescued other businessmen from their follies and mistakes. He could always cook up a good business plan from the scraps of other people's shattered ambitions. Dad had taught him well to look before he leaped, to gauge a situation from all angles, above all to avoid wishful thinking, and to know a business for its fundamentals using his own research or researchers he could trust. He was beginning to get a handle on showing up at an executive board meeting, knowing more about their business than they themselves knew. It was almost too good to pass along to Geoff, who would have to do his own business in parallel. Or Geoff would decide to take his own show on the road. That was how it was in this business. Water flowing downhill, seeking its own level. It worked. It was good.

Then, there was his personal life. As always, not so good.

He had been in New York City, where a thin first snow lay melting on the bushes and trees in Central Park. Slush briefly made the streets run brown before drizzle washed it away. New York was a city of umbrellas.

Rick had just dated an assistant fashion buyer at Mondorf's on Sixth Avenue. She was a beautiful, warmly pleasant Londoner of Iranian extraction named Pari Shahnas. Everything was right about her, yet nothing quite clicked, and they both knew it. She was graceful and endured a lunch at an expensive restaurant. After a large glass of wine, she admitted that she was in love with a man from Belgium who kept breaking her heart and then coming back to her. Rick relaxed inwardly, knowing that nothing more could come of this. He appreciated her honesty and her languid search in life, and was not frustrated with her. He could endure a lot of things, including perhaps even an instance of infidelity (he had no idea; he imagined he could get over it with a lot of work) but not a woman who was like a boat that kept bashing itself to pieces on the same rocks with every incoming tide. Pari, for all of her glamor, her café-au-lait skin and flashing black eyes and white teeth and rakish grin and long black hair, was a train wreck in motion. He sensed danger about her, and she understood she was no good for any man as long as this Brussels sprout kept working her over on every business trip from Brussels to New York City.

Rick and Pari had found an end to their lunch rather gracefully. "I don't like Brussels sprouts," he told her.

"Me too, Rick. I think I am beginning to acquire more of a taste for good old American hamburger," she said while finishing her after dinner coffee and glancing at her watch. "You know," she said with a wink, "red blooded meat, made in U.S.A. Maybe a nice cowboy type, all sizzle and all steak."

"I am afraid that I'm just a meatball," he told her. "I hope you find that right guy who will take care of you better than Mr. Endive."

They parted company with a handshake on a street corner in Midtown, and knew they probably would never see each other again. It went like that a lot, when Rick tried his hand at dating in the City.

It was finally with a sense of relief that Rick once again arrived in steady-state, slow-paced, reliable Emery Township. He had no friends or roots here, but the little place was beginning to feel more and more homey.

Crossing the border from New York State into Connecticut was, first of all, always a relief for him, going from concrete to greenery. Upstate New York, New England, Pennsylvania, backwoods New Jersey, they were all green regions with pastures and trees. New York City was for him a nice place to visit, and a nicer place to have in his rear view mirror. Maybe he would let Geoff take on a bigger role after all, which Dad in his wisdom apparently had recognized. He said to the dashboard: "You were right, Dad, I was too full of wild oats to get a good running start. I'm racing in top form right now, but I am just not me. What I mean by that is that I am a man without a woman, I mean without a good woman, which is like pencil without lead in it, or a pen without ink, or a wallet without money, or a pizza pie without pepperoni, or a library without cards."

It was raining hard when he pulled into Tony's gas station. Old Tony. There he was, wearing a plastic poncho that didn't fit quite right, working his batootee off as always. The poncho was see through, and he wore those same oily, gray and white striped overalls under it. He counted money, negotiated with customers, pumped gas, answered the phone, yelled instructions to his mechanic, and waved hello to Rick Moyer, seemingly all in one blur of motion. Things were hoppin' and poppin' here in Emery, land of black sand and mysterious librarians.

Tony was doing high jumps in the rain. "I caught the triple payoff at the track! I won a thousand dollars at Belmont!"

Rick pulled him under the aluminum overhang, where the air was a fine mist of whirling droplets but the ground was only damp. "That's wonderful, Tony. So you can close up the station and retire now?"

Tony's face streamed with rain and joy, but his eyes were hard and practical. "With a thousand bucks, I can retire maybe for one day. Are you crazy, Rick?"

"You have to go back every day and win again." They were shouting because of the noise of wind, rain, traffic, and a backhoe raising hell nearby.

"I can't do this again, maybe ever in a lifetime, Rick."

"You have to know your horses, Tony. You have to study them."

"They all look alike to me, Rick. And their rear ends too."

"Then why do you risk your money on them?"

"Because want to feel like a million bucks sometime."

"You don't make any sense."

"It happened to me one time and I will tell everyone for the rest of my life about the day I won a thousand dollars at the track."

"Let me be the first to congratulate you."

"Thank you, thank you, thank you my friend. We should be this lucky with women."

Rick looked at him while the pump hose at his side gurgled and throbbed with gasoline. "Is it luck with women, or do you have to study them like you do race horses?"

"I've been married five times, Rick." He patted Rick on the cheek. "I am the wrong man to ask."

Rick followed him around in the rain. "You mean you just keep gambling. You meet a woman and you marry her a few days later."

"Weeks, months, Rick. A decent span of time to make it look good." He pumped gas, yelled at a passing taxi, waved to a police car who emitted a siren fweep and briefly flashed his lights, and ran to answer the phone in his office.

Rick ran after him, hoping for something more.

Tony turned and patted him once more on the cheek, in the entrance to the gas station with its smells of oil and rubber and glue. "The truth is, my boy, I marry them the first time I lay eyes on them. The ceremony and the alimony come later. That is passion. The hell with the consequences. The first one cleaned me out so I have nothing for the next ones to go after. You see how much energy, how hard I work, not even stop to take a sang-gwich." He pronounced it the Long Island way, home of the Belmont track where he had made his win. "What good is life without passion?"

"If I find the answer, I'll text you," Rick said.

Minutes later, Rick drove across the street and pulled into the library parking lot. There was a book in there, and he was going to check it out. He wasn't sure what it was, but he was going to find it today. It was a book he had been looking for all his life. It was pouring sheets and buckets as he pulled his raincoat over his head and made a run for the main entrance.

Inside, he found himself amid the same welcome smells of perfume, books, and wet umbrellas. As he shook his coat out, careful not to splash, there was that woman at the counter who resembled a prehistoric hen, missing only talons (unless you counted her long acrylic pink fingernails). "Mr. Moyer," she said in a reedy but commanding tone. "What can we do for you."

"I need to check out a book."

"Do you have a membership here?"

He stepped up to the counter. "No, but I would like one."

"You have to be a resident of Emery, Mr. Moyer." She reached under the counter and, with trembling hands perhaps symptomatic of early onset palsy, she took out a book with a rubber band around it, and a yellow form slip. "This is that book on dinosaurs that you wanted. I'm afraid I cannot lend it to you because you need a library card."

He put both hands on the counter, palms down. "What is your name?"

"Mrs. Rose Otto."

"Mrs. Otter—"

"Otto," she said with flaring little eyes and a horrified red mouth.

"Mrs. Otter, what if I bought a house here in town today? What if I paid cash. What if I bought a whole row of houses here, just so I can check out that book."

She trembled with horror. "I don't know."

He slapped his hand down on the counter, gently but firmly. "What do you mean you don't know?"

She raised one trembling, talon-like hand and pointed at him as if her arthritic fingers were a chicken beak. "Mr. Moyer, you can buy all the houses here that you want, but that doesn't make you a resident. It doesn't mean you really live here."

It was Rick's turn to look horrified. "Am I having a nightmare? Is this a rainy day dream?"

She continued holding that trembling, bluish chicken head-hand in the air, with one large, flat, yellowed fingernail pointing at Rick like a staring eye. "Mr. Moyer, your soul is not here. You drive through here in your car, stop for gas or pizza, and order a book about dinosaurs. You do business deals in New York and you reside in Boston or wherever you reside, but you are not living here in Emery. You see, buying an address makes you a resident, but it doesn't mean you live here."

Rick sputtered: "This cannot be for real. We are not having this conversation. I must be asleep in my car. That's it. I am going to wake up any moment and realize that I am home in bed. This cannot be happening to me."

At that second, a woman's voice intruded. "Rose, dear, it's time for lunch."

Rose kept her hand in the air, but turned halfway to face a pleasant lady who had emerged from an office. The sign on the office door read Mrs. Linda Damien, Chief Librarian. "But I am not done with Mr. Moyer here."

"That is okay," said Mrs. Damien. "I am going to send you off to lunch, and I will take over here."

"But."

"Go."

Rose meekly turned and sort of hopped away in little odd steps.

"I am sorry," Mrs. Damien exclaimed genially. She was a heavy set, imposing woman with very dark reddish-copper hair. She was an Earth-mother figure swathed in Earth colors including a kind of light tomato sweater, a sort of cocoa wool skirt, some very English looking cereal-colored wool hiking socks, and sensible brown shoes with thick caramel rubber soles. She wore a pretty white blouse with vivid tiny green asparagus (or something) motifs all over it in a tasteful distribution. "I am sorry. Rose has worked here since the English settlers arrived, or maybe earlier. She tends to get very fussy and philosophical. Now what is your problem, young man?"

Rick pointed to the book.

"And?"

"Residence."

"You live here?"

"No, and I do not reside here."

"I'm sorry."

"Me too."

She blinked, long and deeply. "Huh? What did you just say?"

Rick cleared his throat. "The lady said…"

"Oh, that's just Rose. Not to worry. Do you have a library card, Mr. -?"

"Moyer. Richard Moyer. Rick."

"Mister Richard Rick Moyer, how do you do. Let's solve your problem."

He showed her his library card, which was from an hour out of town, and actually nearly out of state, though not out of date thank God. Harford was nearly in Massachusetts. Connecticut being so small, it was a lot like Luxembourg or Andorra, if a bit larger. Drive two hours in any direction, and you were no longer there.

"We have a form you sign, and you pay a dollar, and you get an inter-library loan good for three weeks. We run it against your home library. If you don't deposit the book with them for return to us within three weeks, we send teams of armed assassins to water board you. Can you work with that?"

"I will try to read the book on my lunch hour tomorrow and have it back here within two days—no more."

She clapped him soundly on the back. "Just kidding, my friend. We do the inter-library loan, it is a dollar, and I am sure you will return our book to us one way or another."

"I promise."

"Good." She raised her face and said loudly: "Marian!"

A voice wafted from somewhere. "Yes."

Or: Ye-e-e-s-s.

"Marian, kindly take care of this gentleman's needs."

Rick turned, and nearly had a heart attack.

There, rounding a corner, was the most beautiful and perfect woman he had ever seen. It was She, the woman who had nearly caused his heart to stop before, She for whom he scanned in the windows every time he drove (slowly) through Emery, She in fact who was the only reason he even knew Emery existed, and the little Town of Black Sand had become a mythological paradise in his feverish imagination.

She had that dark, rich hair—a mystery in itself, the way it tangled and hung somehow in generous, shiny swirls over her neck. She was almost tall, and willowy, and maybe a bit thin. Yet, she was no emaciated and bony fashion model, but a woman, filled out just right, and curvy where she needed to be so. She wore a rainy day outfit, consisting of expensive, soft leather hiking-type boots, crew socks, jeans pants that looked comfortable yet fit snugly on her curves and points; she wore a white blouse with rounded collar wings, a blouse decorated with fine periwinkles; and over that a richly corded, expensive looking sweater braided in some sort of fisherman's weave; and a pair of gold earrings like an odd little lump or rock on each ear lobe.

Her facial features suggested a typical rich American mix of Mediterranean and Irish or German, perhaps. Her eyes seemed crisp and vaguely almond-shaped, almost epicanthic, her cheekbones faintly high and sharp in a remarkable, pleasing way. Her facial shape was slightly exotic—fine boned, finely honed, hard to describe: stately, magnificent, handsome, sculpted, all without being exaggerated or overly sculptural. She had a girl next door quality that fit perfectly with the jeans and the sweater, the periwinkles and dusky glances, the pearly teeth and the pink tip of a tongue captured between them in a moment of shock. She was so perfect that he wanted to cry. He could look at her forever.

Her skin was pale, but with a rich creamy understatement as if her maker had thrown in a little extra melanin for pigment. For a moment, he thought it was her eyes that caused him such paralyzing joy and admiration, being a vivid caramel-green, but today tinged with a blue almost violet, and shiny as a dark blue sky on a stormy rainy day (like the one outside right now). Or was it the way she bit her lower lip, sucking it under her upper lip and teeth? No, it was the shocked, almost shamed look of recognition that said everything. Her look said that she longed for him. Her look, without a word said, was filled with an admission: she had coveted him, thought about him, and wanted him from the first moment they had laid eyes on each other several months ago. He knew that much about women. He had coveted, and been coveted, many times, but never anything like this. She came around that corner, never suspecting a thing, and came to a petrified stop before the man whose knees she would kiss if he let her, and here was Mrs. Damien commanding her to take care of this man's needs. He read all this in her expression, and his heart melted within him. He was a kick or a shove away from being putty in her hands, if only she knew enough to seize the moment.

6

For a moment, confronting the mythological sociopath and New York playboy known as Richard 'Rick' Moyer, Marian Charles felt the floor sink beneath her feet. She thought the earth was going to swallow her up.

There, life-sized but not larger than life, stood the man who had saved her life without knowing it. Lillie had painted him as a figure of terror like that giant tomato dressed in a bed sheet that was in one of the Hallow E'en stories she read to the children at Story Hour.

Instead, he looked—as the expression went—like he put his pants on one leg at a time, same as everyone else. He looked rather sweet. Very. And a bit confused. Or lost.

"Can I help you?" she asked.

She had put her wedding band on this morning from old habit. Now she put her hand over that hand so he would not see it.

Why, then, were her legs trembling? Why were her knees knocking together? Why did she feel like a little girl at her first school dance?

"I am lost," he said. "I hope you can help me."

She gathered her wits and her courage, and stepped forward. "Yes?" She hoped he did not hear the faint little *yeth* in her *yes*.

He opened his mouth, and out came a voice that sounded like a nice strong coffee tempered with the finest cream. "My name is Rick Moyer, and I was looking for—" His eyes seemed larger than they should be—the whites were showing. He seemed to stop and swallow, as if she were on fire.

Marian stared at him with a mixture of fear and desire. "Yes?"

"A book." He said the word in a higher, strained tone.

"No." It was the irrepressible humor in her, even at a moment of sheer terror.

"Yes."

She raised her arms to encompass the large hall all around them. "Well, here they all are." She added a nervous laugh. The humor was spontaneous, and helped break her paralysis. "Which one do you want?"

He got it. "Yeah." He laughed in a mix of surprise and disarmament. "Now we just have to find the right one." His voice sank back down to its more normal, seductive (at least, she found) tone.

She moved her hands defensively behind her back and stood like a grammar school child. "You have to pick one."

"Maybe you can help me pick just the right one for me." His eyes were not on the books, but on her. He looked flustered, and she wondered if it was a lascivious sense as his eyes roamed up and down her starved figure. His eyes did narrow back to a normal dimension as he apparently found his own wits back as well.

She said: "You are allowed to check out up to four on a cross-library loan."

"I only read one at a time."

"How nice," she said. "A one book at a time gentleman." She was holding her own in the cleverness department, though her knees were knocking together. She hoped he could not hear it—bone on bone, she imagined, just in time for Hallow E'en. At least her teeth were not rattling, and her tongue was under control. She did not believe for a moment that this charming, handsome man could be a one woman at a time guy. He probably had open books scattered all over his mansion.

"I had been thinking about dinosaurs," he said, flicking a gaze toward Rose Otto nearby. His gaze returned to her, roving between her face and her mid-section. Then he looked her squarely in the eyes: "Now I am thinking maybe I should read about something more—warm-blooded."

"You mean like mammals?"

"Yeah. A mammal," he agreed. If gentlemen wore hats these days, he would be jauntily spinning his hat on one finger. "Please, take me to your mammal department." From his eyeballs, it was not hard to figure out that she was the mammal in which he was suddenly most interested.

She had run out of funny things to say, choked up a bit with embarrassment, and turned. With her shoulders, she made a gesture for him to follow, like this way.

Together, they walked down the short, wide hallway from the main lobby, past the children's rooms, and into the main adult reading room. From the experience of past guided tours, she pointed like an airline stewardess, gracefully to the left and then to the right in one rolling motion. "Fiction on the left, fact on the right."

He stopped and waited. His turn to hold his hands behind his back, like a little boy waiting for story time. "You show the way. I'll follow."

"Mammals," she said. "This way."

"I am wondering if you have anything about horses."

"Horses?" She felt a jolt of surprise. Coming from Oklahoma, she'd grown around farms with horses.

"I don't know if there is much interest in horses around Emery," he said, as if preparing to be told they didn't have such books.

"Let's go have a look."

"Sure. Okay."

Together, they ambled—not really walked, more like two kids off on an exploration when the adults were not looking—down the aisles until they came to a section titled Nature and Pets. For a second, she was having sheer fun. For a second, too, he touched her back with his hand. It was a playful, gentle touch, lasting just a second, but it sent a jolt through her. For a moment, it was all fun. Then it became awkward. Something in her stiffened, making her afraid. She was afraid to let go, to trust, to really let herself enjoy.

For his part, he reacted in the same instant by pulling back— surprised at his own brashness, perhaps; startled that she seemed to react with such stiffness all of a sudden. He just managed to say: "Thank you" in a voice full of wonder, as she fled away.

"Will that take care of all your needs?" she asked, with mischief in mind. Lillian had so innocently said to take care of the gentleman's needs.

"For the moment," he said. "My needs are complex."

"You seem like a complex sort of gentleman." As she turned to run, she called busily over her shoulder: "Let me know if you need anything else."

She felt his eyes burning into her back, and it was the kind of heat you got from a warming pad—blissful. *Please, look all you want. I hope you like what you see.*

Yes, more than anything else, she wanted to explore his needs— and hers. He scared her to death, frankly. She felt doors and windows flying open in her soul, and fresh air blowing in, long forgotten. Could she let him get closer to her? That part would be easy. A woman did not worry about that. But could she let herself get close to him? She'd already had that conversation with her husband in her thoughts falling asleep alone in the king-size bed in her little house by the lake. Tommy would grin and say *Go for it*...

She remembered Lillie's admonition to beware of a man this handsome, flirtatious, and self-possessed. She ducked into the Ladies' Room and washed her face with lukewarm water. Just waiting there, leaning over the sink with her elbows on the cold granite and her wrists dangling under the cold water, waiting for the water to turn warm, she felt a sense of relief. She knew she was not yet ready for that kind of relationship. Maybe she never would be. The idea scared her. But she was grateful that someone—especially that man—had come knocking at her door. So what if they went to a movie or walked by the lake. Maybe they'd hold hands or even kiss. She wasn't sure if he would turn out to be anything more than a brief flirtation. He seemed like just the type who would enjoy the thrill of conquest, but hold back from anything resembling lunch or commitment. If he was just a fly by night prince, let him fly away. He had already twice brought dawn to her night. Only he did not know it yet.

7

Rick felt relieved to watch her hurry away. He was fresh out of jokes, and feeling awkward. I've done well so far, he thought. I didn't bungle it totally. I spoke, and words came out of my mouth. I didn't stiffen up, and I was not a robot.

He was also confused. She was not wearing her wedding band. Or had he been hallucinating days and weeks ago when he thought he saw it on her finger? She always wore the black ribbon, which looked sort of cute on her in a ghoulish way. Hallow E'en was past, and the Munsters were back in their haunted house until next year. She was just so disarmingly, charmingly herself, so direct and guileless, except for those clouds moving across the otherwise clear skies in her eyes. She was sending mixed signals, which was scary. He had never, ever flirted with a married or even an engaged woman; or even some other guy's girlfriend. Something about this lady kept drawing him back to her when his inner mom and dad told him to grab his rear end with both hands and run for his life. If he looked back, he would turn into a sodium chloride monkey-shape.

Because he was not a born actor or seducer, Rick had developed a way of listening to the other person and responding rather than pushing. It worked wonders in business as well as in friendships and in matters of the heart. He had money, looks, and poise, and could ride that car by just keeping his mouth shut and acting attentive and slightly, humorously bemused. People liked to think they were important, and he reflected their desires back to them like a mirror. It was also a defensive technique because he really preferred sitting alone in a room with a book and a beer or a cup of tea. With his somewhat overbearing parents and a weighty destiny to carry forward (the family business), he had developed the ability to retreat inwardly to a place of peace. For the most part, except for his insecurities and awkwardness, he liked himself and got along with himself well. He'd thought about being a musician (but fingers of clay), or a singer (nice voice, don't call us, we'll call you, *next!*), or an artist (slightly color blind). That left writing and teaching. He imagined he might have been a history professor or some such thing; but Moyer LX Holdings was the ticket Fate had handed him, and he would be a fool to say no.

He had the feeling this Marian the Librarian would not say yes, but she would not say no. He was not looking for anything more than friendship. If he could get close enough to study her, to know her, to savor her, maybe he would understand how not to open himself up to another pratfall like Cindy. He was a reserved, sensible guy, who kept his hands, his mouth, and his appetites to himself. He could be friends with a girl, and never let hormones get in the way of a good laugh. The greatest joy in life was to be friends with a good girl, because there was a warmth in that—he knew from experience—no man could offer. There was always a distance, since doors had to be kept shut that were never in question if he was swilling beer and tossing jockey shorts and raunchy jokes about with a squad of half-bombed bozos. That was a good time also. Being with a nice woman was like having a sister. The right chick could be so warm and companionable, as long as each party kept up the fundamental understanding: no touching, no smooching, no falling for the other. It was hard. He'd had a lot of romantic and sensual relationships, but maybe just a half dozen to a dozen close friendships with women over many years. Of those, maybe a third had ended when she moved out of town and lost touch. Another third ended when she'd found Mr. Korrekto for her life. The last third had ended awkwardly in bed and with regrets for various complex, guilty reasons (like with Louise, who was bi, but committed to a relationship with her pastry chef friend Margo, who did not dig guys *at* all and might take a cookie cutter to Rick if further provoked). Takes all kinds to make the world go round, Rick thought. His toleration was global except for dingdongs and dingdongettes.

Marian the Librarian would say maybe to lunch one day, and he could work with that. He wanted to study her, to ask what a girl like her wanted in a man. If they became chums (chum and chumette), he could explain his dilemma and ask her for solid advice. What was Mr. Marian the Librarian like? Did she have any girlfriends who might be available—oh god, or sisters? Was there hope? I have the bagels and the cream cheese, Rick thought, but I am fresh out of lox and looking—trying to keep it casual, without missing any stones that should be turned over, or any hedge under which a worthy Easter egg might be hidden.

She seemed a bit harried today—probably busy with a million tasks. He liked that in a woman—strong, busy, determined, but kind and nurturing without smothering.

He closed his eyes and inhaled the scent of her that remained on the air. Oh God, she was so perfect. Too bad there was a Mr. Marian the Librarian already. Oh, good for her and him. He wouldn't begrudge the lucky pair.

Rick opened his eyes and watched her back receding from him. He took in the swaying sweater and jeans, the bobbing mass of thick hair, and the long arms with those intriguing hands. Her hands had a softness to them, almost a bit of Mediterranean cream color, with a tapering of the fingers rather than boniness, which described her entire figure: sparse but generous, tall but well-proportioned. He watched her elegant stride in those soft boots, and could only imagine her in an elegant gown with high heels.

He glanced across the worn, mostly out of date books and saw nothing that appealed to him. He would have to select something to make it look good. He had come here for a moment of delight, the way a man walking into a garden will stop to smell a single, special flower in the entrance with his eyes closed and an expression of indescribable enjoyment.

The world was filled with tall and short, wide and narrow women in gowns and high heels. Rick Moyer had lived in a world surrounded by such women and their doting fathers and husband-hunting mothers since adolescence. Growing up amid wealth and power, he had been the object of endless advances, sometimes clumsy maneuvers, sometimes clever but cold-hearted stratagems, often brutal and calculating tactics. He had learned to spar with women of all sorts the way you played at judo or jiu-jitsu. Actually, the women he remembered best were the ones who had been more like sisters to him rather than lovers. Yes, he had scored plenty with beautiful and exotic girls and women over the years. He had plenty of notches on his gun. Then again, the debacle with Cindy had proven to him that he had learned virtually nothing about women over all these years.

He sauntered along the aisle, out of Mammals, past Dinosaurs, and crossed the central aisle to Fiction. He felt more at home here in the land of make-believe. He glanced at his watch and realized, also, that he must get back on the road again.

Business was calling, as usual. The movie ran in Rick's head, an endless re-run: Dad's stern eyes and military haircut loomed from behind that desk in West Hartford. *Did you close that deal in Manhattan, son? Why not? Take Geoff with you—he'll line them up before a firing squad if they screw around on us any further. And Mom says not to forget your lunch—there is a boiled egg for you in our fridge, along with an apple juice. Keep up the Vitamin C! Love ya. Now get zipping and zooming! No time to waste. We have a legacy to maintain, and we are always falling behind. Whoosh! Off you go.*

Rick had satisfied the modest desire that had brought him here. He had hoped for nothing more than just to catch sight of her once again, maybe amid scattered children's books and helpful kids, or bent over her carrel sorting books—looking up, surprised, with that blush, that wild look that had drawn him to her in the first place, now several months ago. He had actually spoken with her now for the first time ever. It had seemed fun for a fleeting second, then awkward. He wasn't sure if it was his own clumsiness, his racing pulse and stammering paralysis, that had driven her away from him. It had been a relief to see her hurrying away so that he could take time to collect himself, take a deep breath, and pretend to look for a book.

Here, finally, he picked one. It was a novel titled *The Stars Shine On Us*. Its cover depicted a cowboy--gun and hat and all, leading a horse into a barn. On a fence nearby sat a gorgeous woman with a generous and perfect figure in tight jeans and a leather, fringed top. The cowboy was just tipping his hat to her, with glint in his eyes and a kind of raw, hungry grin. The woman appeared to be applauding with both pale, soft hands in the air, while making an admiring face at him. From the angle of their looks, it was evident the artist meant to portray them at that moment before they ever made significant, romantic eye contact. Aside from the woman's figure, what Rick admired most was the clear, blue country sky and the sun shining over a backdrop of distant trees. Come to think of it, there was kind of an Emery quality about the place. All they needed was a lake, some boats, and a 400 year legacy. Although there was of course at least a 10,000 year legacy across the whole continent if you counted the Native Americans...

As he strode toward the main desk, bemused with such stray thoughts, Rick tossed the cowboy book from hand to hand. He intended to glance inside, but was not sure he'd actually go so far as to read it. He just needed a book as his excuse for coming; almost any book would do. He'd feel awkward leaving here empty-handed.

Silly thought—if she saw him, he did not want her to think he'd been ungrateful for her help. Better to make her feel he'd found what he was looking for.

I found what I was looking for, he thought. She cannot be free. She simply does not have that available air about her. This would be too good to be true. But I can study her. I can see what a woman like that is like up close. She must have a husband, that lucky stiff. Maybe if I can dance around her like a butterfly, I can inhale her scent and figure out how I can find a flower like that of my own.

As he approached the Check Desk, he saw with a mixture of relief and disappointment that this woman Marian Whatever was not there to assist him--Marian the Librarian. Instead, it was the older woman he had previously sparred with. The Chief Librarian had gone back to her office, and at the desk once again sat Rose Otto.

He approached, prepared to do battle, but she smiled at him with a surprising amount of warmth. "Hi," she said as if they knew each other.

Rick was relieved that it was Rose and not Marian. He would be spared the stress of confronting the woman of his dreams (how do you act? how do you not make a fool of yourself?). He was simultaneously disappointed, like a coffee addict who is handed a glass of watery diet lemonade instead. Rose Otto's friendly, humane welcome almost unnerved him.

Rose raised her glance upward as she called into the air: "Marian!"

Was it possible.

Ye-e-e-s-s-s? answered that angelic voice from somewhere in the ether.

"Can you please handle this?" Rose Otto gave Rick a glance as she slid from her high stool. "Excuse me, I have some business in the office." With that, she walked off.

"Hello again," said the divine woman as she appeared from around a corner. She seemed more relaxed. "Are you ready to check out?"

"Please, check me out," Rick said.

She swiped his West Hartford library card without looking up, but with a knowing, chummy glow. "I will check you out," she said. "We go through all the check-out jokes here."

"Your humble servant," he said, with a slight bow.

"I don't know about humble or servant." She typed some clickety-clicks into that great cloud computer in library heaven, which spoke with government computers across the land. Apparently a message came down from the cloud, saying it was okay for Rick to check out a book in Emery Township. Now that she was done with the licensing formalities, Marian pulled his book toward her. She glanced at the cover. "Well, that's a horse book like what you said you were looking for," she said. She peered at it closely, inclining her head so he glimpsed traces of a pale line of her scalp through the dark tangle of hair. She wore a hair clip in the form of a small pink plastic bow on top. Her hair was really thick and unruly, but also glossy and fragrant. He close his eyes and inhaled.

"Wow," she said.

"Wow?"

"That looks like Oklahoma. I grew up there as a child near Shawnee."

"No, I'm sure you are mistaken," Rick said. "It looks a lot like Emery to me. See?" He pointed to the barn. "There is the library." He pointed. "There is me leading my horse in for some oats, and there you are, waving to me. You are checking me out."

She looked at it warmly. "Looks like I am clapping. What did you do to deserve applause?"

"I probably just stayed out of trouble all afternoon."

"Well done, Mr. Moyer. We appreciate that in our customers." She slid the book across the demagnetizer in a practiced motion, then ran it over the checker that emitted a red laser signal to record the transaction as she checked it out for him.

"You can call me Rick if you wish."

She gave him an enigmatic look as she pushed the book toward him. Her mouth was slightly open as if she were about to say something (maybe clever) but nothing came out.

Had he frightened or offended her? Talk about mixed signals. Hot one second, cold the next. He felt his stomach lurch. Had he been too forward? Mortified, he drew back. "Forgive me."

She gave him a frank look, distant but warm, a mixed signal that scared him suddenly. "Come see us again—" (she seemed to struggle with what to say for a second)—"Mr. Moyer." Was that struggle about his name or was it about the 'us' that she really maybe meant to come out as a 'me'? Or not?

Unable to speak, he laid his palm down on the desk for a second, gave her a nod, a hum, and a pair of raised eyebrows, and then he scurried out of the library. He almost tossed the book into the

Return slot, but did it only because he did not want to send any signals, intentional or not, especially not rude ones. Instead, he tossed the book in the trunk of his car and forgot about it.

Pulling out of the library driveway, waiting to find an opening in traffic, he reflected how foolish he was. Inadvertently, was he doing something he never did—flirt with a married woman? Or was there something else going on? Please, send me sanity, he prayed.

It took him a full twenty minutes, driving robotically in heavy traffic, to soothe his ruffled feelings and forgive himself, then to put everything in an acceptable perspective. The empty seats around him seemed to listen sympathetically.

"I screwed up. I probably offended her. No wonder she was stand-offish. Trying to be polite to me while I probably made her squirm with discomfort. I mistook her warm, simple, beautiful nature for a come-on. I am an evil person. She is probably a married woman after all. A happily married woman. No wonder she was looking at me so strangely, and acting so nervously. What a fool I have been again." Then he comforted himself: "She is the kind of woman I would like to meet some day if I ever can trust myself again. I have paid my dues in life." The sting of what had happened with Cindy remained a fresh wound on his soul. "I carry a thick book of Be Silly and Get Out of Jail Free coupons. I am allowed to fumble a bit, as long as my intentions are pure. If I were married, I'd want a wife who is just like her. Generous, warm, dignified, with that kind of superior librarian air about her. I don't want to spend my life with a glamour queen or a high-maintenance society babe. I want to meet a nurse or a librarian. Somebody true blue with a simple life to share. Somebody real. Oh Lord why can I never grow up? Why must the woman I want always be someone out of reach? Why do they have these loyal, home-body Penelope types in these little towns? Maybe I just have to move here to find one like her."

In a way, he felt heartbroken. He'd developed such a crush on her, driven by the library windows so many times, and all for nothing. He said out loud to the empty seats all around him: "Lesson learned. Thou shalt not covet thy neighbor's goodies, just as you don't want him coveting or coming on to your goodies. You know," he told the seats, "I am not a shmoe. I am not the kind of guy who screws around with other men's wives. I have dignity. I have integrity and honor. I will never be stopping in Emery again and bothering that poor woman. What a sap!" He slapped himself hard on the thigh, two or three times until it stung. "I am a idiot. But I learn my lesson and move on in life."

The empty seats around him agreed completely amid the river of passing headlights and taillights as he hove into familiar home territory. Ahead, a rambling house of empty rooms awaited him. He could throw a party and fill it with women. He could splash in the pool with bikinis, dance with gowns, chat with clowns, sip champagne with high heels and lipstick—but he'd done that all his life. It meant nothing to him. There was no *there* there.

It was just elevator music.

8.

Rose Otto, a woman of surprises, had called Marian over to give her a chance to meet him at the Checkout Desk.  Marian could kick herself. She had clutched. There he was, Adonis, and all she had to say was "I have checked you out" (meaning him, not the book) or better yet "I wish you would check me out sometime" but instead her whole head had become one gigantic lisp and no words came out. He looked at her as if she were on fire, and left hurriedly with the book hanging from his thumb and index finger as if it were plague-material.

Rose stepped back up after Mr. Moyer had left, and told Marian: "You scared him off."

"What do you mean?" Marian was baffled. Was this another of Rose's odd mannerisms? Ever since Lillie had broken the ice, and Linda Damien had shown a protective side of Rose, there was a new sense of acceptance about the older librarian. For her part, Rose, somehow, inexplicably, seemed to have grown more sensitive to those around her. It was nothing major or definable, just something subtle and noticeable in the air around Rose. She even seemed to dress in a less dowdy and spinsterish fashion.

"I saw him looking at your hand," Rose said as they stood side by side, passing piles of children's dropped-off books through the checker-inner machine as Lillie called it (who was off from work this evening due to a child emergency, a broken tooth on a playground).

Marian looked at her hand with shock. She touched the gleaming golden-yellow band with the fingers of her other hand. "You mean—?"

"He thinks you are married."

"Oh my god." Of all the things she could say just then (but I am married; I am not married; I am a widow; I cannot bear to part with this ring) she said nothing.

"I don't want you to cry, honey." Rose had a little tremble in her rouged lips. Her glasses looked massive and owlish, like church windows. "If you cry, I'll have to cry with you. It's terrible, I know. It is contagious."

Marian was determined not to cry, but she vividly remembered the events of the day her world had been shattered, so suddenly and cruelly.

She felt the tightness in her chest that she'd become so used to—that cruel, unexpected, very real clutching like a nightmare fist around her heart, which she had gotten that moment which was engraved on her soul the way their names (Tommy & Marian) were engraved inside this ring. A black car with Federal plates had slid into a parking spot before the house. It was odd how they knew to engineer that. Unbeknown to her, 'they' (the dactyls or fingers of Uncle Sam) had contacted the local recruiters, who had many duties besides signing boys like Tommy up for war. The recruiting sergeants looked through their records dating to Tommy's visits to them before he ever left for the induction center far away. He had given his new bride as a point of contact, as well as his parents, her parents (located in distant Oklahoma), and a neighbor lady.

All of a sudden, one morning about eight o'clock, Marian's phone had rung. She was in the middle of ironing her clothes to go to work later that day at the library. It was Annette next door—Annette DeFrancesco, a housewife ten years older than Marian, who worked at a salon as a manicurist, while her husband Rocco worked as a machinist in Waterbury. How odd. "Honey, can you be home for the next hour or so?"

"Sure." Marian felt puzzled. What could this be about? "Is everything okay?"

In retrospect, what could Annette say? Yes? No? "I'm not so sure, hon. Please, this is really really important. I will be over to meet you in a short while. Okay? Give me a few minutes to get my face put on and some decent clothes."

"What is this about?" Marian said. Annette had several children. Was there an emergency? She had babysat the Second Grader, Amy, a few times late afternoons at the library, while Annette or Rocco rushed to pick her up after work. It was all the kind of thing you did in a small town where everyone knew each other.

"Put yourself together and wait for me. I'll be there as soon as I can," Annette said and abruptly hung up. How else could she handle what she must do, and what was coming next?

Marian looked at herself in the mirror. She had showered, and needed to apply a little makeup and comb out her endlessly demanding hair. Without a clue, she changed from her nightgown into a summer dress that happened to be handy, since she didn't have a house coat handy. She pushed her big fuzzy purple slippers under the coffee table and stood bare legged, barefoot, ironing until a frantic rapping came at the door. It was Annette—a dark-haired, small, wiry looking woman with dark eyes and growing jowls in an otherwise still attractive, pleasant face. She was on a cell phone, pushing her way in through the door as Marian held it open. "Yes, yes, she is here." With that, she slipped her cell phone into the pocket of her dark blue, loose house coat. She took Marian's hands in both her hands, and looked into her eyes with a sense of tragedy that suddenly conveyed to Marian that her world had just been destroyed.

Annette could not speak. She simply squeezed Marian's hands, and stood looking into her eyes until her lips started quivering and tears flowed freely down her cheeks, bouncing on her bare neck, on Marian's hands, and on the coffee table nearby.

Overcome with a sense of catastrophic, paralyzing, horrifying dread, Marian began to sob as well. Over Annette's shoulder, she could see Rocco's red pickup truck slamming to a halt against the curb. What was he doing home at this hour? He was a regular man, who was always driving off to work at the machine shop just after six a.m. Rocco, a small, muscular guy with a shock of gray hair, a tough-looking reddish-brown face, very Italian, came jogging up the lawn toward Marian's open door. Annette had called him home from work that day to help her help Marian. Rocco was a decorated U.S. Marine Corps veteran himself.

By now, Marian's legs had grown weak. The air around her head seemed hard to breathe. Annette took her by one hand, while Rocco put an arm behind her back to steady her. They led her from the back door to the front door, where she could see—through the big window left of the door—the Federal sedan that pulled up. There were three men in it, all in uniform. One was the recruiter sergeant who had signed Tommy up. He was driving, and stayed in the car. From the front passenger seat, an older Army Reserve sergeant with much gold on his dark uniform sleeves stepped out. He held the rear door open for a tall, grizzled old colonel, also in dark dress blues, who stepped out. They looked very grim as they walked up the driveway and rang the door bell.

At the sight of the sergeant holding the door open for the officer,

Marian *knew*.

Before they reached the door, she turned her head toward heaven and emitted a wail of sorrow and pain that must have echoed through the neighborhood. Her legs gave out and she fell over backwards into darkness. Rocco caught her, she was later told, and together with Annette laid her down on the living room couch.

Annette opened the door.

The men stepped into the small house, respectfully removing their saucer caps and putting them under their elbows. Each wore white gloves. Their trousers were knife-creased. Their black shoes gleamed as if they had lights inside.

Marian refused to be seen lying down. She stood erect, but not at attention. Through the haze of shock, she balled her fists at her thighs, and hollered hoarsely, over and over again: "No. No-o. No-o-o…" until her voice broke and she sat down abruptly as if all the energy and tension had gone out of her body. She felt as if she were made of numb, unfeeling rubber.

She heard the colonel's voice—sharp as a cutting knife, hard as a flint grind stone—say: "Mrs. Thomas Charles, it is my deepest sorrow and regret to inform you that your husband, Sergeant Thomas Charles, has died in the service of our country. He was killed in action near…" He mentioned some forsaken road stop on the other side of the earth, went on to say a lot more words that made no sense after that. Marian sat like a rock letting it all wash over her. Annette sat beside her, and took her in her arms, and Marian cried heartbrokenly on Annette's breast. Big cries, big sobs, like she had not felt since she was a little girl, from deep in her convulsing gut; her cries just went on and on while the men waited silently like broken statues.

Later, the colonel sat beside her and held her hands. "I was a field commander once in battle, and held more than one brave young man while he died. Your husband passed away surrounded by his comrades, who were able to comfort him. He was unable to speak, but they say he showed them his wedding ring." He reached into his inside jacket pocket and took out a plain sandwich baggie, in which was Tommy's wedding ring. "We have other effects in the car for you. There will be a special service with an honor guard at Arlington…"

Back to reality: "If you are going to cry," Rose Otto said in her usual direct but sincere manner, I will cover for you here at the desk for as long as you need me to. You can go into Linda's office."

"I am not going to cry," Marian said in a very small, quiet voice. "I have cried enough. Thanks though, Rose."

Rose opened up for the first time. She took Marian's hands into her own. "I was married once, long ago, myself. It isn't the same thing, but I just want you to know that I feel for you, hon. I made a bad choice, like I often do, and married a man who drank and hit me. He could be quite pleasant when he was sober, but he drank more and more and got more abusive. Finally, one day, someone came to the office where I worked—that was the water company office downtown—and told me they had found him in the park. He took his gun there with him, and shot himself in the head. He died instantly. I don't mean to say it's the same—"

Marian gave Rose's hands a shake. "No, it is something terrible that happened to you in your life. I understand. I had no idea because you are always such a mouse about things."

"I don't like to talk about it," Rose said in her bland, ever surprised looking manner. "I can't." She suddenly started crying. "It makes me cry."

Marian held Rose, and rubbed her back while Rose cried. Marian saw that Rose would never heal from the things that had happened to her. Marian just as instantly understood that she herself was going to grow beyond her sorrows and start a new life. Poor broken Rose. But...

Later, Marian did cry a little bit in the bathroom, alone and privately. She washed her face and put on fresh makeup. Then she slid the ring off her finger and thought about where to put it. She held the ring in her hands, bouncing it lightly on one palm, like the precious relic it was. She must not make this mistake again. She stared at it, kissing it several times. It gleamed yellow-golden on her palm. "I love you, Tommy. I will love you forever."

At last, she opened her purse, which had among its compartments a little leather change pocket, which had a nice secure zipper. She put the ring in there beside Tommy's ring, which she had been carrying with her all along. On her lunch break, she walked three blocks down along the main street to the bank, and rented a safety deposit box.

"What size would you like?" asked the dapper little old bank manager in a gray suit and pink tie, who was the. He had a kindly manner about him, and a patient air.

"The smallest one you've got," Marian said. "I don't have anything big to put in it."

"Must be very important," he said with a sober, respectful attitude. He must have sensed the air of gravity about her.

"Yes. Here." She reached into her purse and handed him the two rings.

Just my heart, she thought.

Winter

9

Richard Moyer became very busy, and very frazzled over the next few weeks. He forgot all about the library book, although he drove through Emery Township on the thruway at least once a week. Each time, he would dutifully take the exit ramp onto the frontage road, and drive slowly past the library.

Once or twice, he thought about stopping in, but reconsidered. She appeared to be married or otherwise spoken for, and he had no business flirting with her or courting her. With all the stress going on right now, he had best let that all cool off for a while.

Mom was seeing a doctor about a possible cancer scare. Her liver was waving for help after years of quiet Chablis. Dad was on his high horse, trying to settle two huge estates in Pennsylvania, so he was throwing Rick at one and Geoff at the other, while working himself to death eighteen hours a day behind that desk of his in West Hartford.

Rick had been doing penance now for how many years? He slammed the stick shift of the car through its gears, and ground his teeth as he thought about it. *Where am I?*

He couldn't help it. Dad controlled the finances. Rick earned a relatively modest salary, although he had a corporate expense account equal to his salary, so he really had a lot of income to play with. But Dad was of the school that you plowed everything back into the business, so there was a floor (rather low) above which Dad reviewed Rick's expenses with a green eye shade, so to speak. It was rather humiliating. Rick understood enough about business to start his own firm, toss the old man overboard, and kiss Moyer LX Holdings goodbye. It was very tempting to do so. His parents were wonderful and loving people, but severe and smothering. With the snap of a finger, Rick could walk and probably be a millionaire in his own right within a year, year and a half. He had enough connections of his own to do deals without bumping the old man. What kept him in this harness was pure loyalty. He felt obligated to his mother, to his father, and to the firm that represented over century of family endeavor. It was a legacy. Also, to be brutally honest with himself, Dad was going to retire in about ten years if he did not drop from a heart attack or a stroke first. He was already on blood pressure medications, and borderline diabetic. The stress of running a tight ship would take a toll. Rick wanted to be more helpful, but the old man was a control freak.

Filled with anger and frustration, Rick drove between the City and Hartford or Boston many a day, listening to overly loud music on the car stereo and trying to put off the fact that he was increasingly doubtful he could stand waiting. He was becoming more and more tempted to chuck it. He was not sure his parents would ever forgive him. Things would not be the same again, for sure. And yet how could he go on being a trainee, more or less? He'd soon be in his mid 30s. This other old guy, Geoff, was being groomed for some role that Dad had not made entirely clear. That was the other huge, frustrating factor. Rick had no doubt that he would inherit the firm, and control over it. The assumption was that he would take his father's place one day. But when, and under what circumstances? He had no idea what his father had in mind. Until that became clear, Rick was living in limbo. He did not lack for a fine car, the best suits, or a nice home. It was all good for business—no questions asked. If he decided to take a two week vacation and go surfing in Hawaii or sailing in the Bahamas, the old man would be all over him. Money and time wasted. *Gaaaad!*

Rick almost side swiped a Greyhound bus pulling up from the entrance ramp near Meriden as he was ready to tear his hair out, thinking about all this. He felt tears of rage and frustration welling up in his eyes at the thought of how badly his marriage had turned out, and how his old man was treating him like a kid, and how his love life consisted of elevator music dates and a crush on a married chick in a small town library.

Recovering, he swerved to avoid the bus, whose driver emitted a long, angry blare of the horns behind Rick as dusk fell on the busy highway.

Although he knew the near accident would have been his fault, Rick made a frustrated gesture to the rear window. It was something he'd learned years ago while on vacation in Santiago, Chile. It was the open palm, held face up as if containing a large object. These are your *cojones, amigo*—very large.

Actually, the gesture was as much meant for Moyer LX Holdings and its Chief Executive (Mister Daddy-O) as much as for the poor bus driver, who probably figured who is this gadzook tearing around in the Jaguar?

Over the next few weeks, Rick got his deal done, and Geoff got his in the bag. They reported back to Captain Bligh and were put back in their eternal holding pattern under Dad's controlling hand. Rick could see the questioning and confusion growing in Geoff's eyes. He had a feeling Geoff was starting to look around for a better position. He couldn't blame him.

Amid all this, time fled by, and Rick did not see his librarian angel again for a few weeks.

Thanksgiving came and went, with all the obligatory office parties and family get-togethers. The Moyers were a small clan, and did little partying at home. Rick's sister flew out with her husband because of the diplomatic reason that, if they visited her family in West Hartford for Thanksgiving, as the holiday season launched, they could spend Christmas in Santa Barbara, California with his family. Rick's sister had married into Chicago money, and Rick's brother-in-law by now had set up a corporation in Santa Barbara. Rick had never been as close to his sister as he might have liked, and accepted the terms of this strange arrangement. He only hoped it gave his parents pause for thinking about their priorities in life.

The season's first snow fell, a light dusting that was quickly churned into mud by thousands of automobile tires in the city and on the freeways. The lights looked pretty at night, especially the colored lights of Christmas. On New Year's Eve, Rick attended a company bash in Boston, paid for by his father, and attended by some of the bright young investors whose every waking (and maybe sleeping) moment was dedicated to the glory of their personal aggrandizement. Rick cautioned himself not to be too cynical, since he already had his personal nest egg, handed down through generations of Moyers, and could afford to float around in the ether of Abraham Maslow's 1943 Hierarchy of Needs at the fifth and highest level of self-actualization: the spiritual, at which all of a person's more earthly needs had already been satisfied. Most of the strivers around him at the costly party in Boston would go on to greater wealth, because Dad had chosen them carefully like the great Gatsby bringing people to his parties on Long Island. The difference was that the Gat in Gatsby most likely referred to a Gat, which was slang for a gun, and Fitzgerald's desperately phony, sad character had been modeled on a gangster (Rick's theory about this, on which he'd written an A+ paper in college English)—whereas

Dad was the most up-and-up, straight-arrow, Eagle Scout guy Rick knew, and the attendees in Boston had been carefully vetted by the near apoplectic man trapped so painfully and hyper-diastolically at his desk.

The holidays passed tolerably. Rick made all the prescribed stops, and saw a few women. Actually, he was selective and only dated two or three old friends.

One was a high school classmate from long ago, who was separated from her husband and not available but good for lunch and some hearty laughs.

Likewise, he spent a day in Manhattan with an old college friend who had been the girlfriend of a girl he had dated during junior year—more for old times' sake than anything else; with a promise to visit each other again someday, all very cordial, but no commitment even on when that might be.

Last, he'd actually dated a Japanese-American cellist who was doing her Ph.D. work at the University of Connecticut. It had been a bland, forgettable date, though they'd shared a glass of wine, and he'd listened to her playing some adagios in a key of blah.

Taking nothing away from the woman's talent or beauty, he'd been glad to drive back from the main Storrs campus on I-84, feeling unfulfilled and in need of a cold shower. And a hot toddy. And an hour or two throwing darts in a dark dive of a corner bar while pool balls clicked in a nearby corner, and down to earth people dropped quarters in a juke box full of old rock hits.

January arrived—unseasonably warm and rainy. It looked to be a mild, boring winter, which was fine if you spent zillions of hours driving in your car on crowded turnpikes. Emery became a memory.

The book with the cowboy and the girl on the rail lay forgotten in the trunk of Rick's car.

As the days ticked by, and the book lay in the darkness next to the spare tire, its license expired, and the Emery Township Free Public Library—as promised—was organizing a Ninja assassination squad to find the missing Mr. Moyer, waterboard him, and then return him face-down and hog-tied on a horse along with the stolen manuscript, to be delivered to Mrs. Otter, who no doubt kept looking out the window of the library at the traffic and wondering where her novel had been hijacked to.

Had Rick remembered the book (he later thought), it might have occurred to him in his most dismal nightmares that the girl on the cover had stopped clapping, gotten off the fence rail, and walked away in a huff.

Actually, things were not about to happen in quite that manner. But the book was to precipitate a crisis within Moyer LX Holdings—and in Rick Moyer's life.

It was something with which neither Mrs. Chicken nor Marian the Librarian would have anything to do.

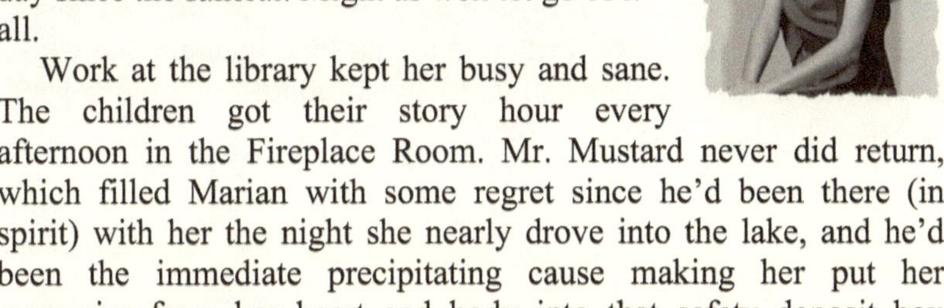

10

Marian had Saturday off, a few days after opening her bank safety box account. She had left her rings there, as well as the black ribbon she had worn every day since the funeral. Might as well let go of it all.

Work at the library kept her busy and sane. The children got their story hour every afternoon in the Fireplace Room. Mr. Mustard never did return, which filled Marian with some regret since he'd been there (in spirit) with her the night she nearly drove into the lake, and he'd been the immediate precipitating cause making her put her memories from her heart and body into that safety deposit box instead. Life went on. Marian often sighed.

It rained a lot that January. There was a light dusting of snow, which stayed longer in the chill, windy valley but turned to slush as it fell on the thruway. As always, the library glowed like a lantern along the road, and she hoped maybe her new friend would stop in again sometime. She thought about how she was the girl on the fence, clapping, and he was the cowboy leading the horse into the barn. She smiled to herself at how she had checked him out. Now where was the book? He'd better come back soon and check the book in and maybe check her out. She was ready and waiting, though the idea of making such a break from her past scared—no, petrified—her.

She slept in, went out for lox bagels and cream cheese, had coffee and read the morning news on her tablet, ran some errands in town—down by the lake—and returned home just as the mail truck was pulling away down the block. That meant the mail lady had already been by, so Marian checked the mail on her way up the driveway to the front door of the little house she and Tommy had bought, it seemed just months ago.

She rifled through the bills and advertisements, separating two or three items that deserved an immediate look. One of them was an odd piece of mail that she at first thought to discard. It was from an unknown sender, out of state, with pretty letterhead. The Farmouth Company. Never heard of it. Probably an advert. She was going to toss it aside, but noticed the expensive First Class stamp. It could not be some ordinary promo thing. She sliced it open and unfolded a single sheet of expensive letterhead. She stopped before the house and almost forgot for a moment to unlock the door.

A photograph fell out and dropped onto the flagstones amid moss and stray bits of grass. She bent down to pick up the little three by three photo—and saw with a shock that it was of her, taken by Tommy's aunt somebody at a party about two years ago. How much younger I look, she thought. How innocent, and proud, and happy, and naive. The letter was written in a light blue fountain pen with a few little ink spatters here and there. It was addressed, in long hand, to Mrs. Thomas Charles, and read:

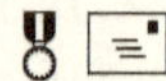

Dear Mrs. Charles:

My name is Ernest Farmouth, of Islin, Nebraska. I hope I have the right Marian Charles here. If not, please forgive my error, but please call me collect to let me know so that I can locate the widow of my former service mate, Tommy Charles.

I never met you, Marian, but Tommy always carried your picture and always talked about you. We single guys in the outfit were impressed and jealous. In a strange kind of way, those of us who were not married, and did not have a steady girl back home, we all felt like we were sort of married to you.

I hope you do not find that offensive. I only mean to say that when things got rough, and it was pretty tough at times, you were one of the things that kept us going. Maybe you were like a sister or an aunt to us, I don't know. You were there when it was raining bullets and bombs, or when it was hot along the road and we were kind of scared and nervous. You were there with us when we went to sleep at night, and when we woke up for yet another desert morning.

When Tommy took the IED, and I am sure you know all about it at this point so I am hopefully not being indelicate, he handed me that photo of you. I never thought about it until I returned home just a few months ago, and went to work at my father's accounting firm.

I'm doing okay now, made my high school sweetheart my fiancé, and we're getting married soon. I lost my left leg, but you get on the winning side if you figure out how to get past things, pick yourself up, and move on ahead with life. It's nice for me because I have a strong woman by my side. She keeps me going when I want to give up, which is no longer so often because I don't want to let her down.

I have a photo of my fiancé with me now, and it occurred to me that sending you this would be more like sending you something of Tommy, rather than just sending you a picture of yourself. I hope you understand what I mean. My fiancé read this letter and promised me you would not be offended by anything I say. I did want to say thank you for being there with us out in the field and taking heat with us, just like you were there in person rather than this beautiful photo.

Tommy loved you with all his heart, and actually all the guys in my squad did. I am not the best writer in the world. My fiancé helped me. But I wanted to tell you that Tommy died in my arms, and we both said your name together. It was the last thing he ever said—your name. He smiled a little, although a dying man's face goes through some changes. Forgive me, I am so sorry, but I thought you would want to know the exact truth, just like it was, because you surely deserve to know exactly how it went down.

We had some anesthetics with us, and a medic arrived soon after the IED went off. I don't think Tommy suffered more than he had to, and I held him the whole time. That is something I will live with for the rest of my life. I wish it could be a better memory, but it could be worse. I thought you deserved to know the exact truth.

If you ever need anything—no matter what—please contact me or my fiancé Theresa Skybow.

Yours Truly, Ernest Farmouth.

Marian resolved to read the letter many more times, but not more than once a week. Maybe one day it would be once a month, or once a year. Then it would migrate to her bank deposit box. Or maybe by then she would be able to keep the rings and the letter in the house with her. Maybe, nor maybe not. Like Ernest Farmouth would forever carry his memories with him, so would she. Ernest had moved on with life, and was settling accounts, like writing this letter that had to be sent.

She wrote him a brief, heart-felt letter in reply, saying she hoped they would meet someday, and thanking him for the information about those boys she had never met. She hoped she had been of some comfort to them, and that they all got home okay to their loved ones. She was sure Tommy would have wished that for them also.

She went outside with a glass of lemonade, and sat for a long time amid the weed field that Tommy's beautifully kept lawn had turned into. She thought about everything, and realized that the old adage was true. As many doors as close in your life, so many new doors open ahead of you. The world was full of men needing a woman, and she imagined that maybe somewhere out there was a man who would not take Tommy's place, but surprise her. That man, if he existed, and if she found him, might just open a new world of unexpected joys and pleasures for her. She would surely love him to pieces and take good care of him. She did not cry as she sat there holding her frosty glass of lemonade, twirling it slowly and pensively in her fingers, while her bare feet ached on the sun parched stubble of the dead lawn.

She still wore the fine, gold filigree anklet Tommy had given her on her 24th birthday, just before shipping out. It looked pretty on one tanned, bony ankle. He said it was very sexy. She wiggled her toes, and thought she must get down to see Annette at the beauty parlor. She decided on a bubble gum pink toenail color for herself. Her chest was not tight, and she did not cry.

She briefly thought of the beautiful man who had come to the library. What was his name? Rick Mustard or something.

Would she ever meet a guy like that for real? And would he be real? She wondered what had become of Rick Meister.

Probably going through women like a cake cutter through devil's food, with those smoldering looks, that boyish air needing rescue, offset by that master of the universe attitude, that gray suit and those quadzillions of dollars he probably had in his bank account.

Speaking of Mustards of the Universe, she imagined herself pretending she was he, speaking in a deep like voice (woman imitating man's voice, with chin pulled close to chest and big comical eyes): "I have come to buy your library and all the buildings around it. You can keep the coloring books if you want, but I'm going keep to the rest."

She imagined herself rubbing her hands together and cackling like a dark mage: "Bwoo-haw-hah-haw!"

She laughed quietly at herself. Time for a glass of wine. Maybe she would call up one of Tommy's girl cousins and see if they could go to a dance place that evening.

It had been a long time.

She was turning in to a real recluse.

Time to get out of the cave and back into the sunshine. Tommy would want this for her.

On her way to work, she stopped at the bank.

There, she added the letter from Tommy's comrade to the contents of her heart in that little safety deposit box.

11

Rick Moyer sat in a conference room high above Manhattan. He was looking downtown, toward the Empire State Building and the new World Trade Center, among masses of tall and taller buildings making a gray field under miles of scudding clouds. It was nine a.m. on a rainy day, the kind where you want to be indoors. At least they had a little heat going in this otherwise chilly conference room. Even so, Rick had his tan raincoat with dangling buckles draped over his shoulders as he sat in the high-backed luxury office chair someone had borrowed from Mahogany Row, now a ghost town down the hall.

It was February—a month not of snow and freezing cold, as was traditional, but of huge charcoal clouds floating across the Manhattan skies like battleships, and of tidal seas of rain and drizzle that rattled and pressed ominously against thick plate glass windows far above the city streets. Way down there, where pedestrians and their umbrellas looked ant-like, and the usual rivers of yellow taxis flowed, street lights seemed to glow day and night. People with money had long since left for vacations in Florida, Los Angeles, Barbados, Australia, Ibiza—you name it. Only Rick Moyer (so he felt at odd moments) was stuck here with a leaky pen, reading coffee-stained contracts written by Lilliputians in microscopic ink scratches.

A secretary brought a new stack of papers to be signed and examined.

Rick joked: "We should just weigh them by the pound."

"That would make our lives easier," the woman agreed. She left them by his side on the gleaming mahogany desk top. She was a tall, pretty lady—with a wedding ring, of course. "Can I get you some tea or coffee, Mr. Moyer?"

He smiled. "If you had a donut, I would rejoice. Thanks, Agatha."

The woman named smiled back, her face crowned in blonde ringlets. "I think I might be able to arrange something in a jelly donut." She was the host business owner's executive assistant, a stylish New York City woman in her late thirties. As in Paris, Milan, or London, Rick noted, women working and living in a fashion center managed somehow to acquire a higher taste in clothing and makeup. Her hair style was perfect for her. Without makeup, she might be an average looker in small town USA, but here in the Massive Mackintosh she was a looker wearing hot-magazine jewelry and clothing right off the fashion runway.

"Raspberry."

"Sorry. Grape." She was diplomatic, too.

"Grape is my favorite."

"You are so diplomatic. No wonder you do such big deals."

"In my heart I wanted grape. It just seemed like such an impossible thing to wish for that I didn't bother trying, so I merely hoped for raspberry, thinking it would be easier for you. My heart was with grape."

"If you want something, you have to ask for it, I always say." She opened the documents to the marked pages and made sure he had a working pen. "Did you say coffee?"

"I think I am in a tea mood." He took out reading glasses. The light in here was a bit dim and yellowish. He put on the glasses, which had dark-brown horn rims and made him look intellectual. The light reminded him of something. Home. He wasn't sure what. He was about to sign the papers for a ten million dollar merger, in which Moyer LX Holding would acquire two underperforming mutual funds that were all that was left of an otherwise gutted and bankrupt firm. The firm's proxy board members had been in the office, agreed to Rick's reasonably generous terms—since the principals had been indicted after running their firm into the ground. Everyone would walk away with a piece of something, even the two executives now serving time and wearing khaki prison garb to better mop the halls of Sing-Sing with. The light reminded him of the library in Emery. He would drive by there later today, yearning for its lantern comfort, and the Vestals inside, who languidly tended to its sacred mysteries. He did not relish the long drive home, during which he would again have occasion to resent Dad and his life. Which was unfair, and he knew he'd have to make a confrontation about it soon or do something crazy like take up bungee-jumping off the Empire State Building with a paragliding kit. Or tearing all his clothes off and running down the street screaming until the police captured him with a big butterfly net and locked him up for his own safety.

"I'll bring you a fresh pot."

"I think I saw a nice Irish breakfast tea out there on the table, with a little lemon and sugar please."

"You don't miss a thing," the secretary said with that cheerful glow.

Rick watched her sway from the room, admiring her shapely figure in the black and white speckled wool dress, along with her dark nylons and black high heels. So many women in the world, so many satisfied men. He shook his head, picked up the pen, and turned his attention to the misery before him. Not that making money was misery, just that it was—well, again—elevator music if you had nobody real and solid to share a dreary Saturday afternoon at home with over popcorn and beer, a ball game on TV, and maybe a blanket big enough for two.

Inside Rick's jacket, his cell phone made a noise. He had it programmed to make a rather professional, but still fun, ringing noise like an old fashioned phone. Sometimes when he was free on a weekend, out and about in his shorts and sandals, maybe sailing on Long Island Sound, or jetting up to Montreal for a good theater in the Old City, he changed the ring tone to his favorite: a woman yodeling. But not now. Not here.

"This is Rick Moyer," he said in a businesslike manner.

"Mr. Moyer," said a woman's voice full of laughter and sunshine.

"Yes? No lemons?" It had to be the woman with the curly ringlets.

"Wha-a-a-?"

"I'm sorry. Is this Agatha? Is there tea?"

"There is no tea, but I want to know where you are keeping the book."

"I am sorry. This must be a wrong number." If it were a guy, he would have hung up already or thrown the phone across the room into that trashcan in the corner by the window overlooking the Chrysler Building. Something about that voice made him keep the phone cocked to one ear. As he did so, Agatha entered—pushing the door open with that delightful rear end—carrying a tray with delicious looking things on it. The woman on the phone was therefore not Agatha, unless Agatha had a twin sister or some crazy thing.

"Am I speaking with Mr. Richard Moyer?"

"Yes?" He felt puzzled while Agatha poured tea and fussed about him with crumpets, butter, jelly, and what not. He nodded thanks, brightly, Agatha made a saluting motion with bright blue eyes as she left the room to let him sign all the legal trash.

"You probably do not remember me—the pesky librarian from Emery."

"Oh, Mrs. Otter. How are you and all the little otters?"

"Not Mrs. Otto. This is Marian McLaughlin."

As he stirred sugar into his tea, he said: "You know, I am confused, frightened, and puzzled. I have no idea who you are. From England?"

"Emery."

"We must have a bad connection. Are you calling from underwater?"

"Yes, I am in a submarine off New York City."

He was beginning to recognize the voice, and filled inwardly with delight, but he kept up the banter. Was it possible? The married woman he had flirted with? Surely this was just all a silly, funny, pleasant little joke. She had liked him after all, and didn't hate him for being a flirtatious, inconsiderate cad. Now he realized what the cozy, wan light reminded him of—libraries everywhere, in his home town growing up, or in Emery Township where the cars flew by without ever stopping to smell the roses or check out a book.

"The compartments are flooding, so I must swim to the surface."

"Those must be bubbles I hear. That's why we have a poor connection."

"And the porpoises playing saxophone nearby."

"Yes. Marian, is this you?"

"You remembered my name."

"How could I forget? I was so embarrassed."

"I know why you are embarrassed." She managed somehow to seem like she was sitting next to him. How did she do that?

"The ring."

"It never occurred to me you saw it. Rose Otto told me. She saw us talking."

"When I saw that ring on your paw, I could have crawled under the Help Desk and died."

"You poor man."

"It's a good thing I didn't have a baseball bat, or I would have beaten myself unconscious."

"Well, I called about my book."

"What book?"

"The cowboy and the chick on the rail. You know. *The Stars Shine On Us, by Ruff MacDuff* or somebody."

"Oh my god in heaven. I screwed up again. It's in the trunk of my car, sitting in a parking lot right here in Manhattan."

"You can drop it off on your way home."

"And your husband? Small detail."

"I never thought to explain to you—I am a widow."

Rick was stunned. He felt as if a hard, cold fist had just tightened around his heart. After a shocked pause, he said:

"I am so sorry."

"Naw," she said with a philosophical, accepting little chuckle, "It's my life. Or was. Or is."

"I am so sorry if I offended you in any way."

"Offended me? I was hoping you'd stop back and check your book in and check me out."

He felt tongue-tied. Before he could speak, she said:

"I like you, Mr. Moyer. No need to feel sorry."

"I like you too."

"Mind if I call you Richard?"

"Rick. No. Yes. Call me anything, but call me. Please."

She laughed. The last ice had been broken. "I am calling you, am I not?"

"Oh my god. You are. And here I am."

"There you are."

"Marian, I feel like—Christmas all over again."

"Me too. I have to confess. The book thing is real. You are in huge trouble here in Emery. But I wanted to take the excuse to hear your voice again."

"Oh my god." He felt helpless and terrified—could this be a dream, a delusion, a sign of impending insanity? Had the stress flipped his wig for him?

"I'll make a deal with you if you are interested."

Rick patted the multi-million dollar package before him with his palm. "I am pretty good at deals."

"I am sure you are." There was sunshine in her voice.

He said: "I have a ten inch packet of contracts, worth zillions of dollars, sitting here awaiting my signature. Somehow, Marian, I have a feeling you can trump that."

She laughed. "Oh, I don't know. I was just going to say that you could bring that book back. It's overdue and the fine is up to twelve dollars by now. So I was going to suggest that we go out for dinner when you drop the book off. I thought I would offer to reduce the fine to, oh, say fifty cents, and you could treat me to a burger and fries—unless it's not payday yet. If you are broke, I'll just steal the money from the small change here by the used book sale."

"You are a wheeler and dealer at heart, Marian. Were you always Marian, or did you change your name when you went to work at the library?"

"Always Marian—maiden name McLaughlin, as in you funny man and you always keep me a-loffin."

"I am sure you did not just make that joke up."

"No. Kids used to tease me in Kindergarten. McLaughlin?"

"I get it, Marian. They are ruthless, those Kindergarteners."

"That wasn't half so bad. We had a girl named Lifshitz. You can imagine what they said to her."

"I dare not think of it. Hey, so it's like 9:30 a.m."

"You usually come by late in the afternoon."

"It's been a long time."

"You thought I was married and you were mortified. Aw."

"I must confess. Yes. I do not mess with ladies who are married or otherwise spoken for."

"You are a shining knight. I'll save my appetite if you are interested in my offer."

"Your offer is the most exciting thing that's happened to me all day."

"And your zillion dollar doo-hickey?"

"This is just paper. That is coins, real money, that you have there. Look, don't steal the kitty. I'll pay my fine, since I am a good resident of Emery."

"But not a soul dwelling here."

"That was Rose's gig."

"Poor thing. She has had a hard life, but she means well. She set us up, you know."

"Really?" He raised his chin and imitated Rose's holler: "Marian!"

"*Ye-e-e-s-s?*" she imitated herself right back, in that same ghostly wail he had heard in the library.

"Ah, that voice floating in from the stacks. Okay, so if you could be there, we'll be square."

"I will wait for you by the entrance if it's late."

"Keep the lamp on for me."

"Mm?"

"The lamp of your soul. Light my way."

"Bring the book, cowboy."

"Wait on the fence for me."

"You picked that particular novel to send me a message."

"Busted."

"I will be clapping my paws as you drive up."

"Will you check me out?"

"Only if you promise to check me out first."

"I can't wait."

Suddenly, the banter ended. After a moment's silence, she hung up as if some other, dark emotions had gotten the better of her. Rick knew by now that he had not once again said or done the wrong thing. She was trying to hard, and she was so shy. She'd had a panic attack—he could tell.

12

D id you call him about the book?" Rose Otto asked as Marian hung up the phone.

The two women talked while working at the desk, sorting library overdue entries on the computer system, in preparation for sending out the latest crop of notices.

"Yes." Marian raised both hands as in What Have I Done, and rested her forehead in her palms.

Rose's small, pinched face did not show a variety of emotions too well, especially behind her gigantic, pink-rimmed glasses. "And you are so happy."

Marian had not realized Rose could be capable of sarcasm.

"Have courage," Rose said dryly. "Turn into the waves."

"He is coming to take me to dinner."

"And you look like you are DNR, end-of-life."

"No, I am starting a new life, and I will insist on being resuscitated. Specifically, by Mr. Moyer. We are having dinner."

"No!" Rose breathed.

"Yes. I hope to live at least long enough for desert."

"You deserve somebody nice," Rose said. "Just make sure he is not a gondolier."

"You sound like Lillie. What is a gondolier?"

"A man who puts your heart in a gondola and paddles around with you until you get sea-sick and it falls in the canal."

"You have been to Venice." It was a question.

"No, but I have fallen in the canal. Not recently, but I was a wild chick long ago. I know, it seems hard to believe."

Marian did not have the heart to ask if that was before or after her tragic marriage. "You were a hippie?"

"I am that old, yes."

"Now, Rose. You are young enough to remember."

"That makes absolutely no sense, but I'll buy it." Rose managed that elusive little smile again. "I had my share of flings, plus five years of hell. I mean being married. I dated after that, but it was never the same again." She removed her glasses with a flourish and looked at Marian with a kind of palsied shaking that suggested she was about to say something very weighty, or start crying, or both. "Honey, you are still young and you have it all in front of you. Don't waste your life away grieving. Get over it."

"I am making progress, Rose. Thank you."

Rose was still shaking. "I grieved over that no good so and so for years. I don't know why. He hit me whenever he was drinking. He was passable when he was sober. But he drank more and more as time went by, so you know where that all goes."

Coincidentally, later that day, Marian happened to encounter Linda Damien, the Chief Librarian, in the break room. Rose had gone to lunch.

"Yes," Linda said, "Rose has had a difficult life. She is fragile, and I like to keep her under my wing."

"You think my being young has brought back memories for her?"

Linda nodded. "I think so. She has been opening up a lot more. I have had a lot of young women working here over the years. None of them has ever had quite the effect on Rose that you have. Or wait a minute—that playboy who came here asking about dinosaur books. I hope you realize that was just an excuse by him to see you."

"It never dawned on me." Now she was being sarcastic. Thanks, Rose.

"I've been around the block more than my share of times in life. You're young. It's all kind of predictable."

"You think he is a playboy?"

"He is handsome, rich, cocky, and a bit boyish. I would say—if I were your age, and single, and had the nerves of steel a young woman has, like one of those Indians that can walk on girders a hundred stories up without any ropes or safety nets—I would say I might be tempted to go out to play with him. Or if I had any common sense, I might be inclined to grab my skirt with both hands and run for my life."

"I don't know how much common sense I have right now. I think my supply is low."

"Your supply will fill back up, don't worry. At your age, that's what life is all about. Taking chances." She patted Marian's wrist several times with one hand. "You know we are all rooting for you."

They were alone in the break room. Linda was having a plum

yoghurt from a container, with a plastic ice cream spoon, and drinking tea. Marian had made herself a strong cup of French roast, and was eating a package of cookies from a vending machine.

Marian had never opened up so much with her boss, although they had always been on friendly terms. But Linda Damien was like that with all her employees. Now Marian felt as if she had gained another friend. "I love working here. I like the steady pace, the nice people, the books…"

"You don't miss Oklahoma or California?"

Marian shook her head. "You know…it's like this. I came here, in love with Tommy, and fell in love with this place. It's such a wonderful little town. So close to New York City, Boston, Montreal, the Atlantic coast…and yet such a little hideaway."

"It's a little heartland place," Linda agreed. "I have lived here for thirty years. Came here from the boonies in upstate New York when I married my husband. He passed away from a heart attack two years ago. I transferred here from the high school library soon after to become Chief Librarian. The move helped me get over it and continue on with life."

"So you are a widow too." Marian had known this about Linda, but only in a distant way.

"Oh yeah. It never goes away. But life goes on. The train leaves the station, and you better be on it. So we move to the next adventure."

"Are you still—alone?"

Linda nodded. "Yep. I am dating a professor in New Haven, and having a nice time. I have kids, he has kids, they all get along fine, and we sometimes think about making it a permanent party. We're in no rush. The chance to really be with someone comes rarely in life. If you have that bird in hand, go for it."

"And if it's a mistake?"

Linda laughed out loud. "Just don't sign any papers or get pregnant. Take your time."

"That's it in a nutshell," Marian said quietly.

"Roll the dice," Linda said. She added: "Just keep your car outside with the motor running, in case."

"In case he turns out to be a gondolier, this Moyer."

"What-*evvah!*" Linda said in New York City dialect.

"I must be out of my mind, but I think I can do this. Unless I get all nervous again, and can't talk, so he thinks I'm an idiot."

"If that happens, just pretend you are thinking really important thoughts. I know a trick.”

"What's that?”

Linda held up one finger, with the pad of the tip pointing toward Marian.

"Huh?”

"That's what I mean. It's a trick I learned. If you are baffled, just hold up your finger. It makes the other person shut up, and they think you are having a brilliant brainstorm. You're waiting for the whole brainstorm to download, and you can't talk at the moment. They will wait for you to tell them. Then you look away suddenly, like it's a secret and you can't tell them or you'd have to kill them. You can kill several minutes that way, save yourself from paralysis, and distract him from whatever he was saying that made you choke up in the first place.”

"And never make eye contact,” Marian improvised. “Or you burst out laughing and spoil the whole thing.” *And don't lithp*, she secretly reminded the little girl inside her.

"You got it.” Linda waved the little plastic spoon. She had yoghurt and plum on her upper lip. “See, you are an expert at it already.”

Afeeling of desperation suddenly grew upon Rick Moyer. The day would be over before he could get away here—and he would fail to show up for his very first date with Miss Wonderful. He could not allow this to happen. But what to do?

As noon rolled by, Rick finished reading and signing the contracts in the pile before him. The city had grown slightly more rainy and gray outside, meanwhile. Thick charcoal clouds rolled across an otherwise light, mother-of-pearls sky.

It was a beautiful sight. Sunlight penetrated through the clouds in a few places, and painted an orange glow on glass and metal surfaces. Superimposed on that was a quadrille of fine white and yellow rectangles fine as sugar grains. Those were lights on in myriad office and hotel windows as millions of people went about their daily works and lives.

Rick glanced at a wall clock, checked his cell phone and pad clocks, and decided it was time for decisive action. He was not going to make the long, tiring drive to Emery in a rain storm. He wouldn't make it in time.

Dad would choke like bloody murder when he reviewed Rick's accounts, but this was it. Rick had had it. He was going to fulfill the Marian mission today or die trying: Operation Marian the Librarian, ho!

He'd been up since early in the morning. He'd enjoyed a fine hotel room, as well as a chef's breakfast, and frankly something just came over him—a kind of lethargy of the soul. He had worked his brain into a frazzle, working these documents. He'd scanned and faxed copies back and forth with legal teams in Manhattan, Boston, and home base in West Hartford. There were always endless little knicks and knacks to iron out, to change, to initial after printing, to go over and over in review. Most of the time, after working a case, he had the whole package couriered to the Moyer LX Building in West Hartford. This particular deal had been on a time element, and required signed approval today. He checked the time again. The last thing on earth he wanted was to miss his date with Marian. He had no idea if she was playing with him, or even lying—he'd seen everything in his time. A friend of his had dated a woman who said she was divorced, only to find out through back channels that she was an opportunist who was still actually married, but playing around behind her husband's back, looking for a better deal, and prepared to dump him if a wealthier man came along. The friend had almost fallen for it, until his lawyers had insisted on a steel-jawed prenuptial agreement, and the gold digger had dropped him like a tired old shoe. Her strategy had been clear: to divorce him after a year or so, and get a huge settlement with alimony for her year's play acting job. Rick Moyer had seen all the games. He felt something real, burning in his gut, for this woman. In a way, maybe she was too good to be true. But she seemed so real that it was worth playing along (cautiously) to see what might happen.

He pressed an intercom button in a gadget on the table. "Agatha, Rick Moyer."

"Yes, Mr. Moyer."

"I need you to put me through to my home office."

"Yes, Mr. Moyer."

In five minutes, Rick had Helen Dupuy on the line. Helen was a love. Helen was his father's executive secretary, a woman in her sixties given to cream colored suits, big earrings, her fine lips struck with bright red lipstick, and thinning hair poufed into a slightly orange ball. Rick had played at Helen's feet in his father's office, when Rick was maybe two, Helen was probably thirty, Mom about 35, and Dad was maybe forty. "Yes, Rick?"

"Helen, I am running out of time here and need some quick assistance. Can you take some notes please?'

"Yes, Rick. Of course."

"Don't ask, don't tell."

"What?"

"Please."

Hearing the mix of command and pleading in his tone, she said: "Whatever you say, dear." There was also a tone in her voice that suggested she didn't want to know for fear of getting sucked into something.

"First of all, let's get this package couriered over to the right persons, with a copy to our office."

"Okay." Helen was an old hand at taking all sorts of wild requests, understanding them, and making things happen.

"I am going to need the following. I need a courier to stop by the Ace Ali Baba Parking Garage in Manhattan. The street address is on the credit slip."

"I have it here. It arrived by email."

"I need the courier to open the trunk of my car, and remove a book. I'll give you the title. I need the book hand-carried by whatever means necessary to the Emery Public Library."

"The what, dear?" She pronounced *what* like *h'chwat*.

"Emery Township Free Public Library in Emery, Connecticut."

"Oh yes, been through there."

"Me too."

"Lovely little town. Absolutely nothing going on there."

"Nothing at all," Rick said, "until today. Use a chopper service. I think that would d be best."

"A what, Ricky?"

Rick gave her the address.

"Got it." Helen never lost a beat. It was just another business deal.

"I also need a chopper on the roof here ASAP to take me to the same location in Emery. Most likely there is not a landing pad near the library, so we'll make it the nearest commercial strip or pad as close as possible."

For the first time, Helen appeared a bit confused. "Wait a minute. I am not following you exactly. You want two helicopters?"

"Right. We don't have a lot of time to work with. I am meeting a client at five p.m. at the Emery Public Library. This is a major deal for me."

"Gotcha. No problem. Daddy won't blink?"

"Don't ask, don't tell."

"I am going home early right after I set this up. I don't want to be here."

"He no longer reviews all my logistics and deal sweeteners. Either that, or I quit and start my own firm."

"He doesn't need to know yet. I'll make sure. He will know soon enough."

"Excellent. We'll cross that bridge when it comes our way. I will be on the roof waiting for my chopper."

"I'm sorry, love, but why don't you have one chopper fly the book to you, pick you up, and take you to the library then?"

"It's two operational legs, Helen. No time to lose. Leg A-B takes us from the garage to the roof on this building. Let B-C takes me from here to Emery, which is going to be about a forty minute flight going at cruising speed. If we go A-B-C, I'm afraid I my miss my deadline. If we run the two legs in parallel, it means they can run independently and we might shave a half hour or so off."

"Must be a very important client. Or a special woman. Or both. Well, okay, dear. Anything you say. I'm on your side. I'll get right on it."

"Thanks. I'll need a rental car waiting for me at the destination. And separately, hire a service to drive my car back from Manhattan to West Hartford."

"I'll take care of all the details," Helen said. "That's your expense budget for about six months."

"I don't give a rat's whisker."

"I completely agree."

"Please, Helen, keep me on this line and use the other lines to set it all up. I need to know from moment to moment."

"Gotcha, Ricky. Here we go…"

Rick waited while Helen made phone calls on several other phone lines simultaneously.

"I have a landing place configured for you."

"What is it?" He had his phone pad in hand and checked her arrangements as she posted them on his mobile calendar for him.

"Emery Field. It's a private air club where they give lessons and store small planes for members. They have a public pad that is leased by the city and county for emergency services like fire and EMT. Shall I book you?"

"Book away, please." He sipped tea, waving the cup in one hand, while waving the mobile before his face, speaker mode, and swallowing distractedly.

The redoubtable Helen continued: "I can have your book flown there separately to meet you."

"That's perfect."

"And they will have a rental car ready when you land."

"Excellent. Thank you, Helen."

"Anything else, dear?"

"Tell dad I said hello, and New York City went very well today as it usually does."

"I will. You fly safely now."

"I always do my best."

After ringing off, Rick wrote a note for Agatha to take care of the contract package with Helen. He gathered his coat and his briefcase.

He stuffed his cell and his pad into various pockets. Juggling a paper tea cup, and holding a scone in his teeth, he made his way up to the helipad on the 90th floor of the building. There, he waited behind a plate glass window while sleet and hail silently hammered the glass on the other side. After some minutes, a helicopter with twirling orange running lights flew sideways onto the apron. Pushing the rooftop door open, Rick entered a maelstrom of churning wind and water. Pilot and co-pilot, in orange jumpsuits and helmets with microphones, pulled him up in to the dry, upholstery-smelling passenger compartment of the chopper, and off they went, sailing into the elements half a mile above Manhattan.

In the courtesy refrigerator of the small but efficient luxury aircraft, Rick found a variety of foods and drinks. He chose a fresh banana and a bowl of granola with whole milk to tide him over, along with a seven ounce container of fresh grape juice. He wanted to save some appetite for his date with Marian, but he'd had a busy morning and needed a little pickup on the way. If it were a few hundred miles more, he would have hired a jet, but it wasn't clear where you landed a Lear jet in Emery. A person had to make do with materials available in a pinch--the right tools for the job. Within the paneled, sound-tight walls and doors of the small but luxurious compartment, Rick put back his plush easy chair recliner. There were two such seats in here, along with a complete entertainment center with video screens, plus the wet bar, small fridge, and microwave/convection oven. After eating, he disposed of the containers in a small compactor and lay back. Pulling up his raincoat like a blanket, he closed his eyes and got a brief nap. Except for an occasional small air pocket, or a buffeting air gust, Rick was blissfully unaware of flying a mile high in the sky. Eventually, the pilot announced he was descending for a landing approach at a small private airfield on the outskirts of Emery.

14

Rain fell steadily in Emery, and the library was at its lantern best. It was quiet and dry inside. The children were still in school next door. Lillie, Terie, Rose, and Marian were busy reordering shelves that had been messed up by a lunchtime rush of kids. Linda was in her office, interviewing a high school boy for a possible intern job. Two high school interns were learning how to sort through the drops in back, where passers by could deposit returns into a shute that landed the materials in a bin.

Marian wore jeans, a green, floral blouse, and a heavy cream cable sweater open in front with three low buttons. She wore gray track shoes with dark-pink shoelaces because of the cold February rain. The damp weather made her hair frizzy, so she wore an ivory stretch band to capture it for future reference (brushing). The band ran from her neck in back, at the base of her skull, behind her ears, up, and across just above the forehead leaving an inch of dark hair pinned before it; behind it rose a tangle of dark hair with two small baby-blue bow clips—one toward the crown of her head, the other slightly off to the left above one ear, following the major, natural whorl of her hair. Sometimes, as she sat among the children at story time, wearing a denim coverall dress and cream blouse with periwinkles on the collar, she might hear passing grandmothers whisper dotingly among themselves "adorable," and she would turn red as a potato steamer knowing they meant her; because you could tell sometimes whom people were talking about by the way their voices followed the angle of their eyes' gaze, even when you did not look at them. Marian had been a reasonably adorable child most of her life. As a widow of 28, she hardly placed it among the top of her desired qualities. More and more, she felt an occasional urge to stop in the tavern across the Green downtown, drink several stiff whiskies, and stand near the pond yelling obscenities at night; but it was usually a passing urge. She was the sort of person who could tolerate about one glass of wine, after which it was anything goes, luckily almost always ending with her falling sound asleep while snoring like a diesel truck going up a grade. The 'almost' referred to a night, about ten years ago during college, when she and three other intoxicated girls had walked along a downtown city street in suburban Oklahoma City, loudly singing Gothic Rock tunes and toilet papering police cruisers until they were arrested. Lectures had been received, notices sent to parents, and promises extracted never to repeat the offense. Marian had gone on to earn her B.A. in English with a Minor in Library Science. Since it was a first conviction (and the last ever) on record for Marian, she'd gotten off with a warning. Her life after that was not without sin or blush, but she'd graduated on time, held responsible jobs, married, and tried to live an acceptable adult life; which included this delightful relocation to New England; until her plane had crashed and burned with the arrival of those grim looking Army guys in the black sedan. Friends and family both in Oklahoma and Connecticut commented that she'd developed a faintly sarcastic, humorous curl of the lip and a slightly crazy sense of funny after that.

At about 2:30 like clockwork, the afternoon rush hit. Kids were getting out of school. On a rainy day, this involved extra logistics including umbrellas, raincoats, and other gear. There were a few fender-benders out on the thruway, meaning spots of flashing red or blue lights. Tow trucks from local garages were having a field day. Marian noticed one ambulance passing by with lights and sirens.

Marian kept working steadily inside the dry, comfortable halls of the library while the world passed by around her, outside. Sometimes she felt suffocated. Here she was with married women—wait, I am married too; no, I was—and older women. She was young, and bursting with hormones and ambitions. She had just driven through a huge tunnel, had her world pulled out from under her, all those clichés and metaphors— and her heart was telling her it was slowly getting to be time to make a fresh start. It was just such a let-down and an empty feeling after having a whole life laid out before her. She was sure if she thought about it long enough, dwelt on it, that she would cry again. There was no end to the tears, but she was all cried out. It was more of a reflex now. There were moments—not days, but hours, or even just minutes—where she felt overwhelmed. At such moments, she felt sorry for herself; but such feelings got you nowhere. You had to process them and admit to them, but you had to move them along the stacks and carrels of your soul. The sun rose every morning, it was a new day, and here she was—all those clichés suddenly made sense.

She thought about the strange man who seemed so focused on her library. Was he really so interested in her? Or was he some devious real estate pasha who planned to use the library for his acquisition schemes? You never knew. Between Rose, Lillie, and the other women around her, Marian was having prudent doubts. She would not let herself go with this strange man she did not know. She would let herself enjoy dinner and take it a step at a time. That gave her a sense of inner equilibrium.

Somebody had once told her that you needed a good five years to recover from a major life event. But there was something else she knew from gardening, which she thought about now. The rule of thumb was that, if you planted a tree, when it took, usually in a few years, you could expect that the root ball was about the same dimensions as the crown. You could eyeball a tree, and sort of imagine what its root ball looked like, hidden in the earth, just from how its crown spread out.

Here she was, having a kind of silly, disjointed thought. If she'd been married two years, then the leafy crown of her marriage spread across two years. That meant the roots were buried in the soil of her soul deep enough to require at least two years for the soil to turn over, life to renew itself, and a new start to open up. But then again, how many years did it take to arrive at those two years of marriage: how many years of learning, growing, day-dreaming, lousy dates, misunderstanding, buck-toothed boyfriends with ill-fitting suits, and painful dates you couldn't wait to be over did it take until you met Mr. Right? Not many women had Mr. Right—no, Mr. Perfect, Mr. Forever—taken from them so abruptly.

"Marian," Terie said. She and Marian were walking into the break room together. Marian wanted to replenish the near-empty coffee cup in her hand, and Terie had to wash her hands at the sink, then dry them with a paper towel.

"Huh?"

"You are stewing again." Terie tossed the paper towel into the trashcan under the sink

"I'm sorry."

"Don't be sorry. Just stop doing that. You should see your face."

Marian laughed. "I'll bet I look like a toad."

"You are very pretty, but it's scary when you look grim."

Lillie bustled into the break room, to the microwave oven, carrying a plate with stuffed peppers and a can of soda. A spicy, steamy aroma grew around her as the microwave cooked her dinner. Lillie said, aside, "How is Mr. Dinosaur these days? Heard from him?"

Marian made a mysterious face and Lillie shrugged.

Terie and Marian went into the children's section, where they sorted reshelf books in adjoining aisles as they talked. It was noisy and crowded today. The air was humid and smelled of damp kid clothes. Lillie wrinkled a lip nearby as she resorted the shelves of teen adventure books.

"To the point, actually," Marian said nerdishly, "he is supposed to be coming by to drop off an overdue library book."

Lillie made owl eyes at the rain and gloom outside. "He could pick a more sensible day."

Marian shrugged. "I was making my round of calls to all the delinquents, and got a hold of him at some business meeting in New York City."

"New York City, huh?" Terie held an armload of Golden Books. She was from Brooklyn, descended from Puerto Rican roots. Her hair was frizzy, and her skin coffee, which made Marian's skin tone seem less custardly.

Lillie had once explained during a bullshoe session that, although she was blonde and blue-eyed, she was part Algonquin Indian. Everyone was a mix these days.

There was a new library policeman on duty—a young, muscular man who looked as if he lifted weights and practiced boxing or martial arts, judging by the way he carried himself. He was a bit rough looking, Marian thought, though handsome in a street sort of way. Speaking of whom, Mr. Michael Chesney threaded his way amid piled backpacks of all colors, from table to table, in his dark green uniform with yellow braid insignia, shooshing Third Graders. Chesney, who looked to be about Marian's age, had a nice way with children. He was a pale, freckled man with short red hair and humorous light blue eyes. He certainly had eyes for the younger librarians, it was quickly noticed as well. Marian enjoyed bantering with him, as did Terie who was two years older than Marian. Terie was a married woman, however, and Marian given Mike Chesney some stern looks to warn him off. He did not seem to like that one bit.

He was inquisitive, pushy, and persistent though. In a way it was cute. He was so self-assured. On the other hand, it got annoying fairly quickly. Linda had already given him one strong verbal hint, since she henned over her employees. The guard staff were not directly affiliated with the library system, but with the schools department. There were two tiny branches besides this main library. One was the Lake Branch, and the other was the Valley Branch, also known as the Downtown Branch. The Main library happened to land here on the thruway because the town's grammar school had been built here over 130 years ago, when there had been a winding dirt and gravel post road running sort of vaguely between New York City and Boston, with stops in Hartford and Stamford and the like. Literally, unless they got stuck in axle-deep mud, only the occasional stage coach made the journey, including a daily mail coach authorized by Congress.

Mike Chesney was a wide-shouldered, powerful presence, replacing Mr. Perez. Chesney managed to keep order. The kids respected him, and he was good with them—easy going, humorous, but firm. He was a single man (Lillie said) and a veteran of the U.S. Marine Corps (hence the globe and anchor tattoo on one bicep).

To explain the absence of Mr. Perez, and his replacement by Mr. Chesney, Linda had called the staff together for a meeting. "Mr. Perez is on leave because his wife, unfortunately, is gravely ill and I am afraid it is now terminal. The end is near. Most of you know she has been pretty much in and out of a coma for the past year, unable to recognize her husband and children." A stir of sympathy passed through the dozen employees present, all women, who sat around on kid desks after hours for the meeting. Linda continued: "She is now in home hospice care, and the end could come any day now. We are going to have a substitute guard on loan from the schools department. I understand he is young, charming, and good at his job." She looked around. She laughed and made a wry face. "How do I say this?" Everyone snickered because they had already been hit upon by Mr. Chesney and knew what was coming. "Ladies, we will all conduct ourselves professionally, right? Goes without saying since most of us are married. A few of you are single, and I remind you that—how shall I put this?" They all laughed. "The guard must be able to focus on his or her duties and not be distracted by flirting, excessive joking, or whatever. You are to refuse all offers of lunch, drinks, walks, talks, or any other form of fraternization with the guard staff, consisting of Mr. Chesney. Have I clarified myself sufficiently?"

From the hum of approval, it was clear she had.

"So about Mr. Perez," Linda continued. "His wife Rosario is 55 and very ill with breast cancer." To the ensuing rustle of sympathy, she responded: "I know, it's very sad. He is such a nice man, and it is a shame to see this happening to him. Although—Rosario has been in and out of consciousness for over a year now. She has not been lucid much, and they have had her in a care facility for a year since the dementia showed up. That's from the metastasis of her cancer to the brain." Linda made a sorrowful face.

Marian, sitting in a back corner, found herself dabbing her eyes. She teared up and cried so easily these days at the slightest sorrow or sentimentality in anyone's life, and there was so much of it. She glanced across the room, and sure enough, Rose Otto was dabbing her eyes with a hankie.

If Linda noticed Marian's hankie and the sniffle, or the honk as Marian blew her nose, she did not react. "Mr. Perez took a leave of absence with pay last week when Rosario was moved to a hospice, and of course that is the end of life place where the care changes from saving to just making them comfortable on their last journey."

Marian could picture Adolfo Perez: a tall, wiry man with dark, short, almost kinky hair and reddish-brown skin that glistened in the library's lights—extra bright, bluish where you read books, and that wan yellowish glow in the hallways. Mr. Perez always seemed to care personally for each of the staff, and escorted them to their cars each evening. Rose Otto always seemed extra nervous when Mr. Perez was in the building, and he was extra patient with her.

"How is Cleopatra this evening?" asked Mike Chesney, regarding Marian.

Terrie gave him a *tisk*. "You are going to get yourself in trouble."

Marian turned sharply away. Her thoughts were on her gondolier.

Mike flexed his muscles, maintaining his self-assured, almost cocky attitude, and rolled his tiny behind off a low book case so he stood with his thumbs hooked in his police-style belt. He carried a can of spray, but no other weapons—the town made sure it hired physically fit, imposing men and women for the guard positions. His other weapon, come to think of it, was a special little cell phone with pre-dials for town police and 911.

Lillie also ignored Mike, as the women turned to other tasks and left Chesney standing there looking ignored.

Chesney knew Marian was single, and seemed to be particularly taken with her. Marian enjoyed the attention up to a point. *I must be starved for affection*, she told herself, while avoiding eye contact. No way would she even be at the same lunch counter with this man.

Tommy would have put a hurt on him, karate or not. Oops, must not think like that. She kind of hoped Chesney would not see her with Rick Moyer.

"I'm talking to you, Cleopatra." Chesney seemed polite in his flattery. You never knew if he was joking or if there was some ulterior motive to his endless challenging and attention getting. There was something coiled and dangerous beneath the surface with him.

Lillie swung a cart of books between him and Marian. "I hear they are tagging cars out in the lot. Mike, would you put on your slicker and go out, and make sure they don't tow any employee cars away in their enthusiasm?"

"Sure," Mike said, flexing his shoulder muscles as if they ached. With one last gloomy glance at Marian, he turned and minced off to get his coat and hat. Outside, two tow trucks prowled about with their greenish-orange lights flashing—predators, hunting for their dinner in the form of a juicy towing fee on top of the township's ticket for violators.

The compact, athletic Mr. Chesney minced away, walking like a rock star or a body builder.

Lillie laughed and winked to Marian and Terie. "If his buns get any tighter, he can put hamburgers in his pockets."

"If I were single, I might take a bite," Terie said. She leaned close to Marian, with the whites of her eyes large in her coffee features with pinked lips: "You are too white to be Cleopatra."

"That's fine with me," Marian said. "You can be the Egyptian. You like those muscles?"

"He is a *boy*," Terie said her gaze followed the athletic Mr. Chesney.

"And you are married, girl," said Lillie.

"You have club eyes when you talk like that," Marian said to Terie. She felt weary, and the banter did not come easily today.

"Club you," Terie muttered fondly. She took her eyes of Chesney and returned her gaze to the books on her cart.

Lillie looked at Marian. "Marian, you seem a bit quiet today."

"It's the weather," Marian said. *It wasn't.* She had gone from being elated to being terrified again. She couldn't admit that publicly.

"Oh I know," Lillie said, "doesn't it make you want to curl up with beer and a ball game?"

"Whoa," said Rose Otto from the Help Desk. She pointed with a shaky hand. "Look who is coming."

Lillie, Terie, and Marian whipped around, and looked across the tables dotted with small heads, out through the large plate glass windows, at the whirl of people and cars out in the rain. Wind whipped stray leaves about in figure eight patterns. Tow trucks with green flashers prowled looking for illegally parked victim cars.

"What?" Lillie said.

"I don't see anything," Terie said. "Rose, you have eagle eyes."

Marian felt a strange lurch in her gut. Her face instantly flushed, and she barely dared look up. Outside, sitting in the middle of the parking lot, was a shiny, expensive new car. At the wheel of the not-Jaguar sat none other than Mr. Richard Moyer, looking left and right for a safe place to stash his wheels. He was early. She glanced up at the library clock. It was barely 3:20. She did not get off until 5:00 today. What if—he made a scene? she fainted? he caught her? everyone laughed? he left in a huff? it was all a big mistake? she was being a fool? he'd been joking about dinner? What if? What if? Her legs trembled. He always did this to her. Oh mortification, and then her tongue would seize up and she wouldn't be able to speak. Lisps and wheezes would come out.

"It's the Dinosaur Man," said Rose tolerantly. She clearly knew his initial joke had been on her, which explained her ultra-dry sarcasm.

"He brought your book back," Lillie told Rose brashly.

Marian knew it wasn't a dinosaur book, but the cowboy fable. She felt a bit like a child at Christmas time. Maybe this would be fun after all. He had certainly driven about 900 miles an hour to get here so fast.

"I have been lying awake at night worried about it," Rose said about the book. Her thin frame, big glasses, and shock of orange hair underscored her ironic tone.

"Here he comes," Terie said. "Bring me oxygen."

"Now, now," Lillie said wisely with a smurky, chummy glance toward Marian. "I think he wants to check out a different title."

As Marian watched, Richard Moyer, seeing an available spot, pulled his rather large, luxurious car into it.

"Looks like a rental," Lillie said.

"I wonder if he cracked up that Jaguar he was driving last time," Terie said.

"Kind of odd," Marian said vaguely. Hope he is okay, she thought. Hope nothing happened.

"Here he comes," Rose said.

"Everyone, pretend you aren't looking," Lillie said.

The door opened, and in strode Mr. Moyer. He wore a raincoat, but no hat. His dark hair looked wet and mussy, with beard shadow on strong jaws, and brooding eyes that glittered in the yellowish lobby lights. Marian felt flustered—should she look? should she wave? should she act cool and ignore him? Those chiseled features, those crisp brown eyes under long lashes—they sought her out. She looked up at him as their eyes met in a glance of recognition. She gave him a shy, sidelong look. Are my eyes as big as his? she wondered. It was almost as if his eyes were yelling at her, to her. She quickly looked down. With a flutter of her eyelids, she saw that he had turned to the service desks, where Rose waited.

Under one arm, he had a flat briefcase. Rose moved languidly from Help to Check. Moyer placed his briefcase on it, and pulled out a book from inside. "I am afraid it is overdue."

Rose might as well have been chewing gum, so silently did she ignore him while reaching for the book. She did this many times a day—they all did. Moyer waited like a boy about to be chastised. His face radiated innocent concern.

Rose ran the book over the scanner and said: "Well." Marian was glad she didn't say Mr. Dinosaur to him. "You owe twelve dollars. The fine is fifty cents a day."

Moyer patted his pockets all around. "I think I have change here…" He placed a beautiful walnut-colored leather wallet on the counter and peeled out some bills. Rose's eyes widened. "Those are twenties," she said.

He pushed them across the counter. "I'd like to make a donation."

"I will make change for you if you cannot."

He rubbed his hands together. "My fingers are a little numb from the cold outside."

Rose gave the window thermometer a glance. It read 49F. Hardly a wind chill in there. Marian almost laughed. She didn't know Rick Moyer from the Mona Lisa, but she could swear he enjoyed putting on an act like this.

"Oh here," Rick said, pushing two twenties across the desk. "It's a tax deduction for a good cause."

Rose looked at him curiously.

He looked back emphatically. "Take it. I also get a hundred years off purgatory."

Rose clucked as she put the bills in the register, dropped the change drawer down on them, and handed him an electronic receipt. He thanked her. "I think I'll browse in the fantasy section for a while."

Rose managed a tiny smile. "I hope you find something exciting to read."

"I already have. Thanks." With a glowing grin, he sauntered off toward the Fiction hall. He gave Marian a beautiful-eyed wink. She nodded excitedly, then looked demurely down, with a faint smile.

"Oh my god," said Terie, "Marian, I think he did goo-goo eyes on ya."

Marian put down the books she was holding, said something about excusing her, and went to the bathroom. In the Ladies' room, she examined herself in the mirror. She patted her hair, adjusted the white band, tugged at the two little blue bow clips, and then gave up on her hair. She touched her cheekbones with her fingertips while making an O-mouth, then a D-mouth, then a W-mouth, and finally a big M-shape with her lips. She was not going to add make-up since they would (she presumed) be in the rain soon enough. A glance at her wristwatch told her it was 3:45. What would he do in the Fiction section for over an hour? Maybe he'd take a nap. Should she tell Linda she needed an hour off, and lose the pay? Or she'd—never mind. Let him make whatever move.

But she'd better say something. So, coming out of the Ladies' room, she put her arms behind her, and pretended to be nonchalantly sauntering. She kicked an imaginary pebble to one side, whistled soundlessly, and did a skip-hop with both feet.

Where was he?

"Marian!" Rick whispered from the F's somewhere.

"Where are you?" she whispered, flushing at the thought of her fellow librarians watching them.

"Here."

"Where?" She stopped like a child lost in the woods. The main fiction hall was round, with a rotunda dome capped by a glass oculus. Ages ago, during the Great Depression, talented and imaginative WPA artists had painted the houses of the Zodiac up there, complete with silvery-white stars on a blue-black evening sky backdrop, and then the twelve divisions, each with its own symbol—the crab, the virgin, the water carrier, and more.

"Between Faulkner and Fitzgerald."

"Oh." She looked at the F's, and saw his face in a gap between the books. He was standing in the next aisle over. She laughed. "What are you doing there?"

"Teasing you."

She shook her head. "I will be laughing too hard to get any more work done."

"I will wait for you quietly."

"And behave yourself."

"I am incorrigible."

"You are."

"And so excited to see you."

"Me too. You came early."

"I know. Is that bad?"

"Actually," she admitted, "I am rather glad you did."

"Were you waiting for me?"

"No. I was sorting books." Her laugh that escaped must tell him she was bluffing. "Of course I was waiting for you." She walked toward his face, which was framed by books.

"You are just hungry."

"Yes." She put her fingertips on the shelf and peered at him with her face level with his. "I am hungry for you."

They looked at each other, made faces, and each burst into a laugh.

Despite herself, she felt as if she were in freefall. She did not feel at all as guarded as she had planned to be.

At that moment, a crackling sound echoed around the dome above, startling them both.

"Good afternoon," said Linda Damien's voice. "Due to the rain today, we will be cutting staff. Miss McLaughlin, you can leave now. I will clock you out at five."

It took Marian a few seconds to realize that Miss and her maiden name were intended for her. Linda was acutely conscious of Marian's new preferences. Lillie must have put in a word for me, Marian thought. Linda was being blatantly generous and understanding, letting her go early with pay. She'd expect the time made up somewhere along the line, of course.

"You look ravishing."

"Just call me Marian the Librarian." She remembered his words. "Call me anything—just call me, okay?"

"Go, clock out so we can clock in." He rested his chin comically on the shelf. He made a window with this two hands, thumbs tip to tip, framing it with fingers. "I am going to close the shutters now."

He turned a large copy of The Beautiful and the Damned face-out, hiding himself behind it.

"You are very entertaining," she said. "Why don't you read for a few minutes. I'll quickly get my coat and punch out."

She walked back to the main lobby, and then into the break room. Terie and Lillie were there, preparing a last pot of coffee for the day.

"Did you talk to him?" Terie asked.

"I did. I thanked him for remembering to bring the book back."

"He could have mailed it," Lillie said with pragmatic insightfulness.

"Does this guy have a job?" Terie asked.

Lillie winked. "Good for you, sister."

Terie caught on. "Go get 'im."

Marian unlocked her locker and pulled out her rain coat, umbrella, and purse. "He owns his own business." From a coat pocket, she extracted her fine silk scarf, which she threw over her hair in a triangle. From another pocket, she pulled a see-through plastic harmonica hood, which she tied under her chin.

"Well," Lillie said, "he wants to do more than return a book if he drove all this way in the rain."

"Be brave," Terie said. "Be careful. Above all, be wild."

"I'm not sure I remember how to get wild."

Lillie giggled. "It will quickly come back to you."

15

Rick Moyer seated himself in a beat-up but comfortable chair with green leather upholstery that was partially falling out of its worn spots. He had spotted The Great Gatsby by F. Scott Fitzgerald, which he had not read since college, and now relaxed while rain rattled down on the glass windows in the dome above.

So she is not married but a widow, he reflected, not for the first time. He could not get her out of his thoughts. He would be sensitive and go easy.

"Would you like to check out another book?"

He looked up, startled. There she stood, wearing all sorts of hoods on her head, and a nice olive-drab raincoat with military-style buckles and probably hidden cameras, like spies wore. She carried a long, stylish brown leather purse with gold snaps, and a mauve umbrella with a broken spoke that caused some fraying in the material.

"I dressed for work, not a date," she said. "I had no idea you'd ask me out, but that is so nice. What are you reading?"

He held up the book for her to see.

"One of my favorites," she said. "The writer painted with words. Very nice."

"I have a copy at my house." He jumped up, filed the book back in its slot, and stepped close to offer her his arm. He wasn't ready to tell her he had his own library at home, with over 2,000 books in it.

"A gentleman," she said, pleased. She laid her arm through his, seeming relaxed and at ease. The weight of her arm was light, and made him tingle at the touch, even through their sleeves. When he felt her arm on his, and in the crook of his elbow, Rick savored the contact. This surprising lightness about her touch was elegant. Her hand made a little turning or wriggling motion as if it were a small animal curling up in a cozy nook—his elbow. She leaned into it, as if wanting to pull him along, but waiting for him to lead. She looked up at him expectantly with just a little curl in one eyebrow. She'd added some wine-red lipstick that made the pucker of her mouth humorous and alluring.

Getting over the surprise of her first touch, he patted the hand close to his side, and led her toward the door. "Is there a favorite restaurant I can take you to?"

She shrugged. "I thought you like pizza."

"I do. Papa's is the best. I don't know how the roads are here in Emery when the weather is beastly. How far do you want to go?"

"Papa's has a back room you evidently don't now about."

"I could go for a little lasagna. How about you?"

"I'll have whatever you are having." She pulled her shoulders close in a shrug.

He held the door open for her, and they stepped into the rain and gloom. That fresh valley wind rose up, full of tree smells and soil and flowers. "Wow," he said delightedly. He felt alive and happy.

They stood looking at each other under the worn concrete overhang on the low front steps. She held her purse in both hands and looked up at him expectantly, with a trusting smile. "Mr. Moyer?"

"Yes?" He stared at her, inhaling who and what she was, and the town she lived in.

"Aren't you going to walk me down to Papa's?"

He laughed. "No, I thought we'd stand here and look at each other."

They linked arms again. She popped open her umbrella. The bent spoke nearly impaled him. They laughed together—hers a silvery shriek--as they dashed into the wind and rain and blowing leaves. He put his arm around her and held the umbrella over her, while she pressed her soft, shapely body against his. He impulsively gave her a little squeeze, and she gave him a friendly bump with her shoulder. They hustled down the uneven sidewalk, which now glistened wetly under street lights.

Mr. Papa and his wife and several older children were manning or womaning the ovens. Mrs. Papa waved a large wooden pizza puller. Mr. Papa, still looking corpulent in his evening attire—white shirt, black pants, black Oxford shoes—negotiated briefly with Marian, then ushered them in to a candle-lit, cozy back room with just four tables. Each table had a checkered table cloth, though in varied colors matched with white. There was only one table free, the one with a green and white checkered table cloth. As on the other tables, a candle flickered in a red glass goblet next to the obligatory menu, salt and pepper shakers, and small dispensers of Parmesan and Romano cheese.

"Smells divine," Rick said as he took her coat, while Papa seated her and a young girl in a white blouse, short black dress, and black tights came out with a pair of menus.

"Would you like to start with some wine or a cocktail?"

Rick hesitated. "I have to drive, and it's already been a long day." He looked at Marian, who looked exotic and Egyptian in the dim light.

Reddish light flickered on her features. "I think we should share a glass of Chianti. What do you say, Mr. Dinosaur?" Her smile glittered in the semi-dark. She had a way of curling up on herself, almost a body language of submission—but companionable submission.

Rick told the ready brunette server: "The girl next door has the right idea. A glass of your nicest red. And an appetizer while we look at the menu, if you have that."

"We do," the young woman said. "May I recommend a nice breaded zucchini you can dip in either marinara sauce or ranch dressing?"

Rick kept looking at his new-found friend, ready to accommodate any unexpected request or change in direction, but she seemed to be gazing at him with admiring eyes. She had her forearms folded over each other on the table, and her hands with their red nails sprawled in a relaxed manner. "Yes, that will be fine. So, my friend and I were thinking of ordering lasagnas."

"Full or half?"

"Two full."

"Rick," Marian said admonishingly. "I can't eat all that."

He shrugged. "We'll have doggie bags to take home."

Marian looked at the waitress, perplexed, and the woman nodded as she walked off to the kitchen. She looked at Rick: "It is very generous of you."

"What's generous?"

"I can pay for mine. Or both of us."

He shook his head. "Not an issue. Don't worry about it."

"As long as you don't have to live on left-over lasagna for days."

"I'll get by," he said a bit curtly, trying to steer the conversation toward her rather than himself. He could have told her that he could buy the restaurant for cash, right now, but how crass would that be? It would be a while before he told her, or she figured out, that he came from old money, as the expression went. A lifetime of habits went into how he went about his relationships with anyone, be they a new lady friend or a male associate in their line of work, or anyone. Money was like strong drink. It came between people. It went to people's heads. Money was like a noisy pet or child—it was best kept quietly in a safe place, unseen and unheard. "Tell me a little about yourself."

She shrugged mysteriously. "Not much to tell."

"I don't believe that." He was growing warm, and shrugged off his own coat. The waitress rushed up to take it. "Classy place," he said.

"I'm glad you like our pizzeria in Emery."

"I love your pizzeria."

"Where do you live, Rick? I don't know anything much about you." Her tone suggested that she could have added: "But you seem very nice."

"I live in West Hartford."

"Upscale."

"It has its points. And lattes. And all that."

"Not married," she said. It was a question.

"Oh heavens no. I don't play any of those games. I am divorced."

"Nasty?"

"They all are."

She burst out laughing. "How many have you had?"

"What, drinks or divorces?"

"Silly."

"I was married one time. Together four, married two of those. All a big mistake." He made wiping motions in the air, with his eyes pinched shut as if in pain.

"You weren't meant for each other?"

"I would say so." He picked up a beer coaster and spun it idly between his fingers as they got into the meat of a nice conversation. He felt very much at ease with her. It was actually kind of scary. Was he falling into another situation?

"I'm sorry."

"Now you're sorry. What are you sorry about?"

The wine came—a full glass and an empty one. The waitress held them on the tray for Rick to decide. "We'll share the full one if you don't mind. Seems sort of romantic."

The waitress smiled. "Nice choice. We don't mind washing the extra glasses. You two just meet?" Her name tag read Eleni. Rick surmised that the Papas were Greek, rather than Italian. Eleni was in her mid-20s, a little younger than Marian. Probably Papandreou if he had to guess. He was a keen student of names and the U.S. melting pot, and all of its wonderful, diverse people. He answered Eleni, but looked at Marian as if she were his angel. "Yes, as a matter of fact. Thank you for asking."

Marian unexpectedly reached across the table and put her hand over his. She told Eleni: "We have known each other for almost half a year, it seems. He came in the library and checked out a book about cowboys."

The waitress, evidently a member of the Papa family and quite at ease, said: "I like cowboys. If they are well behaved. Well, they can be a little rough around the edges. Makes them more interesting." She reached out, just as unexpectedly, and gave Marian's shoulder a little stroke of the hand. "Good for you, girl."

"Did I miss something?" Rick asked after Eleni left.

"This is a small town," Marian said as she continued to sit, kind of leaning forward, as if she wanted to wrap herself around the comfort zone between herself and Rick. "They were at my husband's memorial here in town, after the military honors and funeral in Washington, D.C." She had a careful tone about her as she spoke. She added: "I hope it does not make you uncomfortable, but that is my life right now."

He shook his head. "I feel humbled."

"You're ex-military?"

"Yeah. Army. I was stationed in Kabul. Nothing fancy. I ended my three years as a sergeant, managing an office when I wasn't pulling field duty like everyone else--back of the lines, but no real combat and certainly no heroics."

"You are too modest. You could have taken an IED like my husband did." Her voice was low and serious. She was not playful at all now.

"I did have two friends die on me. One was an MP who drove over a mine. The other was a female clerk in my office who was shot by a sniper while visiting her boyfriend, who was a grunt out in a rear CP. Command Post," he added.

She sat up rather rigidly. "Rick. Mr. Moyer. Let's change the subject."

"Okay. I don't talk much about my humble military background."

"Thank you," she said sincerely. "I am afraid that if I start talking about all that, it will take over our conversation and spoil our evening. I am so scared and shaky right now that I could almost run out of here."

He raised his hands defensively. "Okay. Honey, look. I would understand. Anything you do—I will not hold it against you. If this is too much for you, I understand. We can leave."

"I don't want to cry."

"Then you don't need to. But if you wish, I will get a big checkered table cloth for you and hold it while you bawl your eyes out if that is what you need to do. I am here for you."

She took a deep, shuddering breath. Her eyes closed, and she could not look at him. "Go easy with me."

He played with the beer coasters as if they were a deck of cards. "Marian, I ask nothing of you. I want to be your friend. You know I like you a lot."

"I like you too. Just—go really slow, okay?"

"Honey, lasagna is a slow boat. Movie maybe next month, two months, I have time if you do."

She broke into a half smile, a kind of crooked, grateful like broken smile. "You silly guy."

"I'm serious. Slow cooked, sloe gin, slow boat, you name it. Your wish is my command. Cole slaw. Slow motion. Would you like me to make some funny faces to entertain you?" He pulled out a quarter, rolled it across his hand from finger to finger, made it disappear, snapped his finger, and appeared to pull it out from behind her ear. "See? Keep it light."

"Thank you." She sat scrunched in the corner of her bench, away from him.

His biggest fear at the moment was that she would run out and never talk to him again. He was prepared to order to go, and sit in the rain with her sharing lasagna and grape juice or whatever it took. He did not look forward to a painful hour or two if she saw him as the enemy rather than as a friend.

She said: "I really want this to work. Being friends."

"Sure. We'll take it a day at a time, an hour or a minute at a time. Whatever it is, let's just enjoy being together and not make anything more of it than a little light friendship."

"Why did you pick me, Mr. Moyer?"

He felt startled. "Why? Pick you?"

"That day last summer when we first laid eyes on each other."

"Oh, that. I didn't pick you. I thought you picked me."

"I thought you picked me."

He played with the beer coasters, feeling really awkward and sad, afraid this whole thing was going over a cliff suddenly, a huge awful painful mistake. They sat in silence for a few minutes, until Eleni brought two big chafers of steaming (almost smoking) lasagna "Careful," Eleni said. She held the plates in kitchen mittens. "They are piping hot." As she went through her motions, her eyes grew large and serious and she seemed to sense that something heavy was going on. She spoke in obvious metaphors. "Take it slow with the hot sauce," she said. "Don't rush things. No need to burn your fingers. Just go slow, one fork full at a time, one little bite, then the next one…"

"Thank you," Marian said gratefully. After Eleni left, she looked dismayed. "I had no idea I would be such a total drag."

"Don't make it a self-fulfilling prophecy."

"I just want to crawl under my bed and die."

"I won't let you do either thing. Here, grab a fork, put a napkin in your neck, and let's try this nice lasagna. You do like lasagna, don't you?"

"I do."

"You didn't just say it to go along with me?"

"No, Rick. I like lasagna."

"You really wanted a liverwurst sandwich."

"I love lasagna, you silly man."

"I broke your heart and made you eat lasagna. I get it now. I am a failure."

She patted his hand. "You are actually quite a nice guy. Thank you for putting up with me."

"I was looking forward to meeting you. Talking with you. Already, I got to hold your hand, hold your umbrella, and walk you in the rain. That's the most fun I have had in ages."

She gingerly picked up a knife and fork. "I might still run out of here screaming if I have a panic attack."

"I'll take care of the tab if you do. I just hope—"

"I am not going to run out of here," she said with sudden determination. She cut off a square of lasagna with slashing motions, almost angrily, and pulled it onto her empty plate. "I am going to enjoy having dinner with the most handsome man I have met in ages."

"You are very kind."

"Oh, Rick. You know women all look at you and adore you. If you are just playing with me, it's okay. I can use some cheering up.

Honest. I have always been kind of a girl next door type. I can change the oil in your car and bake you a cake the same day. I don't know if I would be Miss Pomp and Circumstance for you. I can be fun to be with when I am not crying my eyes out or being a girl. So you'll have to take me or leave me just as I am."

"I looked forward to just being with you for months. I just want to sit with you and make mozzarella strings in the air with my fork."

Despite her gloom, she choked with laughter. She patted her lips and accepted the water he offered. "You make me laugh."

He nibbled at his lasagna, which was delicious. He had more appetite for her than for food. The wine sat nearby, untouched. They took nervous sips of water instead, and Eleni brought them a pitcher of ice water. 'Wine not so good tonight?"

"We might have it for dessert," Rick said.

"Fair enough. Let me know if you need anything." Eleni walked off to talk with other customers—a middle aged couple, two businessmen with graying hair and thick glasses, and a pair of young women wearing dark blue nylon UConn windbreakers.

Marian nibbled half-heartedly, but stayed put and bravely chopped away at her lasagna.

Rick said: "Look, I'll put my cards on the table. I would love to have something with you. Friendship. What do I know? We should get to know each other before we leap to conclusions. Live for the moment. If it feels good, do it. If not, screw it. At least we get to know each other. That can't be so bad."

"Slow boat."

"Right. Ships passing in the night, unless we crash into each other."

She grinned. "We could hope for that."

"Then we'd have to rescue each other from the frigid waters."

"So what is it about libraries? Do you have a thing for librarians?"

"Yeah, I do. Here's the thing. I always loved to read. I used to wait for my mom or dad to pick me up after school, in the library. I would do my homework as quickly as I could so I could brows through the books and find something more interesting."

"Dinosaurs."

"I just said that to rattle Miss Prim."

"Rose."

"Oh yeah, Miss Otter."

"She's actually quite tolerable once you get to know her."

"For you, I would be friends with Mrs. Otter—sorry, Rose—if it pleased you."

"That's sweet of you. I think you are courting me, Rick Moyer. You would do anything to please me, and if we became an item, you'd suddenly turn out to be—a man." She said that last with a teasing kind of growl, as if describing a bear.

"Okay, I am courting you. I am a man. I hope we could date. We're going slow here, right?"

She laughed. "I'm sorry. We are all over the map."

"I know. I don't mind so much if you don't."

"I'm half crazy right now. My circumstance in life. Not what I created or ever imagined. I don't know how you will put up with me."

"Slow boat."

"I am trying, Rick. I'm just totally surprised at myself."

"I'm not. This is all new for you. Will it help if I am relaxed?"

"Yes."

"Okay." He put the beer coaster cards aside and picked up the wine glass. He pushed their dinner plates aside, since she didn't seem to have any more appetite, and neither did he. He put the wine glass between them so that its blood-red contents caught the scintillating candle light and danced like stained glass on her quiet features. Her mouth had a pleased smile about it, at least around the corners. Her exotic eyes and cheek bones glittered with borrowed shades of light. She had a glow, almost as if she already had drunk some of the wine. She glowed warmly from within. She sat leaning slightly forward, with her hands on her knees and her hair a dark jungle around her pale features. "So this is a glass of wine," Rick said in a slow tone. "We are going to sip from it."

She did not run from the room.

"We are going to sip from it slowly, one little sip at a time, very carefully, because I have to drive home and you have to drive home in the dark. We care about each other, and don't want anything to happen to the other person."

"Because I do want to see you again," she said suddenly. She put her hands over his on the table. "I can handle the slow boat. You are handling the boat just right. You are the captain of the boat, and you are doing well."

"We will hold hands like this, and that is all it is. It is not a scary monster under the bed, or a ghostly outline on the wall. Holding hands like this lets us feel each other's warmth and skin. Nothing more."

"It is nice to hold hands," she agreed, and let him wrap his fingers around hers.

"So that's all it is," he said.

"That's all it is."

"One little tiny moment at a time."

"I would love to taste a little wine now."

"Here." They unlinked hands, and he pushed the glass closer to her.

She sipped carefully. "Nice."

She pushed the glass to him, and he took a little sip. She grasped several fingers of his free hand, and did not let go.

He said: "I was really—I don't know what the word is—shook up the first time I met you."

"I know."

"I felt as if some giant hand had slammed us together. It was an overwhelming, meaningful moment."

"I know." She sighed.

"Did you feel something strong for me?"

"I did." She put both hands out, and he held them with both of his.

"You have warm, wonderful hands."

"So do you. Rick, if we never see each other again, I want to thank you for everything."

"Huh?" He felt a thrill of alarm. This sounded ominous.

"You saved my life."

"No way."

"Way."

"You are unforgettable. I don't know if I fell in love with you the first time I saw you, or what. I felt this overwhelming feeling come over me."

"I know."

"You too?"

"Oh yeah." There was a lot she was not telling him just now. Her eyes glittered in candlelight as she looked at him as if with laser beams. Her mouth looked grim. There was a moment of truth coming, and she was scaring him. "What was that all about?"

"I was suicidal."

"No." He felt a cold shower of acid raining in his stomach.

She removed her hands from his, as if she were taking control of some complicated, powerful machine, like an earth mover of her life, a backhoe of her soul, and bulldozer of truth. She sat like an island, toying with her water glass with red fingernails like big oval droplets of shiny blood.

"I was still in shock. I had not told anyone but my mother, but I was pregnant, and when the news came, I lost the fetus. They rushed me to the hospital the day after the Army guys came to tell me Tommy had died. I nearly bled to death. They had a hell of a time bringing me back. It was widowhood, postpartum depression, and general catastrophic depression all rolled into one."

"Oh wow. Oh wow." He repeated it several times.

He remembered her wild look, the inscrutable look she had given him, like an animal cornered in the jungle by the hunter, who is about to kill it with an elephant gun or whatever. It had been such an incredible, powerful moment—so suddenly and unexpectedly, and he with his defenses down, totally open—that he'd been in a daze long after leaving. Now he understood: It really had been a life and death experience. A life or death experience. He had looked into the wilderness moment of a desperate soul.

"Whatever your soul said to my soul in that moment, Mr. Richard Moyer, it was something as profound as life and death. I was actually planning to go down to the lake, the way Virginia Woolf did in her final depression—"

"—the famous English author in the 1930s—"

" —yes. She filled her pockets with stones, walked into a river, and drowned herself. I drove down there. I was going to drive right down the boat ramp at full speed and plow into the water with the windows open. I had it planned. I figured I would lose consciousness in two minutes and it would be over. It was the lowest point in my life."

He listened, and nodded. "May I ask...?"

"What stopped me? I am ready to talk about it. You are the first person I have told this, and probably will be the only one and the last one. This is strictly between the two of us, right?"

"Right."

"I imagined—I was so crazy at that moment—I imagined that Tommy would sit beside me in the car, or his ghost, and we'd go in the drink together. But he didn't show up. I didn't feel him anywhere near me. He disapproved. Instead, Richard Moyer, you were there."

"No way."

"Way."

"What—How?"

"I saw your face, I think it was that same day, when you stopped in. When I saw you, I was hours away from driving into the lake. Some miracle happened. You walked into the library and looked into my eyes. When I was about to die, I didn't see Tommy. All I saw was your beautiful eyes and your wonderful smile. I couldn't go through with it. I drove home, got into bed without undressing, and slept like a dead person without any dreams for almost an entire day. When I woke up, it was like I had been reborn. You were part of that, Mr. Moyer, whether you know it or like it or not."

"I am astonished," Rick said. "I am happy that I was there. I guess I am not very psychic. I wasn't conscious that you were having a crisis that evening at the lake. But maybe we had our crisis that afternoon when we looked into each other's eyes."

She nodded, looking gray at the memory of her near death.

His hands chased her hands across the table. He caught them, and held them, pulling her toward him across the table. "I felt something so deep and powerful in that moment. I can't explain it. Part of it was your soul talking to mine. Part of it was my own tough luck. You see, I had lost everything myself. Not money. I have plenty of that. I fell in love and married a woman who turned out to be several cards short of a deck."

"Several beers short of a six-pack," Marian added ruefully, squeezing his hands. Her hands felt firm, and warm, and dry around his—and were not going to ever let go.

"Three coyotes short of a herd," he said.

"I think coyotes run in packs, dear. And let's not forget several bagels short of a dozen."

They held hands and laughed. They laughed until tears came to their eyes.

Eleni appeared with a box of tissues and the bill. "No more wine for you two."

They each wiped their eyes with a handful of paper tissues. "I think we need some coffee," Rick said.

"Let's not," she said. "Let's get out of here. I have to go home, and so do you."

Rick felt a wrenching sense as if his heart had been dry-cleaned and pressed. It felt sort of new and clean, but the process involved some stinging, biting sensations. No pain, no gain.

They held hands as they walked out, swinging their hands loosely and lightly between them. "I am so sorry that was awkward," she said.

"It was a start. We had to go through that to get to whatever the next step will be, nor not."

"What is the next step?" she asked.

"What we each want it to be."

"Help me. Guide me."

"I want you to be my girlfriend."

She stood still and stared into his face. Her eyes were large and luminous. "Yes?"

"I want to date you. I want to pick you up and drive you to a movie. I want to buy you an ice cream and watch you lick the cone. I want to see you laugh. A lot. I want to see you laugh and be happy."

"And you?"

"That would make me very happy."

"That's all?"

"It's really all I need. I am a very simple person, really."

"I think I am too. I was, before my life became complicated. I want to be a simple, uncomplicated person again. I loved him unconditionally and totally. I was his woman, and he was my man. That is over now, completely and forever. I can do that again if a man will love me as much as I love him."

"Slow lasagna, baby. Slow"

"I am sorry." She caught herself, and laughed. "I should practice what I preach." Outside, she fiercely put her hand around his elbow and pulled him to her by his arm as they walked back toward the library parking lot. Wind blew up from the valley with all of its fresh, leafy smells. It had stopped raining, except for a few sharp gusts that left whip cracks of fine cold spray all over Rick and her.

"Feels wonderful," she said. "I forgot what it feels like, Rick. You make me feel like a woman. I feel comfortable with you."

"Me too. I think if we can avoid being nervous, we'll get along famously."

"Oh I do believe that." She gave him a squeeze.

They reached the dark parking lot, lit only by security lights. Only two cars remained—his and hers. She had a cute Volkswagen Beetle that looked like an electronic datacycle out of *Tron*. As they walked, she put her arm harshly around his back and dug her hand into his opposite side so that he felt the desperate strength in her fingers.

He stopped and turned her toward him, towering over her slightly by a few inches. Her face was upturned, and gleamed in orangey lamp light. Water, or tears, or both, streaked her glowing features as she gave him a piercing look.

Time stood still as he put his arms around her. She threw herself against his body. She wrapped her arms around him and made herself small against the hard, flat abs of his stomach. "Please come see me again."

"I will," he promised thickly. He wanted nothing more in this world.

"It's all so much at once," she said. "I never thought these feelings would be so overwhelming. But now you know. Now I know."

"You'll take care of yourself, will you?"

"I promise. You don't need to worry about me. I am rock solid." She shook her head. "I was crazy for a while there. That will never happen again. It was the shock, and the hormones, losing the baby, losing him, losing everything. That very day was when you came into my life."

"I fell in love with you right on the spot. Why do you think I stop in Emery every time I go through here?"

She grasped his sleeve and shook his arm vehemently, while her eyes lost themselves in his. "I know, I know, I know."

"Marian, do you have any idea how many times I drove by and didn't stop in, but I'd drive by slowly and look in the window as I was driving by, hoping just to get a glimpse of you?"

"I used to look out the window all the time too. I knew you were courting me. I knew you did all those silly things like say excuse me and cough and pretend to look for a book, just so you could talk to me and be close to me for a few seconds. Believe me, in my heart I knew it. I have loved you all this time. There, I said it."

"I love you too, Marian. I can't figure anything out right now because my head is spinning and it feels like Christmas morning. We will work it out between us."

"We will, Rick. I will give it all that I've got."

He awkwardly wanted to confess all. "You don't know what I did today."

"What did you do?" she asked, touching his cheek with her fingertip, protectively, as if there were a speck or a tear there, or just a drop of rain.

"You think I drove here with that book."

She looked puzzled. "It sure looked like it."

"I was stuck in Manhattan on the umpteenth floor of some skyscraper with a stack of contracts to sign and the clock ticking. I had to get it all done that day. I was miserable. Then you called me."

"I called you," she echoed.

"You called me."

"I called you," she said and laughed a little nervous giggle while staring into his eyes as if she was seeing him for the first time. Or seeing her motivations for the first time.

"You called me," he said holding both her hands against his heart. "I was so scared that I would miss our dinner date that I called Hartford and had my father's executive secretary send two helicopters."

"No."

"Yes. One to fly the book from the garage where I had it in the trunk of my car. The other to fly me from the rooftop of that skyscraper right here to you in Emery."

"No."

"Yes. It worked out so that the chopper with the book arrived about the same time as the chopper I was in. I picked up a rental car right there at the Emery landing pad, and drove to the library with the book."

"And we all thought you drove that way from the City."

"Pretty funny, huh? I was so eager to see you, and so anxious not to miss you."

"What about your car? The real one."

"We hired a chauffeur to drive it to Hartford for me."

"My god, Rick. This all sounds very expensive."

"Money is no object when it comes to you." There. It was out on the table. He made himself vulnerable in a way that old money instinctively did not want to be. Every ounce of his upbringing ran against it, but he had just put himself at her mercy. If she were another Cindy...he might just drive into a lake somewhere. Suddenly, his knees were shaking. He could already hear the lectures back in West Hartford.

She said: "I was worried that you didn't have enough money to pay the library fine."

"Yeah. Well, not a problem so much."

"I had no idea that you are a rich fellow."

"I know. I was going to make sure you didn't know. I got taken for a ride last time, with Cindy. That will never happen again."

"And yet you trust me enough to tell me all this."

"Slow boat, baby."

"Honey." She beat him lightly on the chest with a girl next door fist. "I would not have cared if you couldn't pay the fine. I would have paid it for you."

"I believe you."

"Tender," she said. She laid her cheek against his chest and sighed. "Tender heart."

"You drive home now."

"I will. You get home safely," she said. "I will be thinking about you."

"I'll be thinking about you every minute," he promised. "I have been thinking about you for half a year now."

"Me too." There, she had confessed her secret, her weakness, her desire, her dream. He could do with her as he pleased. She signaled her trust in him. He took her in his arms and kissed her. Her mouth came to his mouth with perfection. Their feelings were like two fires burning as one. Their hands roved hungrily, pulling each to the other. She ran her fingers over his cheek. He took her fingers and kissed them, rubbed them over his lips as if he were making love to them the way he would soon master her, take her, use her, blend his passion with hers until they were one.

It was difficult letting go, but they must. She kissed him a hundred more times before she could tear away. She fumbled and dropped her key ring twice, until he bent, picked it up, took her by the hand—she let him lead her as if she were a child, a stumbling, dazed girl. He led her to her car, unlocked it for her, kissed her languorously and passionately again, and helped her into the driver's seat. Her eyes looked dazed, her face stunned. He squatted by the car and held her hands. "Can you drive okay?"

She nodded distantly. "I will go home and sleep, and dream of you. Will you be there in my dreams?"

"I am already there. You said so yourself. I have been chasing you since that day last August. I think we have been dreaming together all this time, but we just didn't realize it."

"Yes," she said. "I have to get home now in one piece. You don't need to worry about me. I'll get there okay."

"Of course. See you."

Minutes later, she was gone. As he watched her Beetle dash away in the darkness with its cute squarish but rounded red tail lights, he was already living up to his promise. He waved, and she responded with a toot of the horn. She dimmed her lights for a second, and waggled her fingers out the window to make sure he got the message. He waved again.

Then he walked slowly to his car, feeling as if he had just gone through an emotional pepper mill and come out as fine grains scattered all over the table.

On his way home, he heard his cell phone begin to make humming noises. He reached over to the seat at his right and pressed its buttons. Its face lit up and a text message displayed: *Had Fun.* He pulled over at a rest stop along the turnpike, briefly, and signaled back: *Same. LY.*

Her reply came back: *LYT.*

=Love you.=

=Love you too.=

He was going to say something more, like More Soon or Soon Again, but decided instead to let her make that call within her comfort zone.

Oddly, on the hour long drive home, he had a torn, empty feeling. Like the storm earlier, it was a mix of shredded emotions—missing her already; fear that he was getting in too quickly over his head; shock at what she had told him about her Virginia Woolf moment; stunned that he had stepped into her life just then and given her new hope. He was afraid to mess with her delicate, complex storm of emotions. His own emotions he figured he could handle, but hers was a whole other life, another wonderful human being, someone he did not want to put in jeopardy of hurting her tender and bruised emotions. There were still stormy times ahead. One or the other might yet run away in panic. Life had this way of making lasagna out of a man's best laid plans. Slow boat, he reminded himself as he followed the late night stream of red taillights up I-91. Slow goat, he also reminded himself, feeling the blue ache in his loins. She was worth waiting for. She was worth everything.

16

For Marian, the next few days became a new kind of stressful. She was traveling into uncharted territory. On the one hand, it was a wonder that this handsome, appealing man had thought so much of her that he pursued her.

On the other hand, every instinct inside of her rebelled. She had kissed her wedding ring goodbye, and with it some part of the bond with her husband. There would always be the eternal bond they had sworn to each other. How cold and cruel the words now seemed: *until death do us part.* Who ever came up with that? It was true that they would never see each other again, but they were not parted. Not completely. There were still moments when she clung to Tommy in her heart, though she had begun to let go. Her oath to him had been forever. No, she reminded herself, it had been *until death do us part*. In her mind, she knew she must let go and move on.

Even in her heart, she was suffering. She had not lied to Richard Moyer. After losing her husband, her baby, her marriage, her life, her love—she had felt a crazy urge to end it all. She had really come close to walking into the lake with rocks in her pockets, or driving her car into the water like a modern woman would. Tommy did not want her to hurt herself. He would want her to pick up and carry on. She only slowly began to convince herself that her own theory was correct—that by some psychic connection, Richard Moyer or his ghost or spirit had somehow stepped into her life to save her. She was not psychic, and neither was Richard. It was a once in a lifetime thing. Maybe she was imagining things. As stressed out as she'd been, anything was possible. Tommy approved of Richard—that was equally clear. In the hallucinatory quality of that day, it was almost as if Tommy's ghost had sent Richard's spirit to save her from herself.

Honestly, if it had been she who died, she would have wished for Tommy to meet a nice girl and have a new start in life while he was still young. If he loved her as she knew he had, he would feel the same. So it was not Tommy who was holding on. It was her memory of him. It was her memory of the happiness they had shared, and the vows they had made. It wasn't that she was afraid of making a new commitment. Richard Moyer was still just a dream, just a pretty face. He was a fluffy emotion. He was nothing. Nothing at all. Not yet.

Not true, she told herself the next moment. They had embraced, and held each other, and kissed as she had not done with any other man in her life—ever. With Tommy, she had still been an innocent, naive girl. With Richard she was a seasoned woman, a widow, the bereaved mother of a little boy who had not made it even to his birth. Yes, the child would have been a boy. She did not know that until that dreadful night at the hospital when she nearly bled to death and saw what no mother should ever see. No wonder she felt so crazy and bereaved. Poor Richard, what he will have to put up with in me.

Then again, she changed, she tacked the boat to the wind, and felt the opposite way. Could her relationship with Richard become more? At the moment, the thought revolted her. She almost felt as if she were being unfaithful in her marriage, though she consciously could remind herself her marriage no longer existed. It was over. It had ended when Tommy lay dying in the arms of his comrade, Ernest Farmouth. Still, you could not simply turn the page or close the book. Not even a librarian could check that book in before its course had run out. Then again, Rick Moyer had saved her life. She liked to think of it that way. He had appeared during her darkest moment, and locked gazes with her. He must have thought she looked like a crazy person, she thought. She must have seemed like a hunted animal deep in some primeval forest when he first laid eyes on her. And yet, he had fallen in love with her. In love? How easily that word floated up in her thoughts. She pushed it away. She did not know him. Not yet. She must give her feelings time, no matter how she might have liked to rush things.

With a sigh, she turned her attention to a handful of late fees and other matters of momentary importance. She was surrounded by children clamoring for her attention. *Mrs. Charles! Mrs. Charles!* they cried with uplifted faces and anxious eyes. One needed a bandage for a cut finger. Another could not get her pink lunch box open. Another wanted back a pencil that a boy had commandeered from her. Another wanted to call home because her stomach felt queasy. She smiled and turned to their needs, which were so much more manageable than her own.

Already she waited for the phone to burp, ring, chirp, or warble. When would Richard call her? She couldn't wait. Slow boat—a day at a time. She smiled to herself as she walked her children to story time in the Fireplace Room. It would all work out. She had faith in this new man. He would not let her down. That would crush her, and she could not imagine it.

17

Rick's father was a commanding figure, whether clad in his business suit at work, or even a bathrobe at home. This particular morning, Jared Moyer strode into the offices with an old-fashioned newspaper under one arm, and his black umbrella in the other. "Richard, I'd like to see you in my office."

"Sure, Dad." *Oh Jeez here it comes.* Rick was immersed in his morning e-mail. The Goldstein account in Philadelphia was showing signs of tanking. He'd have to contact the broker in Philly and see about getting the Goldstein family trust moved into safer harbors, like some municipals a colleague had just the other day mentioned that were doing really well in Chicago.

Most delightfully, Marian had sent him one of her terse little texts: *Morning.*

He texted back: Sunshine & Smiles.

"Richard."

"Yes, Dad."

"Now--please."

Helen Dupuy looked up from her computer screen in the adjoining office, where she reigned supreme over four secretaries. Her gray eyes, meeting Rick's, had a pained look. "He is on his war horse, but then you knew that would happen."

"Yes, Helen. Thank you." With a sigh, Rick rose and grabbed his coffee. Stuffing a donut into his mouth as he passed the office morning tray in the secretaries' pool, he entered his father's large corner library office. "Yes, Dad."

"You have powder all over your face."

Rick snatched a tissue from a box on the window overlooking early summer greenery. "It's powder sugar, Dad. You'd think it was cocaine."

Jared Moyer was a tall, balding man with severe reddening of the face and neck, big gray eyebrows that always looked like thunder clouds, and a balding scalp. "Ricky," he said. "What was that helicopter business the other day?"

"I knew you'd be on to me."

Dad sighed. "Son, I get nervous when stuff like this crosses my desk." He indicated a stack of flash charges for cash accounts— rental cars, helicopters, petty cash.

"You have to trust me, Dad."

Dad, whose narrow gray eyes were still sharp, put on his horn-rimmed reading glasses in a convulsive motion, only to sweep them back down onto the papers. "I trust you. Trust but verify. As long as I remain the captain of this ship, I follow everything that goes on."

"I generated ten million dollars in gross revenues last month. I needed a helicopter."

"Two, from the looks of it. Son, what is going on?"

"Dad, it's a personal matter."

"Oh, it's a personal matter," Dad said sarcastically. Then he gasped for air and looked paralyzed, not knowing what to say next.

"Yes. I am charging it to my personal expense account."

Dad blinked. "Son, you are not carrying on again with another woman." It was a question more than a statement.

"Yes, I am."

Dad died. Or rather, he blinked and seemed to fall down a laundry chute inside himself.

Rick sat in the wooden armchair Dad had rescued from an old hospital due for demolition in a land deal. He put his feet up on the window sill, and dusted his hands off. "I have met a nice woman."

"Son." The nightmare of Cindy flashed before the elder Moyer's eyes. The family had paid dearly for Rick's mistake. Of course, they had also pressured him into marrying her because she came from a good family and would be good for cementing social relationships. In other words, she would be good for business. It all seemed so medieval now. In the juggling of ledgers following the settlement of his divorce, there was a Cindy Maravich account on the Moyer XL Holding books, from which a healthy sum had flown away on painful wings every month; the Moyers were waiting with bated breath for a copy of her new marriage certificate to arrive from an Argentine court to terminate the stipulations of Rick's alimony payments.

"Father."

Dad toyed heartbrokenly with his eyeglasses atop the bills. "Your mother and I love you very much."

"I appreciate that. I love you both very much. Dad, I am 32 years old. I contribute a great deal to this company. Can't I cash in for my needs once in a while?"

"I suppose so."

"Then what is the problem?"

"Don't get huffy."

"Do I hire helicopters every day?"

"No need to shout."

"I'm not shouting."

"If you are to take over this corporation when I retire, you have to show restraint."

Rick stared at his father. He felt elevators of bile rising up his throbbing neck. This was not the first time they had a discussion like this. Dad looked at him with that same sad finality and puritanical judgment he always did at times like this. Mom, were she here rather than at one of her ladies' clubs saving the world, would look at them both with pain in her eyes. He was sick of it. Now that he was coming out of his Cindy tunnel, he wanted a new life. He had been riding on autopilot for the past few years. He'd buried himself in work, possessed by a furious urge to prove Cindy wrong.

Cindy Maravich was not a horrible person. She was just wrong for him. They'd been wrong for each other. Cindy Maravich was what you would call a Piece of Work. She was gorgeous, stylish, and subtle about being a complete bitch. She was from a wealthier family than his—or so she liked to make out. They were old money dating to someone's investment in whaling ships from Boston and Providence back in the 1700s. Maybe Ahab had sailed for them, searching for Moby Dick. Whatever. And then some other flinty-eyed Maraviches had built yet another fortune upon that in Maine lumber, Pennsylvania canal construction, and other venues of the early 1800s. The problem was that a few more recent Maraviches had been bigger spenders than earners. The family was on its downhill side, but beautiful Vassar-educated Cindy had not yet gotten that memo. Her only job to date had been as some sort of nebulous go-to girl at a New York City fashion and marketing promotion firm managing movie stars, opera singers, and glamorous personalities who did nothing but appear constantly in the news. She had lowered herself to marry Richard Moyer of the up and coming Moyers, whose money was less than a century old, and dating to manufacturing contracts during two world wars, plus a 1950s investment empire built by Rick's great-grandfather and grandfather. He understood his father's anxiety. Dad had been brutally regimented and made to feel inferior by those two glowering men who stared at them from wall paintings in Dad's office. If it were up to Rick, he would burn the paintings, or at least stash them in basement storage. This was the conversation he had often thought of having with his father, but did not have the heart to lay on the old man: *Dad, do you suppose for one moment I am going to take a painting of you, when you are constipated and having heartburn, and hang it in this office one day when I am sitting in that chair? It's bad enough you have two generations of Captain Bligh staring at you. You want to become Captain Blight III? And then I suppose I will torment my child, should I ever have one, and become the heir to your telescope and officer's sword? No fracking way, daddy-o.*

But of course, Dad had a heart condition and must be treated with kid gloves. "Dad, we've talked about this before. Cindy ran up all that credit card debt without my knowledge."

"This is not about Cindy."

"Oh? Then what is it about? You are afraid to lose control. It's about the fact that I married a high society princess whose only sacred duty in life was to spend money and show off."

Dad shook his head. "I am going to be turning this ship over to you soon. Can I rely on you to have the sense to drive with the car doors closed?"

Rick stared at his father. Why was he in so particularly nasty a mood this morning? "Dad, we made millions last month. The curve is up over last year. I drive a four year old car, and buy my suits off the rack. You know, Cindy wanted me to fly to Paris and Milan to spend $100,000 on tailored clothes for both of us."

Dad closed his eyes in pain.

"You didn't know half of what went on, Dad, because I didn't want to put you through it. That hundred grand you spent on New York City divorce lawyers was for a good reason. She had million dollar Chicago and St. Louis attorneys working around the clock to screw us. I'm sorry about that. I would take it all back if I could."

Dad shook his head. "Son, I didn't mean to stir up the past."

"Then what is this about?" Rick jumped up and started pacing. "I am too old to be treated like a kid. Dad, it's the 21st Century. I'm a grown man. Have you noticed?"

"Yes," Dad said with rueful pride and love. "Sit down, Richard."

"No, Dad, I am going to pace up and down. I am not going to sit when I am told, roll over when it pleases you, beg for a cookie, whatever."

Dad raised his hands to his face, and covered it with his palms. "You were trying to impress a woman."

"No."

"It was a guy."

"Dad, I am a straight man. I need a warm body in bed with me every night. I don't play around. I screwed around royally when I was younger, I admit it." He'd been expelled from three colleges, including Harvard and Oxford. He'd finally managed to get his act together in the Army, and return with his G. I. Bill to finish a business degree at Yale. He had not needed the Federal money, but he'd been proud of his service. The Army had helped straighten him out. The Army had unfortunately not prepared him to deal with a totally lawless, undisciplined element of upper crust society like Cynthia Maravich. "Live and learn, Dad. You never made any mistakes, huh?"

Dad looked at him frankly. "I never had much chance, son. Your grandfather held me close by the bit."

It was true. The two men looked at each other. Father and son, they shared a lifetime of knowing one another as such. Dad had been raised during shaky times, with a mother (Rick's grandma) who was drinking too much, losing her mind, and had to be institutionalized where she drowned herself in a massage bath while stoked up on stolen pain killers. Granddad had responded by drinking heavily, and relying on Dad to carry the load as a young man in his 20s. Eventually, after Grandma's death, Granddad had somehow settled down. He had remarried to the stern Frances Rinaldi, a somewhat older banker's widow from Boston. Whatever it was he needed, maybe a substitute mother or nun or ninja, Frances had provided it. She was now 101 years old and living in a kind of seaside castle in Newport, Rhode Island, amid the ghosts of Vanderbilt and Astor, among other saints of billionaire vintage. Frances had been hard on Dad as well, until Dad—well, that was the Moyer story.

"Dad, you told your old man to go fly a kite."

"I did, son. Are you going to tell me to fly a kite?"

"Some time soon, yes. Probably."

Dad held his hands out as if it were going to rain and he were doomed. "I could retire today, son. Nothing to stop me."

Rick was startled. "Dad, are you feeling okay?"

"I am tired, son." His voice rose in anger, and Rick sensed it was not entirely at himself. "I am tired of riding this old mare of a company all by myself."

"You are not riding it all by yourself." Rick thought of all the cold, uncomfortable mornings in gray, rainy Manhattan or Chicago or Boston conference rooms, going over the accounts of firms that were sinking and being taken over or liquidated for their assets.

Dad slammed his hand down hard in a tantrum. "Two helicopters, you whazzoo. What is wrong with you?"

"Nothing." Rick whirled and faced him with his fists on his hips. "I am on drugs, okay? I am a friggin' hippie. It's the sixties all over again, which you missed because you were too busy getting peckered by your old man."

"You better leave now."

"I am, Dad. I am leaving."

"We can talk later."

"No, I do not want to have this conversation again."

"Richard."

"I am sick and tired of going in circles. Every time I close two or three million bucks' worth of business, you look at me like you want to praise me but can't because you are too constipated."

"Son."

"How about a word of thanks or congratulations some time? Huh?"

Dad looked at him helplessly. It was that moment in the lives of a father and son when the son is ready to fly from the nest at last. It had to be.

Rick turned and stormed to the door. He calmed down and felt an icy peace as he realized his life was about to take another sudden turn, long overdue. With one hand on the knob, he turned and said: "We can talk about this later, Dad. I'm sorry. I can't go on like this any longer."

Dad's face looked utterly pained and inscrutable. Their eyes met and they each knew it would blow over. But they also knew nothing would ever be the same again.

Rick ignored whatever Helen was saying. He snatched his raincoat from the peg by the main door and left the offices, the building. He wanted to leave Hartford, but he was too old to have a tantrum or run off half-cocked to see the world or find himself or get drunk in a random tavern. He had a life now, a stake, that he had worked for. It was time to cash in some chips. Time to make a move toward something positive.

Filled with disturbed, angry, hurt thoughts, he roared out of the parking garage in the old Jaguar vaguely in the direction of New York City. He could make the drive comfortably in two hours. He did not have much to do—just some mopping up on a few minor accounts that he could just as well have delegated to Geoff. And that was another thing. As well as he got along with the older account executive, he was not the man he would have hired to be corporate manager. Dad had hired an old, retired military officer—probably somewhat aware that as a former enlisted man, a guy like Rick would never want to work for an officer type again as he had during his Army years. Rick would have hired someone a lot like Geoff, but maybe younger. Probably someone who had proven himself in civilian life rather than, of all things, the Army. Dad himself had been an Air Force officer as a young man, following a sensible adolescence and a dutiful four years of college at Georgetown. There was this unspoken, subconscious midcourse correction maneuver Dad had made by hiring Geoff, even knowing that if Geoff stayed with the company, Rick would one day be his boss.

I need my own company, Rick thought.

The wind whipped by his face, and tore at his hair, as he speeded along the highway toward Waterbury. It was heresy. A Moyer was supposed to serve his life away in the company that his great-grandfather had built, and all those Moyer men who came afterwards. You had your chance in college to drink, party, dress funny, and act weird. You sowed your wild oats. You got in trouble, but nothing serious. Damages got paid, lawyers mailed out apologies to those whose mailboxes had been flattened by drunk-driving Rick the Harvard freshman, but in the end you settled down and became the next Captain Bligh. Actually, that wasn't so much the problem. The problem was that one Captain Bligh must clear the decks when his time came, to make room for the next. How old was Dad now? Sixty? Too young to retire, but old enough to sit on ten or fifteen corporate boards as a gray eminence and disseminate his wisdom and judgment in remote places like Honolulu, Singapore, Los Angeles, whatever. And take poor old mom out on a date to the beach, dance with her, get her tipsy on good champagne, and run around naked on some beach in Martinique or the Riviera with his gray boobies flapping before both Mom and Dad lost track of things.

As he speeded along the interstate, Rick thought about himself as well. He could very well start his own corporation. He certainly had the seed money, the experience, and the connections. It could be a nearly seamless transition. He'd have his own version of Helen. He'd hire his own Geoff or the un-Geoff. He almost grinned, grimly, at the thought. He'd hire the un-Geoff and the un-Helen. He'd become the un-Dad of his own un-corporation.

Noticing that he was low on gas for the return trip, he looked for the next exit ahead with the usual signs for Food-Gas-Lodging.

It was hard not to think that, subconsciously, he was not making this journey so he'd have an excuse to pass through Emery on his way back from the City to Hartford. He thought about his shaky but wonderful date with Marian last evening. He was no more ready for a relationship than she was. Most likely, he needed to let her go so she could find her way. He might be ready after another two or three years. How long would she need to recover from her terrible losses? Poor thing. He knew this much: the woman he was going to fall in love with must be a lot like Marian. But could he ever find another one like her? He could imagine his mother speaking to him, while light-heartedly waving a cocktail glass: "Oh Ricky, dear, the world is filled with nice girls. You just haven't looked in the right places."

He spotted an exit ramp and veered off to leave the highway. A truck blared its air horns angrily as he cut a little too closely in front of it. He waved *sorry* but wasn't sure if the speeding truck driver had seen his due diligence gesture. He cruised down the ramp into a busy intersection. The gas station was on his right. He turned in, rolled to a stop and the pump, and got ready to pump. While the hose gurgled and the tank filled, he thought more about Marian. Was she really as right as his impulsive heart had been telling him? He understood now why she had looked so wild that first moment. The idea that he had saved her from the ultimate desperation sent shivers through him, even when she admitted it honestly and assured him it was just a terrifying thought, not a plan or an actual deed. Nevertheless, he thought, he was going to take a drive today. Maybe he'd skip New York City for once, and go somewhere to think. Or he might go into the city and talk to a few contacts about opening his own draw accounts to start the ball rolling on Richard Moyer Corporation. That had sort of a ring to it, eh? All paid up, he finished tanking and did a snappy turn on the apron to return to the highway entrance. Waiting impatiently at a red light, he felt driven. He must see Marian again soon. He just wanted to hold her hand and walk with her. Maybe they would go down to that mysterious, beautiful lake he had yet to visit. He wondered if there were black sand along its shores, emery gravel, the kind you used to sand down your sharp edges, soften your troubles, and wear down your troubles in life. He wondered where Cindy was today—probably driving some other poor guy crazy. He thought about the friends he had left behind in Afghanistan. They would not need for anything, because their troubles were suddenly and permanently over. What a poor joke it all was. How unfair life could be to some and not to others!

The light turned green, and Rick shifted into gear. He left a slight screech of rubber and a whiff of smoke behind as he absently accelerated—too fast, and not cautiously enough.

At that moment, a large truck cut across his path from the right. Rick had no idea what to make of it. A semi coming in from the right had failed to slow for a Yield sign, and plowed right into the right side of Rick's car.

The next second or two of Rick's life passed in a darkening blur. Suddenly, he became aware that his car was turning—no, spinning—to the left. His left hand was on the wheel, and his right on the stick shift knob, but nothing mattered now. It was out of his control. Life was just now playing one of its grim jokes on him. How unfair it was, so rude. And why him? That was his last conscious thought as a giant tire rose up, crushing the right fender of his car. He could see huge rubber teeth, coated with bright yellow mud, biting into the metal as if it were paper. His window crumbled in a shower of glass pebbles. Metal screeched as the huge wheel ground his car up like a crumpled paper lying on the road. The last thing Rick felt was a heavy, suffocating load on his chest along with a smell of oil, rubber, and rainwater. Everything went dark.

I nexplicably, Richard Moyer stopped answering her little text messages. She went about her work at the library, puzzled and a little worried if not hurt. Had he changed his mind? Had something happened? Maybe he'd met someone new. Oh silly, she told herself, he is a grown man. Life does not make sudden turns like that. Or does it?

She went home each night to her two-bedroom house down in the valley. What a pleasant life this could have been, she always thought. It was a routine she went through as the custard-yellow VW New Beetle purred along leafy streets out of a Norman Rockwell painting. *Stop it*, she always told herself. *Life has something more in store for me than a lifetime of sadness.*

She drove up her driveway, which needed some major leaf blowing—and these were last fall's dry, dead leaves shoved into sad little piles in corners, amid grass that needed mowing and weeds that needed serious pulling. She began to think that soon, she must really stop waiting for Tommy to come home and do all these things. She must dig out her grungiest jeans and old T-shirts. She must go down to the minimart and buy herself a big soda and some work gloves, and get on her hands and knees here in the garden and make it all grow properly again. Her insides, including her womb, were like this weed garden too. Her whole life was a shattered mess. She could see it clearly. On her days off, she would saunter alone— she spent so much time alone—down to the lake and walk along the round, smooth stones half buried in mud. She might shield her eyes from the sun and look across at the boats. She always liked seeing colorful triangular sails gliding over the water. The lake was about a mile long and a half mile across, with plenty of space during the summery half of the year for water skiing and kite boarding. As the days went by, and the weeks and months, she was beginning to feel more in tune with herself and with life. So what if Rick Moyer had unexpectedly lost interest in her. Well, it had only been a few days. They'd been on such a roll, and now what?

The next morning, at work, she had a nasty surprise. She was just coming from the ladies' room in back, carrying some documents for the shredder, when she saw two men in gray uniforms at the Help Desk. They were speaking with Rose Otto. Linda Damien had stepped out of her office. As a puzzled Marian approached, they looked her. Linda pointed at Marian. The two officers nodded and looked at her. There was no humor in their eyes.

"Marian, can we talk for a minute?" Linda called out.

"Sure," Marian said. She felt an instant pang in her gut. She was not fond of uniformed men showing up with nasty news. "Yes, what is it?"

As Rose Otto stood in the background with her usual mysterious little smile and half-absent look, Linda introduced the two policemen. They were both young—in their 30s—one chunkier than the other. The lean one was Trooper Benoit, who nodded. He had small, flinty eyes and the look of a man who had seen much—she imagined mangled bodies in highway wrecks, shootings on the streets, all sorts of emergencies. The other man was Trooper Johnson, an African-American man with a slightly wandering eye and a broader face; he was chunkier, like a body builder. Both men were state troopers, in gray uniforms with blue trim, gray shirts with blue ties, and gray Stetson type hats. Each wore a black gun belt studded with leather pouches, handcuffs, a stick, and a 9 mm automatic pistol in a holster.

Linda escorted Benoit, Johnson, and Marian into the privacy of her office, and shut the door. It was a large office, which doubled as a conference room and a storage along one wall. They sat down at a long wooden table, while Linda excused herself to check her coffee maker.

"You know a Mr. Richard Meyer?" said Johnson, who was the corporal and thus the senior of the two.

Marian nodded, feeling a sinking sensation.

"Have you seen Mr. Meyer around lately?"

She made a conflicted yes-and-no shake of the head.

"Let me explain carefully what we are about," said Benoit. He had kind of a hard, stony face and cold eyes that intimidated. "If you will be up front and honest with us, it might save you a lot of trouble down the line."

Marian sat with her hands folded nervously on her lap, and her legs crossed below the knee. She wore a modest, below the knee, plaited brown skirt that day, a nice dark-rose colored silk blouse with a generous butterfly bow, nylons, and chocolate leather flats. She had slept well the night before, was well rested—until this happened—and had taken her time that morning putting together her makeup and some nice gold jewelry. Not that she had a lot of gold, but she had a few light, elegant things that looked nice on her, like her filigree necklace, and a wrist bracelet with little beaten gold charms on it.

"Miss McLaughlin," Benoit said. How odd that he called her Miss. It was kind of refreshing and deflating all at once. It took her married life away from her, but left her sort of new and free, or so her muddled and slightly scared thoughts ran. "Miss McLaughlin, do you indulge in any form of drugs? I mean recreational, illegal substances, specifically cocaine, heroin, that sort of thing?"

Astounded, she slowly shook her head.

"How about prescription pills without a prescription? You know, like codeine, oxycodone, anything that is illegal like that?"

She kept shaking her head.

Johnson chimed in, with his deeper voice: "We will find out the truth, Miss McLaughlin. You can make it easier on yourself if you help us out here. We need your help."

She gesticulated. "I will help you in any way I can. No, I don't even drink alcohol much, because I get headaches."

The two state troopers looked at each other, then at Linda, who shrugged. Linda came over, stood by Marian, and put a reassuring hand on her shoulder. This was one of those rural areas of Connecticut that did not have a local police force, but a resident trooper or two. State Troopers, the elite of the State Police, were the primary law enforcers outside the cities. They were highly respected, and conducted a broad range of investigations and operations, aside from chasing down speeders on the highways or assisting stranded motorists. They were trained in riot control, scuba diving, and all sorts of specialized fields. Their duties included some detective work, though they had a plain clothes branch as well.

"Here is the problem, Miss McLaughlin," said Benoit. "The school police conduct regular sniffer operations with dogs they borrow from us. We generally find out when the dogs pick up a scent of drugs around the kids' lockers—or even in returned books. So here's the thing. Your friend Mr. Moyer checked out a book not long ago."

Johnson read from the paper printout: "*The Stars Shine On Us,* by Stanley Murfree. Have you heard of it?"

"Before you answer," Benoit said, "think very carefully. We know you have been friendly with Mr. Moyer for some time. We know you were present when he checked this book out. So when we tell you this next bit of news, please think very, very, very carefully before answering. We can ask you to come with us to the nearest State Police office, and get you a lawyer."

"A lawyer?" Marian said. She nearly laughed at the absurdity of it all. "Am I under arrest?"

"Not at the moment," Trooper Benoit said.

"We do not have a warrant for that, although we have a warrant to search these premises, and I can have a warrant in five minutes via Internet to search your house and your car. It's just that it would look better for you if you volunteered to help us."

She shook her head slowly in amazement. Her head was spinning. "I don't know anything."

"Miss McLaughlin," Benoit said, leaning forward and clenching his heavy fists together. She felt hypnotized by the power in his arms under those long gray sleeves, and the hairiness of his big hands. Johnson, likewise, darker, exuded a sense of crushing power as he leaned his massive body toward her as well. Both men made their ordinary plastic conference chairs look tiny as they sat on them. "We found definite traces of cocaine on that book. Nobody had checked it out after Mr. Moyer brought it back. In fact, it was still sitting on the carrel where the duty librarian left it that evening, waiting for someone to replace it on the shelves."

"I guess that can take a long time," Johnson said.

Linda looked a bit puzzled. "We aren't ordinarily that slow. I mean—" she looked quizzically at Marian, who felt just as baffled—"normally a book goes back within a few hours. This one must have gone into some kind of loop. I'll have to ask Rose if she knows anything."

Marian shook her head. "If Rose had known about the book, she would have returned it to its shelf."

Benoit made fluid motions with his big hands. "Well, stuff does happen. You have so many thousands of books here that one could go astray, right?"

Johnson's open palms and wide eyes reflected the same thinking as Benoit's.

"Yeah..." Linda said slowly. "I guess one book could sort of stray from the pack. It happens from time to time." She said to Marian:

"You remember that copy of *Robinson Crusoe* that we couldn't find for a month, and it was right there on a window sill in the children's room?"

"Yes, I remember that," Marian said.

Johnson smiled fondly. "One of my favorite books when I was growing up."

Benoit looked at Marian closely with his red, small-featured face. "Do you know anything about the cocaine and how it got into that book, Miss McLaughlin?"

She stared at him, realizing with horror the implications about Richard Moyer. Once again, it seemed as if someone was trying to pull the rug out from under her feet. Could Richard Moyer be too good to be true? She felt mildly nauseated. All the terrible events of her recent life swarmed around her like a pack of nightmares, nipping at her, laughing fiendishly, and threatening to spoil what little joy she had gotten in her recovery.

"I am sorry to put you on the spot," Benoit said, "but I am afraid your association with Mr. Moyer has put you there."

Johnson said: "What are we supposed to think? We find definite, blatant evidence in that book that he might have used it to snort lines on it. It happens at parties where those sorts of people get together."

"He is a very wealthy man," Benoit said. "He goes to the City a lot, and he sees all sorts of wealthy clients."

"Well," Marian said, "I don't know. I just met him recently. I have had dinner with him once—a few evenings ago."

"Have you seen him since?"

She shook her head. "We were texting each other a little, just funny sweet little messages, but that stopped."

"Is he seeing other women? What kind of people does he associate with?"

"I don't know," Marian said, feeling more harried now. They were trained in interrogation techniques. They could tighten the screws slowly and make you feel as if you were losing your mind. "I don't know," she repeated, with more of a wail in her voice.

Linda intervened: "Have you spoken with Mr. Moyer about this?"

Benoit shook his head. "We have someone checking up on him. We do have his address and phone number. He is with an investment banking firm in Hartford, owned by his father."

"To be honest," Johnson said, "the way we do this, we kind of circle around and narrow the circle around a subject, rather than walk up to his door and knock. Gives us an edge of some surprise, as long as we work with warrants and do all the right things."

Benoit said: "We have desk people and undercover working this and probably a hundred other cases. We work our leads as we can with available manpower and resources."

"That is why," Johnson said, "we would really appreciate your full and honest cooperation as this case develops."

"It's a case?" Marian asked numbly. "A case against Richard Moyer?"

Both troopers nodded: "The law works kind of slowly sometimes, but this isn't going away."

Linda, as Chief Librarian, stood neutrally by and opined: "I really am very upset to think that someone is getting cocaine and other drugs into my library. We have hundreds of children coming through here every day. That book might be checked out by a high school girl or who knows what."

Marian shrugged and said in a small, sad, disappointed voice: "I will help in any way that I can, but I don't know anything."

Johnson held out a recording device. "Would you mind if I take a statement?"

"You can have a lawyer present if you wish."

Marian felt it was time to be really worried. "If you don't mind, I would like to have an attorney present. I have nothing further to say."

Her mind was racing. Had Rick Moyer ever seemed intoxicated or stoned? Had he acted weird? He was a funny man with a good sense of humor. Was that from drugs, or naturally? In her heart, she really wanted to believe in him. For her own sake, she knew she must be extremely cautious now.

Linda remarked: "He is still innocent unless proven guilty, right?"

"This is America," said Trooper Johnson with a hearty smile, revealing a gold tooth deep on one side of his mouth. It made Marian remember the gold rings in the bank vault. Oh, if only things could be simple again.

19

Connecticut being a small state, it took Troopers Benoit and Johnson less than an hour to drive from Emery Township to Greater Hartford, and thence to the business park in West Hartford where the Moyer Holdings building was just one of a farm of glass and steel clones ranging from four to eight stories tall. Many of the glassy buildings had a green or beige tint designed to modulate the baking summer heat. Today those features were not necessary, since the skies were gray and a light drizzle drifted on a hesitant wind.

"You buy her show?" Johnson asked as Benoit drove.

Benoit shrugged lightly. "She seems very sweet, but you never know."

Johnson took out his cell phone, which was making a warbling sound. "Johnson." He listened for a moment, then reached sideways with his left hand to touch Benoit's shoulder. "Right," he told whoever had called. "Please do. I will. Thank you." He snapped the phone shut and told Benoit: "Our man is in the hospital. He's in the ICU in critical condition."

"What?"

"Yeah. They are not sure if he'll make it." As Johnson spoke, the Hartford skyline loomed ahead. "That was headquarters. She told me that they are in the process of getting toxicology back on the victim, and she'll call me the minute they have a result."

"I can almost bet you he's stoked up. What happened?"

"Kind of a garden variety mishap. He was at a highway entrance, stopped for a red light, all legal and nice. A big semi on his right ran a Yield sign and chewed him up."

"What are his chances?"

"Like I said, he's in the Intensive Care Unit on life support. That's all I know."

"What do we do? You are the boss. I hope he lives so we can interview him."

Johnson bit his lip. "The tox report will tell us a lot. Other than that, there are too many variables going. I'd say we drop this and get on something else until we have more to work with, but cocaine in a public library is a pretty big deal. I mean, they get it in the inner city and places, but Emery is like Mayberry." He was referring to the famous Twilight Zone episode in which a harried businessman commutes from the ulcer-inducing nightmare of modern life, back in time to a long-ago small town paradise (and passes blissfully away in the process). "So let's continue with Plan A and go visit the suspect's place of residence for starters." He waved a flat pad, whose display showed a digital warrant to search Richard Moyer's home. "Then we swing by his place of employment. They are within blocks of each other. Say, with a company name like Moyer Holdings, do you suppose Mr. Moyer owns it?"

Benoit grinned. "Unless it's a colossal coincidence."

Johnson laughed. "That would be like you or I being named Connecticut State Police, right?"

"Yeah. These people have money, and where there is money there is usually cocaine."

"And where there is cocaine, there are suppliers. Too bad our boy is stretched out or we could put a tail on him."

"If he's buying, he's buying from small time punks. Unless he is a conduit and is passing it along for the cut."

Johnson said: "We'll find out soon enough. We can always have someone pick up the librarian and shake things up."

Benoit said with savage humor: "Waterboard her?"

"You are a harsh man. She is too cute. I was staring."

"Yeah, me too. She's a doll. Too bad a chick like that gets into the clutches of a monster like Moyer."

"Dude's got money." Johnson sat back and fanned his hands together over his stomach, as if satisfied with his own insightfulness. "Never fails." He sounded a bit wistful.

"If Mr. Moyer ever wakes up from his coma, maybe he'll find himself handcuffed to the bed."

"I'll loan them my cuffs," Johnson said with vindictive enthusiasm. "I'll roll him on his gurney right over to Club Med." He meant the Medium Security Federal prison at Danbury in the state's northwest corner, where a guy like Moyer, with no known priors, might land.

"Makes you want to go out and enforce laws, huh?"

"Beats being a school crossing guard."

"You are too funny."

Shortly, they rolled to a stop in a gated community. "Not bad,"

Benoit said as they stepped out of the car, onto the curb, putting on their gray Stetson hats and adjusting their service belts. "Ready?"

They strode carefully through a side door guarded by a small, elderly man in a private security guard uniform. The guard supervisor was a retired Hartford policeman, or so he told them. Shapiro had grizzled, tightly cut and curly hair, a red pinched face, and a shnoz. He sported brawny arms with old, faded U.S. Marine Corps tattoos amid a dusting of white hairs. After looking at their warrant, Shapiro led them along a network of concrete paths criss-crossing manicured lawns. The houses all around looked spacious, expensive, and secure. Each had its small pool behind a high stucco wall. The overall stucco tone all around, of walls and buildings, was beige, with chocolate trim and roofs. Many of the windows sported playful circular or cathedral window shapes.

"This guy smuggling weapons? drugs? slaves?"

"We are just here to check the premises," Benoit said. "There may be a Hartford PD forensics team here later to sniff for drugs."

Johnson told him: "We suspect Moyer has a habit of snorting cocaine from library books."

Shapiro looked baffled. "Just when you think you've heard everything. What next?"

"Any suspicious activity around his house?" Benoit asked.

Shapiro guffawed. "Are you kidding? This place is like a synagogue or a church. Nothing ever happens here. I worked the graveyard shift in East Hartford as a detective. I know excitement when I see it."

"Some of these holier-than-thou rich folks are the worst," Benoit agreed.

20

Troopers Johnson and Benoit did not ask Marian any further questions. Evidently, they had been bluffing just a bit. They excused themselves, saying there would be future consultations, and off they went—presumably in search of Richard Moyer and further evidence to build their case against him or whoever had spiked the cowboy book with cocaine.

"Are you okay, honey?" Linda asked Marian after the two men left.

"What now," Rose said as she stood behind the Help Desk with her usual bemused look. She always looked as if she knew something she wasn't telling others, Marian thought. Terie and Lillie had made similar comments in the past.

"I'm okay," Marian told her boss. "I'm at my best if I just keep my head down and stay busy."

Linda smiled. "We will certainly do that to you."

Linda returned to her office. She turned in the door and said to the staff in general: "Mr. Perez will be back to work later today. Everyone...?"

Rose nodded without looking up, but seemed to flinch just the faintest bit, Marian thought. Marian nodded her acknowledgement to Linda. "Is anyone ordering a cake or something?"

"We are going to take him to lunch on Friday," Linda said. "Hope that's okay with everyone."

"That will be fine," Rose said.

Lillie waved from the entrance to the Stacks, and Terie smiled where she knelt at a low book case.

Marian stayed busy all day. As predicted, around 2 p.m. right before the rush, a smiling Mr. Perez walked in. He wore a nice new guard uniform, and looked rested. He looked tan and fit, Marian thought—a handsome man in his late fifties, with gleaming white teeth, short curly dark hair, and a healthy tan on his normally caramel skin. His eyes had a crispness about them, maybe due to the contrast between sugar-white sclera and dark irises; whichever way he looked, there was something incisive and wise about his eyes. He would have made a good politician, she thought. He waved to his fans around the library, and a number of people broke into applause. Marian joined them. It was good to see him back.

The after school rush came and went as usual. It was a dry, windy day outside. That meant overcoats, but no boots, umbrellas, or slickers. Traffic glided by more smoothly, and children poured into their parents' cars for their daily get-away.

Marian paused philosophically and stared at the town beyond the library's big picture windows. Across the busy thruway, and the guard rail dividing it from the drop on the other side, lay the valley and the town. The lake had an extra shimmer today, so that the bluish-gray sky blended in its own pearly reflection on the water. It was relatively clear, and Marian could see red, green, blue, white, all colors of sailboats skimming on the lake surface. Tommy had taken her sailing a lot. He'd been a sailor in his own little right. He'd planned to buy a new sixteen footer when he returned from the service. With the settlements she'd received, Marian could buy herself a sailboat, or a new car, or pay off the mortgage on the house. Right now, the money sat in a CD, earning a small bit of interest. Like everything in her life, that was on hold. She could do a lot of things. She could, for example, say goodbye and move far away to start over. The situation unexpectedly going on with Richard Moyer scared her. She had feelings for him—she wasn't sure how deep they ran. She was not sure she was ready for even the faintest commitment, especially when the man who was courting her was now suspected of being involved in drugs. Some instinct deep inside told her there must be some mistake. But what? Were the state troopers just reaching for some kind of resolution— anything—so they could file a report, arrest someone, and move on? or did they know something about Richard Moyer and perhaps his gang of wealthy Manhattan financiers that she did not know? A man who was doing awful things like snorting cocaine would not tell a naive small-town librarian what a pirate he was.

As she saw the last of the children off to their cars, and the parking lot was largely empty, she stood in the growing evening wind and reflected on her life. She was tired of being alone. It wasn't just being alone, but living with memories. If it weren't for the memories—Tommy smiling, Tommy taking her to a movie, Tommy uncorking a bottle of champagne at her birthday, Tommy lying on his back on the lawn after the branch fell on him and she rushed to bring him an ice pack...all those crazy little things. She was not sure how much longer she could continue to marinate in the past.

Tommy's parents and siblings lived in the Hartford and New Haven areas. When he had brought Marian here from San Diego, he had chosen Emery because it was in the quiet backwoods of the Nutmeg State, not far from the stately, decaying towns of Meriden and Middletown. Here in Connecticut, as across New England, almost every town or city had a welcome sign, and below it in smaller print the word Founded by a number usually beginning with 16, as in 1634, 1688, 1654, and a few in the 1700s. Every town had at least one little white or red brick church with a white steeple dating to Puritan times. Emery dated to the late 1600s, when a land surveyor from Putnam had discovered black sand in a mountain cave overlooking the lake. That was now the site of Worix Corundum, a local firm with a mish-mash name owned by some distant corporation with a U.S. flagship name, but investors in Asia and Europe as well as Chicago and Toronto.

She had an odd feeling about Tommy's family. Her parents loved her, of that they were certain, as much for their son's sake as for hers. But there was something missing or guarded or whatever. There was a certain amount of dysfunction in Tommy's family—the uncle who drank too much, the aunt who was obese and abusive, the sister who acted as if she were jealous of Marian, and so on. Maybe it was natural that they were experiencing a rift now.

As she drove down her street—Montague Lane, named after the surveyor from Putney who had discovered black sand and created the township in 1666—she reflected that she loved it here. She did not consider her feelings bounded by her attachment or lack of attachment to the Charles family. In many respects, she could perhaps change her name back to McLaughlin and make a fresh start. It seemed like treason and heresy, like unfaithfulness and sabotage, but maybe she was just beginning to feel the first inklings of a need for drastic change. She need not feel bound to Emery. New England was filled with small towns like this, as was much of the rest of the USA. As she pulled up in the driveway, and the sun was just setting over the lake down the street, she realized that she was still waiting—for Richard Moyer to tip his hand. She was inclined to give him that much space if he really cared about her. It was scary, because maybe he was a drug fiend or a crime lord or who knew what. As desperate as she had been when Richard Moyer stepped into her life and gave her new dreams, he deserved at least one last chance. He was so ravishing, so gentle yet firm, so kind but cocky and self-assured, with just that tinge of neediness about him that she dreamed of taming. If he had a need, she longed to fulfill it, while filling up her own needs and dreams from the same well. Then again, who could really believe the story he told her about coming in a helicopter, and the book in another helicopter? I must be a real fool, she told herself. Yet here she was, owning her own home, to which she had lock and key, and this gave her a sense of security. Tommy's family had made no claims upon her for the house or any property. She had gladly shared with them any photos or videos dating to their few short years together, their bliss spanning the days in San Diego and more recently their brief home life in Emery. For the moment, anyway, she felt she had both feet planted on the ground. The ground might be a little shaky, so to speak, but it was her ground. She let herself in, turned on the lights inside, and went about the business of making herself at home, making a little dinner. How much more gladly she'd make dinner for two, but it wasn't to be. How much more gladly she would kiss, and nuzzle, and hug, and joke, and curl up before the TV to watch some silly sitcoms or a ball game or the weather report if it were two rather than just one lone woman. The very structure of her life, with its security—her street, her home, her job at the library, her friends—was her prison. Loneliness was the ghost that came at night and tormented her; but that was her private cross to bear. She resolved to make the most of her blessings. Her glass was half full, rather than half empty. *I shall not want.*

21

Fire fighters and paramedics worked for two hours to cut Richard Moyer out of the wreckage of his Jaguar. While the Jaws of Life racketed around the crushed cockpit of the small car, a giant tow truck arrived to carefully remove the multi-ton tractor truck without further injuring the sports car beneath the truck's enormous left front wheel.

State Troopers signaling with heavy black flashlights routed traffic around the grim scene. Magnesium flares burned with red-white intensity on the littered asphalt of the roadway. A news truck came and went—accident scenes were old hat, a brief mention in the evening news. The occupant of the vehicle was briefly and erroneously noted as William Meister by a rookie reporter from Hartford.

As the broken, bloodied body was slowly extricated from the crushed cab, a Life Flight helicopter arrived with flashing lights under it. The chopper danced about, and finally set down in a department store parking lot nearby. An ambulance carried the sheet-draped body the 1,000 feet from the accident scene to the chopper.

The helicopter's engine roared as it took off, turning its tail and rotor for the journey to Hartford General Hospital. Owing to the patient's desperate condition, the flight was re-routed south towards Yale-New Haven Medical Center.

The chopper flew fast through gray, drizzly air. It streaked under charcoal, roiling clouds on its desperate mission, while EMTs worked feverishly in the dark interior to stabilize the patient. That included some very careful, superficial cleaning of a terrible head wound that left spider webs of blood, clots, and dirt all over his face. His eyes were black, swollen lumps amid a shattered face.

The chopper landed atop the helipad in New Haven. Nurses and doctors shrouded in bilious green surgical scrubs, complete with masks and hoods and booties, rushed out to receive the body and wheel it into the building.

The earthly shell of Richard Moyer was wheeled into the science fiction theater of Trauma Bay, where his clothes were cut away and dozens of specialists instantly began the delicate task of salvaging when they could. They worked for two hours under precisely calibrated overhead lights that shed just the right sort of light that made few shadows and was easy on narrowly focused eyes in faces frowning impersonally behind mustard-green surgical masks. Lights twinkled gently on monitors, sine waves in blue and green snaked endlessly and repetitively across radar-like screens. Sleeper bells made regular, low warning sounds like monsters stirring in an uneasy sleep; if the patient's condition changed, they would begin humming and beeping to bring staff running. These would accompany him to his next station as well, if he made it that far. Alternatively, an orderly from Pathology brought an empty gurney and parked it outside the double doors. On the empty gurney was a stack of folded sheets if Mr. Richard Moyer's next, and last, stop were to be into the bowels of the sprawling medical center—to the morgue, if it came to that.

Naked, spread-eagled, trailing tubes and wires, Richard Moyer was then wheeled into the Intensive Care Unit where he was hooked up to life sustainment and calibration machinery. Surrounded by soft winking lights and gently pinging sonar-like sounds, he hovered between life and death. His face looked swollen and distorted, shrouded in bandages. His eyes remained violently purple, swollen plums. The Trauma ICU had its own essential X-Ray and CAT Scan equipment, because its patients typically could not be moved. Radiology technicians now appeared and began assessing the damage inside Richard Moyer's traumatized body.

He was assigned a doctor—a middle aged internist named Dr. Modra Singh, wearing a Sikh turban, and with a dignified gray beard. His trauma nurse was an African-American man named Ray Tillman, who had worked in the ICU for several years, and Richard Moyer would be his sole patient for the next 48 hours—depending on whether he pulled through or not. Everything now depended on the series of tests that Dr. Singh carefully staged, in a succession of best case optimals.

The initial scans told of a significant subdural hematoma—a violent swelling between the skull and the dura mater, the tough pouch inside the skull, which contained and protected the delicate three pound organism known as a brain. More nurse specialists arrived, standing by in case tubes needed to be inserted to relieve pressure on the brain before permanent brain damage or death could set in.

Mr. Richard Moyer, said Dr. Singh to his staff gathered around for an initial team talk, was clinging to life by a thread.

The next 24 hours would be touch and go.

The doctor's expression was businesslike—and grim.

22

Friday was the luncheon celebrating Adolfo Perez' return to work after the loss of his wife. Linda Damien had arranged for several teaching assistants from the grammar school to spend forty minutes manning the library's public spaces. There would be no books checked out during that period, and a school police woman came to oversee the grounds. The police woman was a middle-aged blonde named Stephanie Rasmussen, with a stocky figure and a mannish face. She was handsome rather than pretty, and a bit gruff, but straight-arrow and well liked. As it would turn out, Mrs. Rasmussen became a key player in Marian's life, quite accidentally, for which Marian would always be grateful. Steph, as everyone called Mrs. Rasmussen, was fond of Marian and always gave her a little thump on the back, particularly since her husband was a Navy veteran and she had a daughter named Tina who was serving with the Coast Guard out of New London, on the Connecticut shore not far from Rhode Island.

"You go an enjoy yourselves," Steph called out from the steps of the library as the women departed to ride together in two cars. Marian hardly had room in her car, so she rode in Linda's large blue SUV.

Linda waved as she wrestled the stick shift into reverse. "With Steph in charge, what could go wrong?"

"I'm sure the library will survive for an hour," Marian said, sitting in the front seat. She wore her loose wool dress today, with its fine horizontal stripes in burgundy, charcoal, navy blue, and moss on a light gray background. She wore a custard wrap, yuppie wheat socks, and those shiny mahogany loafers that rarely came out of the closet. The woman complimented her on her little bits of jewelry, including an opal ring with lots of color in it (a gift from her dad back in Oklahoma), and a very light gold necklace that was hardly more than a fine rope screwed together with a clasp at the back of her neck; it matched the ankle bracelet that Tommy had given her.

They arrived at the Chinese restaurant on Fog Street near Lake Emery along with groups from the school and the city administration. Probably forty people in all came to celebrate a somber turning point in Adolfo Perez' life. There would be a minor surprise today, culminating in a stunning realization fueled by a very busy rumor mill.

Marian felt very much at home with her work mates. She enjoyed being squeezed into a corner seat, sheltered among many bodies, while men and women told jokes, bantered, or exchanged information. She had lived here for nearly four years now, and felt at home here. If only she were able to make more friends outside of work. And, of course, if only she could someday invite a nice man to her house, make him a salad and a steak, surprise him with a nice chocolate mousse or cake for dessert, and then just curl up with him and a glass of wine and watch a romantic movie.

She sighed. If only. Richard Moyer, are you in a shoot-out in some drug lair someplace? Are you running across rooftops pursued by police or thugs? Are you thinking of me, or are you sitting in some swanky Midtown watering hole with brick walls and a wine cellar, being waited on by two or three slinky young women in little black dresses and with mysterious faces and alluring dark eyes, who are wrapped sensuously around you while you ask for a martini that's shaken and not stirred? Are you at all aware that I am worried about you and a bit annoyed that you have not sent me any more of those little text messages with doohickeys in them?

Lunch was tasty—*mu shu* chicken breast in wraps, dipped in duck and plum sauce, to die for. She had a lemonade with lunch. She did not like to drink during the day, because it made her sleepy, and the afternoon with be a long drag of yawning and effort. As they waited for dessert—everyone got a little square of some sort of overly sweet lemon cake with a cherry and a green mint leaf on top—there were a few speeches. Linda rose and gabbed. Adolfo Perez, who spoke with only a faint Spanish accent (being Puerto Rican and French Canadian) thanked everyone for their kindness. His wife had been ill for a long time, and in a coma for the last six months. It had been hard on the family, including his two sons and three daughters, all of whom were present in their school best and smiling regally. Only gradually did Marian notice that, sitting on one side of Adolfo was his eldest daughter Maribel, and on the other side was Rose Otto. The hour passed quickly. Marian felt contented with her portions and silently promised to work out fifteen minutes extra on her exercise machine in the basement at home.

In the car back to the library, Lillie and Terie held nothing back. "Did you see Rose sitting there?" Lillie said. She sat in the front seat this time, sideways and facing halfway toward Marian and Terie, who sat in the rear.

"I could swear they held hands under the table at one point," said Terie.

Linda led out a boisterous laugh over her shoulder. "I am not informed or interested." A lot of staff stared as if bursting with questions for their older work mate. Rose kept her eyes down and worked steadily, looking mysterious. She kept a straight face and looked every bit the frumpy, sixty-something librarian with slightly thinning orange hair, pinched little thin features, and just that chicken-peck of a rouged mouth between powdered cheeks. Only her eyes had a bit of a sharp, bluish twinkle. And Marian thought she finally understood that maybe Rose's mysterious, distant smile was really a secretive smurk.

23

We shall be guardedly optimistic," said Dr. Singh to his assembled team— Team Moyer, as they called themselves for the moment. Two days had passed since the helicopter had brought Richard Moyer to New Haven.

"Mr. Moyer has no broken bones and no internal bleeding. He has no ruptured organs or profusion vessels. His lungs are clear and functional; he is off the ventilator. He has head trauma, which is confined to a concussion and the hematoma, which is stabilized and slowly decreasing pressure on his brain. There are still a hundred things that could be terribly wrong, including torn optical nerves resulting in blindness, and many other little hidden things that will only come to light when we have him walking and talking—if he can ever do either thing again. The major crisis is past, in trauma terms. Now it remains to see how the patient will recover toward a full and normal life."

With that, Dr. Singh led his team to another station, another critical patient—a heavy Italian-American mother of four who had been crushed by a toppled freezer in her garage. There was no end to the trauma this big city medical and trauma center as well as a world-class university teaching hospital affiliated with Yale. Richard Moyer was merely a passing blip on a long series of statistical check marks. As with all patients, he was a page or two of cryptic technical jargon spewed out by electronic summarizers from hasty entries made by doctors, nurses, and technicians who recorded everything from his dilation—one pupil slightly larger, suggesting opposite hemisphere tear or swelling, they needed to do more tests—and this stream of input merged with a steady flow of monitor data like pulse, blood pressure, oxygenation, and more.

In a waiting room down the hall sat an elderly man and woman. The man sat with his long, formerly athletic body hunched and his wide shoulders drooping. His elbows rested on his thighs, while his face lay on his palms. He shook his balding head and muttered: "What have I done?" The woman, his wife, had one hand over his hand, and her other arm over his back to comfort him. Her own expression was grim and cried-out. Richard was their only child.

Jared and Sally Moyer had already cried together, lamented, blamed themselves, prayed to the heavens. They had spent every waking hour the past day in that waiting room, having hospital fare brought to them—not caring what it was, jelly or broth, meat or vegetable. They had already summed up their own lives, and made a tally of their shortcomings. At the moment, there were few positives on the balance sheet. Yes, Jared had followed in the footsteps of his forebears. He had become the man they wanted him to be. They had beaten him like a ploughshare, hammered him like a horseshoe on the anvil of their determination and grim vanity. Jared in turn had allowed many of his personal dreams to slip by, in order to focus on tending a thriving business which, like most businesses, was constantly on life support. A wrong investment, a missed opportunity, an overlooked turn in the markets—a lot of factors could send it into a tail spin. That required an ever vigilant, dedicated captain at the helm.

The time was drawing near for the next generation to pick up those duties. Jared and Sally were in their sixties and growing tired. Sally was by now a breast cancer survivor, a recovering alcoholic, and a cautious supporter of progressive causes. Jared had a slow growing prostate cancer that needed more attention than he'd been willing to give it, and himself. He had once been an athlete, but in recent years he'd barely had time for his morning walk before becoming a prisoner of his monotonously gray office in Hartford, surrounded by paintings of scowling men.

"I pushed him too hard," Jared said into his clenched hands.

Sally rubbed his back, somewhat resentfully, but ever dedicated to be with her husband. She would have liked for Richard to pursue his interests in painting, history, and travel. Instead, the boy had married the kind of high-pressure society girl who had all the connections around New York, Washington, and Boston—but none to her own heart or anyone else's. If anything, Cindy Coronato was to be pitied, despite her pitiless machinations in life. Of late, she had been dating an Argentine billionaire twice her age, who liked to show off his young, blonde wife and her knife-edge figure and blue-eyed model face. Cindy would be marrying Augusto Loret any day now, and the Moyers' monthly alimony account for her could thankfully be closed.

With Richard on life support in a dim, cool, impersonal trauma center far from home, none of that mattered any more. None of it. There was no comfort in the Moyer money, or in anything they had done. What mattered now were memories, mental photographs, as well as a tattered old photo album that Sally had brought along for the vigil: Richard, age 3, waving a toy shovel while sitting happily in the sand on a Long Island beach; Richard, age 6, in a little suit, starting First Grade in West Hartford; Richard, age 10, clowning around with other boys at a Cub Scout barbecue in upstate New York; Richard, age 14, as a high school track star at Choate; Richard, age 18, as a promising young freshman who had not yet been expelled from Harvard; Richard, age 22, as a U.S. Army sergeant in the Top Secret Crypto section of a headquarters in Kabul...

When she came to a photograph of Richard, age 26, sitting in a horse-drawn carriage in Manhattan with a coldly smiling, steely-eyed Cindy Coronato one summer day, Sally removed the photo from her album, tore it in half, and threw it into a nearby trash bin.

There was only one other photo taken about two years ago at an office party: a tired, harried looking Richard, age 30, looking up tiredly and distractedly with a wan half-smile from a pile of work in the office in West Hartford, while Helen Dupuy sing-songed "Smile, Richey honey, smile for the camera!" He looked sad, and prematurely old in that photo.

Sally held the snapshot in both trembling hands. She held the photo down low before her, looking down into it, and began to quake. Her look suggested she would do anything—anything at all—to make things be different than this outcome.

Jared, sensing her seismic trauma, looked up from his own self-blame, and put his arm around his wife as she began to cry in a keening, reedy voice that cut through the gloom and silence of the waiting room like a surgical knife.

Jared held her close to him, though he felt a bit of resistance. She blamed him for driving the boy too hard. He knew in his heart that he would never forgive himself, and he did not blame her if she would be cold toward him for the rest of their lives. Nothing mattered now—not his feelings, nor the damned worthless business, nor all the money in the world.

Only Richard mattered, and his happiness after all that he'd already been through. That included friends killed in Afghanistan, a disastrous marriage with Cindy, and a much earlier happy romance with a girl named Mary Hollister, which had been derailed through the machinations of both sets of parents, who had loftier ambitions for their children. Mary was now a housewife in Troy, New York with two children, one of them severely autistic, and a husband who made good money, golfed, but had zipper and gambling problems.

There was a lot for Sally and Jared to cry about.

24

It did not take long—maybe two days—for word to get out that Rose Otto and Adolfo Perez had been carrying on a raging love affair for at least the past six months. Marian was sure the details would be quite juicy.

Of course some people were more shocked than others. Lillie and Terie were abuzz with whispering as they went about their work. Linda kept to her office, emerging only to cast oddly evaluative looks around her domain and its denizens. There was always more going on with mother hen than anyone knew.

Marian stayed buried amid her thoughts and duties and avoided gossip. What did she care if two people found some comfort for their needs, as long as they weren't doing anything really gross? Evidently, Mrs. Perez' wife had been failing for a long time, and hardly recognized him or their children in the final half year of her terribly debilitating illness, which had begun attacking her brain as long as two years ago. Marian only cared that her own troubles with the police over Richard Moyer should not deepen, so she ducked lower each time she saw Linda's door open.

A very uncomfortable thing happened late in the day on that same Friday as Mr. Perez' luncheon. Marian was just leading a dozen or so First Graders from the children's hall into the story hour meeting room when two elderly persons walked into the library.

The man and woman, in their sixties, looked strange, kind of luminous as if filled with emotions. They seemed lost and distressed. The man wore a dark business suit, scarf, and overcoat. The woman was conservatively and richly dressed in what Marian usually called drabs. They marched to the Help Desk, where Rose Otto met their angry arrival with surprise but poise. As she marched the children through the main hall, Marian noted that the elderly man had a marked resemblance to Richard Moyer. She felt a pang of anxiety shoot through her gut like battery acid. The woman— perhaps Richard's mother?—gave Marian a look of speculative recognition and dark hostility. Marian quickly looked away, turning red, and guided the children into the conference room for a story hour involving Dr. Seuss and the Grinch, which always got lots of laughs and attentive arm-waving.

Marian had almost forgotten about the man and woman, so busy was she with the antics of her comic characters, when the door opened and Linda poked her head in. Marian froze. *What trouble am I in now?* she asked herself.

Linda raised a finger to her lips, gave her head a brief shake, and made big eyes. She formed her lips into an emphatic, almost frantic "shoosh."

Marian shrugged and telegraphed with her eyes: *What?*

Linda signaled furiously: *Stay here.*

Marian pushed aside her feeling of unease after Linda left, and continued entertaining the children.

Later, she knocked hesitantly and softly on Linda's door.

"Come on in."

She stepped inside. Her boss was alone in the office.

"I recognized your knock," Linda said with calm humor.

"What was that all about? Doomsday?" She took a seat in an arm chair facing Linda's desk.

Linda came around and sat in another chair beside her. Linda did not like to preside. She liked to play the equals card. "Those were the parents of Richard Moyer."

"Really?" Even though she had suspected as much, Marian was shocked. The older man had an uncanny resemblance to his son. "Why the grim faces?"

"Their son has been in a very bad car accident."

Marian's stomach turned as if rough hands were wringing it like a wet rag over a sink. Was it possible? Was she bad luck? Was there a curse...?

"Happened the day before yesterday, and the father blames himself. However, apparently the police have been to see them about the cocaine issue. They can't believe their son would be involved in something like that. Of course, no upstanding citizen wants to believe that about Junior."

"I believe it," Marian said. "I don't know why, but I like him and I don't think he has anything like that going on. Of course, I could be kidding myself."

Linda shrugged. "They came here to lynch you, frankly. They thought you must be some evil woman. I straightened them out on that."

"Oh thanks." Marian laughed humorlessly.

"They wanted to confront you, but I said no."

"I'm glad you did, although I wouldn't mind—?"

"No," Linda interrupted. "They are too emotional. Their son was nearly killed, and the police are sniffing around..."

"How is he doing?"

"Fine."

Marian shook her head. "What do you mean?"

"He is in Yale-New Haven Medical Center under observation."

"Is he conscious?"

"Yup. So they tell me. He is out of the ICU. He is one lucky fellow. He has a concussion and a huge headache, but no broken bones, no internal bleeding, no whatever else. I'm actually quite happy about it, if only for their sake." She patted Marian on the forearm. "And yours, sort of."

"Sort of?"

"I know you like him. We also don't really know for sure how this cocaine thing came about. He could very easily have a habit."

"I wouldn't like that," Marian said. "I wouldn't want to deal with that."

"Have some sense, girl."

"I'm doing my best, boss."

"I imagine you will be on your way to New Haven."

"It is crossing my mind."

"Well, know that they are no longer out to lynch you. I read them the riot act. I said a lot of positive things about you, and laid it on thick that you are a war widow and how dare they. You could have heard a pin drop. I thought she was going to start crying. He already was."

"Crying?"

"Yeah. She was rubbing his back while he sobbed. I almost ran out of tissues." She waved an empty card stock container, and threw it across the room into the metal trash can with a bang. "You want to leave early before traffic?"

Marian nodded. "I'll make it up to you."

"We'll figure something out. Go."

"Thanks."

Fifteen minutes later, Marian was in her VW, tooling south toward the coast. Rural Connecticut did not have the freeways of California or the other Southwestern states. The landscape here was incredibly green and Disney cartoonish, with black and white cows chewing grass in passing meadows, and hair-pin turns on the narrow blacktop roads that took her toward Meriden. From there, she threaded into congested local roads. Once she was on I-91, the going was faster. She had to see him. This was something she had to do. If nothing else, it was about clearing the air, finding out the truth, and maybe telling him she had made some progress in her ability to let go of the past. Whatever she ran into this evening, she would handle it. Whether it was the last time they saw each other, by his choice or hers or both, so be it.

All hospitals have a quality of sadness, especially as daylight fades and evening pours into the faintly echoing corridors like a dark liquid. Marian strode along in her soft shoes, making little sound except a faint rhythmic squeak. She wore a businessy black dress with a silvery brooch (butterfly) over one breast and a white silk kerchief around her neck. She'd thrown a light wool coat over it, colored a dark butterscotch, with wooden ski-coat buttons. Not an elegant fit, but it would do against the chill night air. Under it, she wore her striped wool dress in drab colors, which was one of her favorites; with black nylons, through which the pale skin of her legs shone.

As she came to the waiting room, the parents rose. There was no hostility in their stance, more like resignation, and a guarded sense of openness. She was not going to let anyone intimidate her. She strode toward them at a normal pace and nodded. "I'm Marian McLaughlin, the librarian. You must be Richard's parents. Linda told me what happened."

"We're glad to see you," the mother said, introducing herself as Sally and the father as Jared.

"We are," Jared affirmed. Both shook her hand. Jared said: "Richard was happy to hear you were coming to see him."

She parted her arms slightly in a brief gesture asking *so where is he?*

Jared Moyer, she sensed, was a keen judge of people, and a tough cookie with a soft center. "I am sorry to hear of your loss," he said.

She was surprised at her own guardedness. She merely nodded to acknowledge his statement. She was not about to discuss her dead husband and war hero with people who had only hours ago wanted to confront her about some scurrilous accusations. She carried her memories with dignity and love, and nobody was going to trifle with that.

"He started talking to us this morning," Sally said. "We have been in shock."

Join the club, Marian thought.

"Thank you for being his friend," Jared said.

That broke the ice and changed the conversation. "I came as soon as I could," Marian said. "Think he'd like to talk to me?"

Sally brightened. "I'm sure it would make his day. You are so pretty."

Jared hopped lamely from one foot to the other, trying to lose some of his gravity. "Our son wants to hang out with librarians—what could be nicer?"

"We owe you a major apology," Mrs. Moyer said with a sincere face.

"Yes, we do," Jared Moyer chimed in, but Marian held up her index finger the way Lillie had suggested, though for a serious reason. The Moyers stopped talking and looked at her expectantly. When she kept holding up her finger because she was too emotional to talk, Jared Moyer said: "You know that Richard had a bad time with his marriage. He and I had words the other day, and he got into an accident. I will never forgive myself. Then the police came about the cocaine, and we assumed—forgive us—that you had something to do with it."

"We were totally wrong, of course," Mrs. Moyer said. "The toxicology report naturally came back totally clear. I'm sorry if we made a scene at the library."

"Think nothing of it," Marian said. "We are all friends at the library where I work. It will blow over."

"We are happy that you like our son," Jared Moyer said. "I am going to make some major changes. We are going to," he amended, and took his wife's hand. The wife pointed down the hall for her to visit her son.

Marian followed their gestures as they made way for her. She stepped into a softly lit single room (of course; they could afford it) and there, behind a half-pulled sheet curtain, lay a person swathed in sheets, with a gauzy white turban around his head. He had the standard tubes and wires trailing from his head and arms, while monitors made sinuous waves around him. She had sat in plenty of hospital rooms in her day, and was not put off by any of it. "Hey," she said a bit shyly.

"Hey," he said just as shyly. "I'm afraid the pasta here sucks."

"Next time, I will bring you some lasagna from Papa's."

He rolled his eyes up. "My prayers have been answered."

She sat down on a stool beside him and held her purse on her knees, with both hands resting on its buckle. "You were praying for pasta?"

He regarded her with two black shiners. "No, I was praying for you."

She reached out and took his hand. "Sweetheart."

He squeezed her hand with a surprisingly strong, dry grip.

She said: "I came as soon as I heard about your accident. I sent you a text the other day, and then I didn't hear from you again."

"A tractor trailer ran over my cell phone. And over me."

She choked up a bit, laughing. "I see he did not run over your sense of humor."

"Seriously," the patient said, "I was in tears until I heard you arrived. My humor came back as you walked in the door."

Sally whispered diplomatically from across the room, where she stood in the doorway with her husband. "We're going outside for a little fresh air. We'll leave you two alone."

Rick waved to his parents, and Marian smiled after them.

He tried to sit up in bed, but held two bandaged hands up to his head and fell back moaning.

"Got a headache?" she asked, stroking his big turban. It felt dry and gauzy, just as it looked. "At least you aren't leaking any brain fluids or anything."

"I am so lucky," he said, taking her hand in his. He lay back with his eyes closed, and she waited for him to regain his composure. "Doctor Singh told me it could have gone either way. I could be dead, blind, or otherwise screwed up for life. Instead, they expect I'll be up and about in a few days. Then, if you are up for it, I will take you for another little outing to our favorite pizzeria."

"I would love that," she said with an inner need and outer warmth toward him that surprised her.

"The cops were here today to talk with me about my heavy drug habit."

"Oh, Richard—" What if he were on drugs? What if he had a problem? What if his life was out of control? What if—?

"Are you serious?" he said. "Am I serious? I have never even tried cocaine. Give me a little credit. Have you?"

She shook her head. "I wouldn't know how to get any if I had the urge, which I don't."

"That's a relief."

"Your parents maybe thought I was dealing from the library."

"Forgive them. They are parents. Plus they are Moyers. You know, all the buttons buttoned from top to bottom, even at the collar."

"They would be poor parents if they didn't care."

"They don't care, they dote. They don't protect, they smother. You may have to get used to it if you hang around with me."

"I would love that," she said. "My parents back in Shawnee will be thrilled to hear that I am starting over. Your parents and I already seem to get along pretty well, I think. So far. One never knows. Unless they change personalities every half hour."

"They are actually werewolves," he said. No problem unless there is a full moon, or raw meat in the fridge." He made a face.

"Honey, you don't need to make a face," she said. "You look like a raccoon."

"Oh thanks." He grimace and writhed in pain. "Every time I try to laugh, it hurts. I am not making faces. I am trying to guffaw."

"You're probably all bones and moans inside."

"That's a new one on me. Is that an Oklahomaism or an Emeryism?"

"It's a Marianism."

"Marian the Librarian."

"Go ahead, tease me." She felt flustered, and there was that hint of a lisp.

"Sweetheart, I don't want to tease you. I want to kiss you but I can't."

"Well, maybe later. Not here."

"I understand. It's not the sort of place where people smooch."

"A peck on the cheek."

"That will do. You'll have to bring it here, because I'm kind of tied up right now." He lifted his bandaged wrists and trailing tubes.

"Hold still." She rose, bent over him, and helicoptered her face over his. He puckered his lips to give her the requested peck on the cheek. *Silly man.* Instead, she gently put her hands on his ribs to steady herself at this awkward angle, and pressed her lips against his. She turned her head a trifle, side to side, in slow motions, to create a pleasant, electric friction between her lips and his. The man was not long in picking up his cue. She felt his hands steal around her back, as she wanted—under the coat, yet. She felt the tip of his tongue part her lips and commandingly seek her tongue. He found what he was after, and she let his tongue chase hers around in her mouth. She found herself breathing harder, and rubbed his poor ribs with her palms. He was nice and smooth and warm. She did not want to tell him yet, but she could not wait to have him slip into bed beside her when the time came. Her tongue did not run from his for long, and she would not run from him either.

It was a long, moist, throbbing kiss before they parted for air.

"Oh my god," he whispered. "Marian, I didn't think you were so passionate."

She touched his nose, then sat back on the stool. "All my systems are go."

"Oh man," he said. "Fly me to the moon."

"As long as you take me with you," she said.

"Two tickets. Always."

"That's what I like to hear. Your parents raised a gentleman, not a career criminal."

"Maybe I do stuff in my sleep that I don't remember when I wake up." He held her hands in his as he bantered. "Maybe I live a double life and don't know it. I could be dangerous, you know."

She squeezed his hands. "Then I'd better get an eye patch and be a pirate so we can go on raids together."

He lifted her hands to his lips and kissed them gently. "I am beginning to think I was not hit by a truck but by a trainload of wonderful feelings."

She admitted: "I have been alone long enough. I made up my mind after the other night. I am going to date you, Richard Moyer, whether you like it or not."

"I surrender totally."

"I still want you to go slow." Her *esses* came out faintly as *etheth*—always a sign that she was stressed.

"Slow boat," he promised, as he had the other evening.

She rubbed his chest with her hand. "I'm going to go now. Enough excitement."

He stared longingly through his shiners. "Slow boat. I will try not to make a nuisance of myself."

She leaned close, eye to eye, and stroked his forehead. "You have beautiful eyes, and long eyelashes."

He touched her lips with a fingertip. "I want more of you."

"You will have all you want. Maybe you'll get sick of me."

"Never," he said firmly. "I have been alone far too long myself. I can feel the gravitation between us, pulling, like the earth and the moon."

"I would love to be in your orbit."

"I will always treat you right. You are a lady, and I will do my best to be a gentleman."

"That I do expect," she said. "And I know you will be on your best behavior."

"I feel so much better already."

"You always have a little comedy going on."

"With an audience like you—who wouldn't?"

"Shall I stop back tomorrow after work?"

He appeared astonished that she would so much go out of her way for him. " I would love to see you. I hope you aren't too tired. I don't want you to get in an accident."

She looked at her bandaged, battered man, and laughed. "I can understand your concern."

"Ouch."

"Don't laugh—you'll cripple yourself. Hey, don't dote and don't smother, okay?"

"I can't wait to see you again."

" I will be here." She said it, and she meant it. She gave him—this time—a peck on the cheek. As she turned to go, she stopped and turned back. "Why don't you take this?" She handed him a pink cell phone. "I have another one at home. That way, if you get bored, you can send me a little text message."

He stared at the pink cell phone. "You don't have a blue one?"

"I'm a girl, silly."

With that, she did a little finger wave and out the door she went. True to their word, Jared and Sally were not back yet from their outing. She felt light as air as she floated down the corridor with the aftertaste of his kiss still buzzing around her lisp.

25

Marian was true to her word, and stopped by each evening for about an hour to see him. Rick had already decided to dedicate his life to her, if she would have him.

On the third day, when the swelling on his head was gone and he was merely stiff all over, his father came to pick him up from the hospital. Rick sat on a bench outside with his suitcase when the dark green Lincoln Town Car glided to the curb. Dad stepped out of the driver's side, careful not to get his door clipped on the busy New Haven street, but Rick waved him back. Rick dropped his small dark blue luggage into the trunk, and climbed into the passenger side of the car.

"Thanks for coming to get me."

"You're my son. I'll always be there for you." Dad pulled out carefully, in that manner Rick had always known, as if his father had some authority over the traffic crawling by; as if he were a captain of the world, which in a way he was. "I love you."

"I love you too, Dad. I need for you to ease up."

"I know, son. I promise."

"That's all I ask."

"I thought we could stop at a nice restaurant for lunch on the way to Hartford."

"I could use something other than hospital food."

"I kind of thought so. Maybe a glass of wine or a stiff shot or something."

Rick shook his head. "I don't do stiff shots in the day time. I get too relaxed. A double espresso maybe. I think my brain is ready for the stimulation now."

"They gave you a clean bill of health?"

"Dr. Singh said he would send me the bill. He was quite casual about it. Actually, he said because of my youth and good health, and my good living habits, I have recovered nicely. He said some people do, and some people don't."

"You're just lucky then. We all are. How is Marian?"

"Marian is a dream."

"I hope it works out. She seems like such a sweet young woman."

"Yeah. I'm due."

"You are. Your mother and I have a very nice feeling about her."

They stopped into a restaurant not far north of New Haven, visible from I-91 on a side street below by its neon lights and jazzy motif. It was one of those long-standing bar and grill places that doubled as a dance place after a good steak on weekend nights. As they parked and walked to the restaurant entrance, Dad briefly put a hand against Rick's back. It was an oddly comradely, loving gesture. Rick was not used to much camaraderie from his usually preoccupied, driven father.

Rick inhaled the smells of food, coffee, and alcohol inside the dimly, reddish lit interior. Busy waitresses criss-crossed each other's paths, waving trays or signaling to each other as the noon rush began. A young hostess with long auburn hair and big almond eyes showed them to a booth. Rick thanked her. Odd that Dad seemed so withdrawn. Or was it something else?

They ordered bread sticks and appetizers, as well as a beer each. The appetizers were breaded zucchini with ranch dressing, which reminded Rick of his recent date with Marian at Papa's.

"So about the business," Dad said after taking a slow, small, careful sip of his beer and pushing the small flute glass away. He wiped his mouth carefully with a linen napkin to remove a foam mustache.

"Ahh," Rick said, "a cold beer. That's one thing they do not serve in hospitals."

"You should have said something. I would have brought you one."

"Yeah, Mom would have had your scalp."

Dad chuckled to himself, then pursued the train of thought that had been brewing ever since he'd picked his son up. "This whole thing had us quite rattled." By us he meant himself and Mom.

"I'm sorry I got you all shook up," Rick said half jokingly.

"It wasn't your fault," Dad said, stating the obvious. "It's time for a change."

Rick fell silent. Yes it was.

"I have decided to hand the business over to you, son."

Rick was stunned. After all these years, all these struggles, all this work—could it be?

"If you want it."

Rick toyed with the stem of his beer flute. "I should probably say yes, of course, how silly."

Dad folded his hands on the linen tablecloth. "Nothing is silly. We should think everything through."

"What are we worth, Dad?"

"Oh...twenty million, walking away money. Give or take a few. Maybe twenty-five. Not much less."

"We have worked hard."

"You have worked hard."

"You've been a wonderful steward, Dad."

"Son...I realized, when I thought you were going to die, that none of it is that important."

"That thought crossed my mind also while I lay there floating among pain killers."

Dad's eyes looked big, gray, and wet. His small reddish lips quivered briefly. "I have been riding you very hard all these years."

"Aw Jeez." Rick patted the old man's hand.

His father did not return the gesture. He said instead: "You decide son. Is it worth it to you?"

"We could double it in another five or ten years if all goes well."

"Or not," Dad said.

The waiter, a blond haired college student named Jacques with a Quebec accent, came to take their orders. Jacques was efficient, friendly, and eagerly innocent aside from a tip-earner's acquired finesse about charming his customers. He was doing all the right things and saying all the right stuff. Dad looked on approvingly. They ordered steak sandwiches with cole slaw and fries for lunch. Nothing overly fancy; just good. Jacques walked off with his dark plastic order book.

"They make a fine New York cut," Dad said. "You'll see."

"I trust you."

"Geoff gave notice the other day. He's bailing out to join one of our rivals."

"I'm not sorry to see him go. He's not a bad guy."

"He's an okay guy. I'm actually glad to see him go because it simplifies what we need to do."

"Which is?"

"Rethink everything.

"I'm for that, Dad."

"I had planned to make him the contract closer to take your place, and bring you up to train you so you could take my place.

Now we are overcome by events."

Rick waited, sensing something big about to come out of his father's face.

"I am going to retire, Richard."

Rick was glad, but it was the type of statement to which no son could suitably reply. It was an opening for a speech, and his father went on to explain. "Your mother and I had words, while you were still in a coma and we weren't sure which way it would go."

"I am sorry she had to go through this. Both of you."

"Stop being sorry. Things happen for a reason. I have no complaints about you as my son. If anything, I have only praise."

"Despite everything?"

"Despite everything." The old man chuckled. "Despite the DUI, despite the goldfish in the bathtub when you were small, despite the playing card in my gas tank that screwed up a perfectly good car and cost me thousands in repair bills; despite the BB pellets in our pears on the old tree—despite Cindy."

"Did you have this sort of conversation with your father at some point?"

"I always wished I had. I never got much chance to talk with my old man. I want to do better by you. He had his stroke before any of us were ready. He was a vegetable the last five years. I was about your age, and had to basically hang up my life and my dreams and take over the company."

"Sounds about like me. You've done a swell job anyway, Dad."

The old man nodded. "I appreciate that. I feel that I am handing a good nest egg to you. It's a funny feeling. I feel kind of like my pants fell down around my ankles. What I mean is, it's so sudden and unexpected, but then it's better now than later. Your mother and I are still in good health and we'll be able to travel a bit."

"You will live longer if you get out of that office."

He nodded. "That's what the doctor told me too. Blood pressure and all that. Need exercise."

Rick shook his head. It was kind of hard to believe. "So you are tossing Moyer LX Holdings into the air to see if I want to catch it."

"Or try something new."

Rick laughed humorlessly, arms folded, staring into this beer. "Yeah. Wow. I got all revved up, came back from the Army, all grown up, and decided to pitch in head over heels to make it work."

"You surprised me. I have been very pleased."

"The question is, Dad. How many years of my life do I want to spend sitting in strange boardrooms in Manhattan, cleaning up other people's messes and failures? The money is great. It's the time..."

Dad nodded. "I understand. I would not have admitted that to you or myself as recently as a week ago. Sometimes I feel like I wasted my whole life sitting in those same sorts of places. We are like vultures, picking over the bodies of companies that were once magnificent, like lions."

"Some were run by shmoes."

"True, but don't ruin my rhetoric. I'm just getting started."

"Luckily, here come our sandwiches."

"I am overcome by events."

"Overcome, but not overdone. Let's eat. We can talk more afterward."

A strange dynamic had moved suddenly between them, like a seismic quake that had shifted their tectonic plates around. Dad was visibly stepping back and letting go. Rick knew he would no longer feel the whip on his back. They ate silently and with gusto. Afterward, they rested over espressos with a bit of orange peel, and a little sweet dessert. Dad went for some pistachio ice cream, while Rick chose a sliver of New York style cheese cake (very fluffy) with a drizzle of cherry syrup and a half a strawberry on top.

"I have friends who would buy us out," Dad said as he wiped his mouth with a napkin after finishing his ice cream.

"For a good close?"

"Yeah. If that's what you want."

Rick took a deep breath. "A week ago, this would not have occurred to me. I was so busy running back and forth between home and the City, always trying to please you—and myself, don't feel uneasy, just sayin'—and lying there helplessly in the hospital after all that's happened..."

"A lot has happened," Dad said. It was his turn to put a hard, cold hand over Rick's, briefly, giving Rick's hand a fatherly jiggle of affection. "You proved yourself, son. We can move on."

Rick folded his hands together, and hunched over the table as if winding up for action, for the future, for something new and different—but he had no idea what.

Dad said: "Don't decide today. Let's take a week or so and think about it. Didn't you always want to study History or something?"

"Yeah. Well, I'm not sure. Maybe. I always pictured myself sitting in an overstuffed chair with a pipe in my mouth, reading a huge book, and wearing a ratty smoking jacket."

"That movie was long ago."

"I know. I'd probably just throw up if I ever smoked a pipe. It's an image. Everything is an image."

"You need to find a nice girl and settle down."

"I thought I found her in Cindy."

"We all make mistakes. You got off easy. No kids."

"Yeah, that was lucky. I'm not sure she even wanted any. She was scheming the whole time—well, never mind. She's going to marry her South American dude—the next victim—and take his money. We're done with Cindy. I may just never marry again."

"Don't say that. Your mother has been wonderful to me all these years. And I never cheated on her. We had our arguments, half of them over you—but we stuck together and made it work."

Rick understood that, despite all the money—old money—families could be dysfunctional. There had been a lot of craziness in both his parents' families, including overly cold grandfathers, spoiled alcoholic grandmothers, favoritism for some kids over others, jealousy, the whole bit. With an only child, and two survivor type parents, a different set of pratfalls had presented themselves, starting with over-protectiveness and various forms of smothering. One good thing about the Cindy episode had been that it leveraged Rick into a chunk of the family fortune so he could buy their million dollar starter town home, which he had managed to cling to when Cindy took everything in it plus the car.

"This Marian seems like a nice girl."

"She came to see me every evening in the hospital."

"I think she really cares about you." Dad shrugged faintly, as if he was surrendering on the female point. He and Mom had done a lot for their son, which amounted to a form of pressure to get him in the right marriage to the right girl, with all the implications that it would look good and set him up as some kind of captain of industry—when it all went horribly wrong from the start. Not that Cindy was the devil so much—it was just that she and Rick had nothing long-term in common after the initial love and craziness had worn off and each once again became the person they had always been.

"She is really nice," Rick said. "I always drove through Emery without slowing down. I might have noticed the lights on my right as I shot through the town's only traffic light on that upper road. There was something about the library—those warm lights, like a lantern always lit. Like an advertisement that said Stop on by. Rest a bit. Check out a book. Chitchat with a friendly, cute librarian."

Dad smiled. "I do think I will begin reading more." He clapped his gnarled hands together. "You know, I am already beginning to enjoy my retirement. And we are going to do gardening. I did plant some apple trees and pear trees years ago, but we hardly paid much attention to them. Your mother would go out once or twice in season and come back with a colander full of these ripe, juicy green pears or apples that had rosy cheeks. Now I'm going to trim the branches and take care of them better."

"You go, Dad. This Emery place is actually a small town by a lake, down in a valley. The library and grammar school and some businesses are just up there along the upper roadway. Maybe I'll go down to the lake with Marian for a walk sometime. I'm curious what her little town looks like down there."

"You could open a business down there, or use it as a base of operations if you get your Ph.D. in History or whatever you want to do."

"I am not thinking that far ahead. It's too early."

"Take your time. Don't rush things."

"Yeah. That is the last thing I want to do."

Dad said: "For her sake as well as your sanity."

Rick thought of his years of unhappy marriage and the divorce and aftermath. "I don't ever want to go through another round like that."

Dad placed both palms down on the table, signaling readiness to leave. "I am going to go back to the office and clean up what I have going. You go find something to do. Take Marian to a movie."

"I have to ask her first," Rick said. He felt all warm inside. "I think she'll say yes."

26

Each afternoon, Marian looked forward to seeing Rick in the hospital. She did not relish the traffic on the way into New Haven, but the hour she spent with him was worth everything. The trip back was usually dark and tedious, made all the more so because she missed him. She wanted to stay by his side.

Today, a Friday, she was happy to hear from him, in a text message, that he was being released from the hospital. He was still stiff and sore, but otherwise on the mend. He had no permanent damage. His father was going to pick him up and drive him home to his house outside Hartford. She imagined she would soon get to see Rick's bachelor pad, the rather sad and stunned outcome of a hopeful but truncated marriage. That woman must have been quite a piece of work.

Rick texted, asking if it was okay for him to drive down to see her that evening, if she was not too tired from work.

She texted back that it was fine with her, as long as he didn't mind if she went home and took her shoes off.

He texted back and said that he would be glad to remove them for her.

She thought about this before replying. She did not want to rush things with him. There was a certain line she was not eager to cross until she felt emotionally ready. She was not a 22 year old college girl. She was a widow who had just been through the mill. As much as she wanted to throw herself into this handsome, charming man's arms and let him ravish her with love, she was not sure how that would work in the space where she had last made love with Tommy not two years ago, before his last deployment. She finally texted back: *Shoes? Okay if you watch for now. Taking things real slow. Can't wait to see you.* That should do it.

His reply came back: Being near you is all I need. Can't wait either.

The afternoon dragged by. It was getting dark out earlier now, though the time had not yet come to set the clocks back. What was that formula? *Fall back, spring forward.*

"Mrs. Charles! Mrs. Charles!" The children kept her busy every moment. They were not yet used to her name change. This boy had taken this girl's pencil, that girl had punched that boy on the head, this boy was looking green and needed to barf, that girl wondered if Marian could figure out fractions for her, and so on. It was like a multiple slice of many motherhoods. Marian rather thought that it would work out really well for her once she got the chance. She could not help but idly think of Rick and she had a little boy, if he would look like Rick the way Rick's father looked like Rick. Rick seemed to have what a friend of hers had once called Sticky Genes, meaning they were a family in which the same phenotype (looks) was passed down from generation to generation, and all the siblings looked alike if there were multiple copies. She and Rick were both only children, so their parents' must be a kind of stop-to-rest generation; but watch out for the next shift coming up.

Marian was in regular touch with her mom and dad back in Oklahoma, where they had retired after Dad's thirty years in the Navy, the last decade or more in San Diego and Coronado. Dad had retired as a Commander, and managed to find a small community of old salts among the land lubbers around Shawnee.

The building's plumbing was backing up, and required major maintenance. That would require closure at least until tomorrow, while a contracting firm and city employees worked overnight to fix the building's sixty year old pipes.

Linda Damien made the rounds about five p.m. "We're closing at six tonight, ladies."

"Fine by me," Lillie said loudly in the Science section.

"My husband is already on his way," Terie said from the Reference section. "We are going to a movie in Waterbury."

"Good for you," Linda said. "Marian? You ready?"

Marian nodded. "I have four little ones left in the story room. Oops, I think I see a van pulling up outside, and they are all excited getting their lunch boxes together."

"With luck, they will all go out the door in one pack," Linda said authoritatively as she swung a ring of keys from a pale, not quite plump hand. "Rose?"

"I am finishing up the week's tardy notices," Rose Otto announced from the business office. "Give me twenty minutes and I will take them to the Post Office on my way home."

"Excellent. The whole crew is on board and we are all rowing together." Linda returned to her office.

Marian escorted the four little children to the main door, where two mothers had come together to pick them up. They were all going to someone's second birthday party at a well known pizza and games emporium in the next town over. As the last of the customers poured out, Linda locked the doors.

The library grew hushed and empty. Linda and Lillie went about shutting off lights. "Leave the main hall lights off for when the work crew comes in about eight. That's when I was told the plumbing contractor will be able to start work."

"Who is going to mind the store?" asked Terie.

"Mr. Perez is going to stay on duty until about ten," Linda said. "That is my understanding."

"You sound like you're not eager to stay," Lillie said from a distant nook, with an echo. More lights went out.

"No," Linda said, "my oldest is part of a school play at St. Boniface School, and I must get going soon." Her children went to a local parochial school.

"I'll go make a sweep," Marian said.

"Check all the doors," Linda said. "Mr. Perez has the keys and he will let the workers in later."

"I'll make sure they are all locked," Marian said. She slipped her sweater on as she walked around the inside of the building. Rick was supposed to meet her in the parking lot and then follow her home. He had never been down in the valley, and did not know his way around. She felt a warm thrill inside. How strange and wonderful it was to start having these feelings again. She'd pretty much forgotten how it was to feel warm and excited inside at the prospect of meeting a guy, and having him put his arm around her and talk nice to her. As she checked each stairwell, and the north or south or east or west doorway at its bottom, she asked herself: *am I rushing things?* And she answered just as quickly: I have been lonely long enough. She had no desire to become a painter in Greenwich Village, or an actress in Stratford, or anything else. She was quite content to stay here in Emery, work at the library, where the township had a decent retirement plan if a person stayed for a million years or so. She felt no need to run away, find herself, lose herself, or whatever. She had done enough traveling with Tommy to know that people were the same everywhere, so the wide-eyed wonder was gone and good riddance. She would enjoy another trip to Europe some time, or a vacation in Canada, and everyone had to go motoring around the United States at least once in a lifetime, so there was that to look forward to once she met the right man and settled down once more. Maybe Moyer would be that man or not. It was kind of more up to him than to her right now to demonstrate if he was that man or not. *So does that mean I am ready for that man?* She asked herself as she returned to the main lobby. *Hah! Probably not, but I am slowly driving in that direction.*

Her lowest moment in life had been the day she was contemplating just swimming out into the lake and not coming back. That had been the day Richard Moyer had walked into her life. She would never forget that wild, deep look they had exchanged. They had communicated at a very deep level, even though neither had understood anything about the other. It was a soul thing, she decided. Her family back home were rock solid and that was how it was done. Mr. Moyer was a good candidate to begin dating her regularly, if he so wished. Or not, that would be fine with her also. Well, not so fine, since she had this growing dream, and this warm, wet something in her loins that he would sweep her off her feet and look into her eyes. He would profess eternal love, which was easy to do, but really mean it, which was the hard part. Marian was not yet sure of her own bearings, but she was rock solid and certain that once she steered a course, she would stick to it and hope her man did not fall out of the boat.

By 5:30, Linda stood holding the door open while her employees filed out. Lillie and Terie went their separate ways to cars waiting with puffing tail pipes and red glowing tail lights. Amid the goodnights, Linda gently pulled Marian out by the shoulder. "Whom does that leave? Rose? Have you seen her?"

"I think she left already," Lillie called out.

"She was on her way to the Post Office with the late slips," Terie called from her family car.

"Oh yeah. Well, she can text me if she is somewhere locked in the ladies' room or stuck someplace." Linda and Marian exchanged laughs. Marian jiggled her car keys. Where was Adolfo Perez? Normally, a school guard came to the parking lot at closing time while the women boarded their transportation and safely left.

As if reading her mind, Linda said: "Come on, I'll walk you to your car."

"And then what about you?" Marian asked as they strode across the parking lot together.

"I'm parked right next to you, so we can leave at the same time."

They walked hurriedly into a patch of darkness.

Linda said "oops" and almost lost her footing in the dark.

"Careful," Marian said. Her own eyes were having difficulty focusing in the blackness under a huge willow tree. Its trailing tendrils hung down for thirty feet all around.

They were alone together—just she and Linda.

There was no school cop, and the only other human beings anywhere near were passing at sixty miles an hour half a block away on the thruway.

Suddenly Linda grasped Marian's wrist with a steel hand. "My god."

"What is it?" Marian said, stunned.

"Hello, Cleopatra," said a man's voice.

It was Michael Chesney, leaning against the driver's side front fender of Marian's car.

"You are not supposed to be on city property," Linda said sharply. Marian heard fear in Linda's voice as Chesney's eyes regarded her with predatory insolence.

"You can take a hike, you dike."

Linda stood holding Marian by one wrist. "I am not going anywhere. We are leaving and you will not get in our way." With her free hand, Linda produced a cell phone which lit up as she started to dial.

The karate trained Mike Chesney almost instantly closed the gap. He launched himself off of the VW and was upon Linda in the same motion. His hard hand made one languid swipe, half open, and the cell phone flew from Linda's hand. It sailed away and shattered audibly but out of sight.

"What do you want?" Marian said, putting her arms protectively around Linda, who was doubled over, holding her injured hand.

"I came to see you, Cleopatra." He stood before Marian, spreading his shoulders and parking his hard fists on his hips. He had been terminated by the city two weeks earlier, and now wore civilian clothes. He wore tight, gray jeans-like pants, crew socks, black athletic shoes, and a blue denim work shirt with a white T-shirt under it. His blond hair was getting longer and unkempt; he did not wear a hat or hood of any kind. "Nobody can hear us, so yell all you want."

"You must be out of your mind," Marian said. He was terrifying. It was like confronting a zoo animal that had gotten loose.

"You don't have your nose in the air now, do you?" he said to

Marian.

As her eyes became accustomed to the wan light, she suddenly realized how his eyes were narrowed with hate and anger. She'd had no idea she had snubbed him that hard. She'd rejected his constant advances, hating that stupid Cleopatra jibe that almost sounded racist if it wasn't a rapist mantra. He regarded her with a smug, violent smile. It was a dirty smile. He licked his lips with a pointy little tongue as if he were already tasting the things he wanted to do to her.

In one motion, he was upon them. He gave Linda a swipe to one side that knocked her to the ground. With his other steely hand, he clamped a vice grip on Marian's shoulder. "You are mine, lady. Get in my car." He pointed to a small, dark station wagon of ancient vintage that had been parked in the shadows a few spots away. "Get in. Do I have to smack your head? I don't have time to waste."

"Leave her alone!" Linda shouted as she rose effortfully to her knees, but stayed on all fours. She looked dazed from his blow.

Marian felt that hand crushing her shoulder. His other hand, fingers like steel snakes, twisted in her hair and pulled. She saw stars and cried out with pain. She tried to hit him, but her aim was off and her strikes were feeble.

Mike Chesney cursed and twisted his hand, so that she fell to her knees. She hardly noticed the gravel bruising her bare knees as she cried out with the pain in her shoulder and now her neck as he expertly manipulated pressure points to force her compliance. "I'm serious, Cleopatra. We can either do this the easy way, or I carry you and throw you into my car."

"What do you want?" Marian cried as she tried to regain some sense of balance, but she flailed around on the harsh, cutting gravel as he turned his powerful grip this way and that.

"Not so high and mighty now, huh? And what about Mister Dinosaur, that dirt bag, huh? Where is he now? Ran away? Can't help you? I'll tear his heart out next time I see him."

So that was it. Michael Chesney, obnoxious and sleazy young street thug temporarily employed as a school constable, had used his position to bully everyone around him. Now Marian understood about his pushiness and shamelessness. To him, the many women working in the school or the library were like chickens, and he was the fox in their hen house.

Within moments, he was dragging her by one arm. She tried to resist, but he knew how to inflict pain to make her go again. So, in fits and starts, he got her kicking and screaming ever closer to his car. What he planned to do with her, she had no idea, but whatever it was, she was terrified. Was he going to drive her down some dark, deserted country road? Rape her? Kill her? His car was a nasty, mean looking like machine seemed to her like a dark green meat grinder and razor blade sharpener out of a nightmare.

Just as all seemed lost, Marian heard a woman's enraged voice. "You piece of trash! You let her go right now."

Mike Chesney put one foot on Marian's back and pressed her down onto the ground while he regarded Rose Otto with arrogant and displeased amusement. "You, the old dinosaur woman."

Rose stood in the middle of the parking lot, her thin features and shock of hair highlighted under a light. Her eyes were large and looked manic. She pointed her purse at him as if it were a weapon. "You are not going to leave this parking lot in one piece, believe you me."

"Oh?" Chesney laughed. "What are you going to do, hit me?" He laughed uproariously.

At that moment, a man's voice cut in. It was a loud voice, almost from a loudspeaker, so firm and rich was it. Adolfo Perez, wearing his school police uniform, stepped out from the shadows. He had his pepper spray in one hand, and a short, stubby day stick in the other. He moved toward Chesney at a crouch, with the two weapons swaying from side to side like cobra heads. Evidently, he knew how to handle himself.

"We are going to issue you guys guns," Linda said. She was sitting up now, sitting back with her bruised palms on the parking lot ground behind her.

Chesney put his left boot on Marian's neck and forced her down. He too assumed a crouching position. Marian squirmed, trying to twist his foot so she could wiggle away now that he had his hands off of her.

Suddenly, Marian felt a stinging in her eyes. She doubled over, choking and coughing as Perez started pepper spraying Chesney.

Chesney laughed. "Are you serious? That stuff is a toy to use on kids and small dogs. I am going to stuff that up your rear end."

Perez tossed the small canister to Linda, who caught it like a pro.

Perez secured the leather thong of his day stick around his right wrist, and held the stick in his fist. The day stick was an old police tool used for prodding, rather than swinging. You could poke someone in the solar plexus, the ribs, the kidneys, or the large muscles. You could do a lot with it, provided your opponent was not a black belt on angel dust.

At that moment, a pair of headlights came swinging in from the street, mounted slightly onto the higher asphalt of the driveway, and paused with both lights aimed at the dueling tableau under the big shade tree. The lights switched to high beams, and out jumped Richard Moyer. "Hey, get your stinkin' feet off her, you piece of trash." Rick jogged toward Chesney.

Chesney made wide, comfortable balancing motions. "I can take down five guys at once. You two jokers are just potato chips. You are snacks, you idiots. Come on, make my day!"

As Adolfo Perez started taking stabs at him with the day stick, Chesney comfortably side stepped each blow. Each time Perez lunged in with a shot, Chesney struck him on the torso with a slapping sound.

By now, Chesney had forgotten about Marian and was dancing with his two fight partners. Perez was taking some serious hits, and looked shaky.

Poor Rick, Marian thought. Just out of the hospital, and this dirt ball had to show up.

27

The last thing Rick Moyer had on his mind as he pulled into the parking lot at the Emery Township Free Public Library was getting into hand to hand combat with a crazed black belt.

As he pulled in, his headlights raked across an amazing tableau. There was Marian on the ground with this goon's boot on her neck. He recognized the attacker vaguely as someone he had seen in the library—a guard or something.

Rose Otto stood by, holding her purse in both hands as if she were zapping the fighter with a futuristic weapon. Her eyes were large, her hair stood out in all directions, and she looked manic. Sitting nearby was their boss, the Chief Librarian, who looked as if she'd taken a hit or two. What on earth was this madman doing? Rose's friend, Perez, stood with a day stick in one hand. As Rick turned on his high beams, jumped from the car, and ran to assist, Perez took a foot strike on the right arm and stood with his arm dangling, and the day stick now hanging from a limp hand. The stick had landed a blow, evidently, because Mr. Crazy jumped away to recover.

Rick had some martial arts training, and was able to land a few slaps on Chesney.

This only seemed to enrage the blond haired fighter, who shook their blows off and counter-attacked in quick lunges. Each time, he would land a punch and then jump back out of reach.

At one point, Perez made a feint to one side, and Chesney stepped into his range.

Perez shot a lightning strike with the day stick, right into the massive muscles under Chesney's arm. It was so fast that Rick, sidling in from the opposite side, could not make out which side of Chesney had been hit. Chesney seemed to turn in mid air, delivering a spinning wheel kick. His small, hard foot just caught Perez on the upper arm before the two men landed apart.

"You'll pay for that," Chesney said as he quickly regrouped.

Meanwhile, Perez stood holding his injured arm with the other hand.

"Here!" Rick said to Perez and held his hands up as if intercepting a pass.

Perez, in one motion with his good arm, stripped the day stick off his wrist and sent it sailing to Rick.

Rick caught the hard wooden stick, which was about a foot long and thick as a hot dog with bun.

"You can play all

you want," Chesney said, "but one of you is going to eat that thing in about two minutes."

While Perez harried Chesney from the far side, using his good arm while the injured one dangled, Rick hassled Chesney from the other direction. Rick held the stick in his right hand, while he made waving motions with his left hand to distract the blond fighter.

"Run," Rick told Marian. "Get out of here. I'll hold him. Run and get help."

Perez said: "I already called for backup. The State Police and Town Constables will be here any second. That's right, Chesney, you piece of prison trash. You are going right back to the main cage where you belong."

Chesney got a look of fear and rage as he danced about.

Rick struck him with a stabbing motion that was aimed at the ribs but landed on his upper arm. Marian, lying on the ground nearby, heard the *oof* as Chesney recoiled in pain.

Rick landed a second blow, hitting Chesney in the mouth.

"I'll kill you both," Chesney said in a wild, blood-choked voice. Blood poured down his front. He made several lightning-quick wheel kicks, flying around the parking lot like a spinning top.

Rick went down, taking a hit to the shoulder.

Perez lunged in and hit Chesney on the neck from behind, trying to get him off Rick—because Chesney was now enraged, but thinking cold and clearly as trained; he was ready to actually kill someone. It was not hyperbole. One kick to the temple, and you could be dead; or have a broken spine and be paralyzed.

Rick managed to dance in and land a full-knuckle, back-handed punch across the blond man's eyes.

Almost in the same instant, the attacker stepped forward and Rick just managed to glimpse the gray, hard knuckles sailing toward him. He just managed to turn his head to one side and avoid being smashed unconscious. He landed on the ground, rolling to the side, and recovered as quickly as he could. His body was still stiff and sore, and he could not move as fast as he normally would.

For a moment, all three men had taken enough punishment that each was bend over, facing the others so that they made a triangle, leaning on their knees with both hands and gasping for breath. Perez seemed to be recovering the use of his injured hand. The blond man, meanwhile, was covered with a fan of nose blood, and wiping his face with his sleeves.

From the look in his face, he was about to mount an all-out, deadly assault.

Somewhere in the distance, Rick heard sirens. The police were coming, but they would be too late. The attacker was still leaning forward, with his hands on his knees, but he was bouncing lightly. He was judging his distances, and planning an attack that would put Pearl Harbor to shame.

28

Seeing Rick and Adolfo hurt, and Linda and Rose standing helplessly by, Marian signaled to Linda.

Linda passed the canister of pepper spray to Rose, who intercepted it while running.

Chesney, was distracted, and watched as Rose cut around his left rear in the direction of Marian.

Rick was moving in from one side, and Perez from the other, so Chesney's attention was tied up.

That gave Rose time, as she ran past, to toss the pepper spray to Marian.

Marian smoothly and deftly caught the can as it made a perfect, smoothly sailing little arc.

Fingering the spray, Marian rose to her feet with her most powerful lunging motion.

She ran two or three steps toward Chesney and launched herself into the air.

She landed on Chesney's back and wrapped himself around him.

Chesney reacted instantly. He pumped his elbows left and right while swinging his body in oscillating motions. The hard, muscular, brutal elbows crashed to the left and right of Marian.

Marian clung all the more tightly, in part to stay attached, and in part to make herself small as those weaponized elbows pumped the air around her. She wrapped her hands around his neck, and her legs under his ribs. She dug in with her heels so he bellowed with pain. She twisted her left fist, trying to crush his windpipe. With her right hand, she reached around. She was already biting him on the back of the neck tasting sweat and blood as well as body odor and dandruff, the disgusting pig. She reached up with her left hand and found his nose. She felt him opening his mouth to bite her hand. She lifted his nostrils with her fingers. She jammed the pepper spray up one nostril with her other hand, and pressed the button.

Chesney bellowed.

The air filled with biting, caustic pepper gas.

Marian coughed and choked.

Tears blinded her.

She held on for dear life, while he swung her body left and right in the air.

She kept her hand on his nostrils, and the pepper spray firmly up his nose.

In a moment, she blacked out—but not before sensing that Chesney was down on the ground yelling, choking, coughing, and trying to tear his eyeballs out to rid himself of the painful spray that filled his sinuses and his eyes like a fiery fog.

The last thing Marian saw, as she sailed over Chesney's shoulders through the air, was Rose jogging past like a quarterback, whacking Chesney over the head with the day stick.

The look in Rose's eyes said that she was about to extract vengeance for a lifetime of damage done to her by someone in her past—her ex-husband, most likely, from years ago.

29

As Rick recovered and rose to his feet—shaking his head to clear it, and inhaling a whiff of that pepper spray—he saw Rose Otto in the process of beating the blond man to death with the day stick. Seeing that he did not respond to her as she hit him the first time—he was busy kneeling and hollering and clawing his eyes—she went back and hit him again. Her strikes were fairly feeble, and he did not seem to notice.

Nevertheless, both Perez and Rick ran to pull the enraged librarian off the creature who was now turning into her victim. Linda Damien and Marian joined in, pulling the fiery-eyed, wild-haired woman off the kneeling, sobbing giant.

Meanwhile, the screaming and keening of sirens grew deafening. In a whirl of multi-colored flashers, several police cruisers swung into the parking lot. A man's voice sounded loudly over a car loudspeaker: "You are ordered to cease and desist. Lie down on the ground with your palms down and your legs spread. This means you, Chesney. We have the goods on you. The game is over."

Rick held Marian closely, and Perez tightly embraced a sobbing, trembling Rose, while Linda Damien summoned all her earthly authority as Chief Librarian and declared: "This is Library property and I am in charge here. Officers, arrest this man!" She pointed to Chesney, who slumped defeatedly to one side on the ground. He was covered with blood from his nose, and his face looked swollen. His eyes looked like a pair of sunnyside up eggs that had been fried in pepper gas.

Seconds later, a crew of men looking sharp and athletic in their clean, untrammeled uniforms were all over Chesney. They had him on his stomach, while holding him at gun point, and one man cuffed him behind. Other men held his feet down, while a female constable had her boot planted on the middle of his back.

State Trooper Johnson stepped forth, coughing and waving a hand before his face. His eyes looked small. "Geez, ladies, it smells like burning barbecue around here." He coughed some more.

Rick held Marian tightly, feeling her pressing herself into his torso to make herself small. He felt her delicate fingers on his ribs, and held her close. Rose and Adolfo were doing similar things nearby. Linda Damien's husband was just then pulling into the parking lot to check on her, since evidently they had meant to caravan together.

Trooper Benoit came forward as well. He read Michael Chesney his rights as Johnson helped Chesney up. "You are under arrest," Benoit Mirandaed him. "Anything you say can and will be used against you..."

Meanwhile, Johnson let two constables lead Chesney away to a waiting prison van. He told Linda, while eyeing Rick and Marian for their benefit as well: "We solved your cocaine case."

"Then I was right," Perez said.

"You can thank Rose," Linda said. As Marian had suspected, Linda knew more than she had let on to. "Rose figured it out," Linda said. "Michael Chesney planted the cocaine in the book. He was angry because he had been fired, and because the women rejected his advances—particularly Marian, for whom he seemed to have the hots."

Marian took this all in with amazement. As an attractive woman, she spent much of her life deflecting the unwanted attentions of men. To her, Chesney had been a noticeable, exceptionally obnoxious annoyance, but she had forgotten about him as soon as he vanished from the library. It turned out that he'd been fired the next day, coincidentally when Adolfo Perez came back to work.

"Somehow, to get even, Chesney sneaked in and took the book that Richard Moyer had checked back in. The book was already back on the shelves, as Rose was able to determine later. He poured one or two lines of cocaine into it and placed it in the offices, where the regular police dog sweep would be sure to pick it up. Chesney knew that this would implicate Mr. Moyer, for whom—in his perception—Marian had snubbed him."

Just then, the van with Chesney inside drove past. He was cuffed, dazed, and bruised looking. Johnson added: "Based on a tip from Officer Perez, we raided Chesney's apartment in Waterbury, and seized a bunch of drugs and paraphernalia--including cocaine, which had impurities in it that precisely matched what we found in that cowboy book. Case closed. Michael Chesney has had some scrapes with the law before—no idea how he got a job with the city, especially working in the school system—and it looks like he will be doing some years in prison. Good riddance."

"You're off the hook," Benoit told Rick and Marian. "Sorry about all the hassle."

"Just doing your job," Rick said. He whispered to Marian so only she could hear him: It worked out fine, because who could ever come up with a better scheme to get myself close to you?"

Marian whispered up to Rick's ear: "My hero."

"My baby," he said impulsively, and kissed her. She writhed happily in his arms, gripping him tightly. Their tongues wrestled like two kittens playing on a rug.

"We will have to return tomorrow and interview you all to finish our police reports," said the two State Troopers.

"Ahem!" Linda said, then more loudly: "Ahem!"

Rick looked up, dazed. Marian had her head tilted back, so that her face looked intoxicated, lying against his shoulder. "Yes?"

"We can all go home now," Linda said. And they all did.

Part Four

Spring

30

Somehow, though premature, the first hint of spring was in the air. Every year, New Englanders engage in wistful thinking as they long for the endless, dreary winter to finally end. Through the drizzle and fog, one could smell a faint fragrance of blossoms. They  had yet to get through March, but April with its mild air and showers was only weeks away. In their hearts, having weathered all that they had been through, it was already spring time.

Marian helped Rick into her car. They decided to leave his car in the lot, parked and locked up. Nobody would recognize it, since it was a rental. Rick's Jaguar had been mangled beyond redemption in his accident, and he was just starting to think about shopping for something new. The gossip mill would be busy talking about the evening's brawl, and probably would not make much of the stray car left there. Chesney's ratty little tank was towed away—he would not need it where he was going. The storage fees would be so prohibitive that it would be auctioned off, long before he was free from prison in a few years, and the money would pay for town expenses.

As a courtesy, the two State Troopers gave Marian an escort home. Partly it was for her protection, and partly it was one of the many ways the community would always have for showing their respect for her loss and blah blah blah—she did not want to dwell on it. They seemed to respect her strength as well. That way, decent people stuck together, society weeded out trash like Chesney, and the world was briefly a better place under the wheeling stars above Emery Lake.

When they pulled onto Emery Lane, her little leafy street, they made the dome lights of their gray cruiser briefly twirl. They let out the briefest of fweep noises from the siren. Then, sure that Marian was safely home with her friend, the car when dim and silent. The two policemen rustled away into the autumn night, like caped crusaders, ready to save other lives and do good; lots of good.

Pleased, Marian joined Rick at the passenger door. "I'm kind of stiff now myself," she said. Her neck ached where she had been manhandled. Her knees and palms burned from being pulled around on the ripping gravel.

"I'm okay," he said bravely, but limped a bit as he shut the car door and followed her.

"You are going to sleep here tonight."

"Are you sure—?"

"It is okay. You deserve a little TLC after all that you have been through. Besides, it will give us a chance to sit down together, with a pot of tea, maybe wrapped in a blanket together, and whisper all night. Would you like that?"

"I must be dreaming."

"You are most certainly not." She unlocked the door, and guided him inside.

He seemed respectful and shy. His face reflected a glow of happiness, and his eyes danced merrily. "I staged all this, you know."

"Oh you are so full of it."

"Seriously. I sat there, thinking, how can I get close to this woman?"

"Well, your nefarious scheme succeeded brilliantly." She dropped her keys and purse loudly on the kitchen counter granite. "We each need to take a shower after rolling around in the dirt. I will make you a nice nest on the living room couch."

"Honestly, I don't want to put you to any trouble."

"Richard, you are the kind of trouble I need in my life. Be still."

"Okay," he said. "Gladly." He walked around the kitchen, eyeballing everything. "What a sweet home you have."

"I'll bet it's not half the size of your house."

"My house is like a barn. It totally lacks that woman's touch. My mother came over and put up curtains after Cindy left, and she bought me a set of bed things, but she finally said it's hopeless and gave up."

"I'll bet." Marian put a kettle of water on the stove. "My place lacks a man's touch. I've been letting it go." She suddenly found herself crying. It wasn't just the idea that she had purposely let the lawn go, thinking Tommy would come back to mow it. That was now so long ago. Her dad had a saying: *there is no cure for your troubles like new troubles*. It was true. She'd just gone through a wrenching situation, where she could have been kidnapped, tortured, raped, and killed. Chesney was crazy enough to do anything. She stood like a child and began bawling great big tears of relief and reaction. Rick held her as she trembled in his arms. She wrapped her arms around him and stroked his back as her poise returned. Poor, dear man. He had thrown himself at Chesney to save her and the other women, aside from helping Mr. Perez. After a while, she was holding him just as much as he was holding her. They stood locked together in an embrace for a long time, stroking and nuzzling each other with growing affection.

"You go in and take your shower first," she said. She led him by the hand, into her bathroom. She handed him a fresh towel from the shelves in the cupboard there. Soap and shampoo were behind the plastic curtain, in their shelves in the tub enclosure. "You'll feel better," she whispered, and kissed him on the cheek. "Go on now. I'll make us tea, and I think I can rustle up some chips and dip."

He looked down at himself. His clothes were dirty. His sweater was caked with drying mud, and his pants had rips on both knees. "I wonder if you'd mind, if I can do a little laundry."

She froze and sized him up. This was one of those moments, and there would be others like it, she knew. She was surprised at how much she was ready to move forward. "I think you and Tommy would be about the same size and build. Those togs are totalled, my friend. I will find you something cute to wear."

"I don't want to look cute," he said. "I prefer to remain manly."

"You are mine," she said, "all mine." She rubbed her hands together fiendishly and said in a fake deep voice: "Boo-hwah-hah-hah!"

"It's Hallow E'en, I take it."

"Take your shower, sweetie. Time's a-wasting." She pushed him gently.

She let herself out and pulled the door shut to give him privacy. She was absolutely in no rush about anything. The time would come soon enough when she'd take him to bed and make hot, passionate love all night, every night, and a few mornings and afternoons to boot. For the moment, this was just right. She headed to the kitchen to prepare a tray of goodies. It was just right, like with the Three Bears. Mama Bear was going to snuggle with Papa Bear and make lip music until the little bears fell asleep—which would not be long, she was sure. And there was always tomorrow; and tomorrow; and lots of wonderful days after that. As she wearily and achingly puttered around in the kitchen, she thought: she was not going to rush anything. She was going to let him do his manly thing and come after her. She would let him court her, every delicious little step of the way. He would take her out, he would take her to the movies, she would make him lots of little dinners and desserts, they would walk by the lake. She was curious what kind of town home a millionaire lived in. She knew he had a swimming pool, unlike her little hovel down here in the valley.

He came out, wearing a nice pair of Tommy's jeans and a gray muscle shirt with maroon trim. He was a shade slimmer than Tommy had been, and maybe a little wirier. She would not make comparisons and contrasts, she promised herself as she served him tea and scones with butter and strawberry rhubarb jam in the living room. She turned the lights low and put a little silly TV on for him. While he ate, she excused herself to take her own shower and change. The hot water and her fragrant soaps felt great, but she wasted no time dressing in her nightgown and heavy merlot terry robe to get back to him. She wore and white towel for a turban to dry her hair. Before joining him, she looked at herself in the mirror. She was still young enough that it would not shock him too much to see her without makeup.

Besides, it was dim enough in the living room that he did not seem to notice that maybe she looked a bit plainer and more natural.

"You do look like a Cleopatra," he said as she sat down beside him.

"Oh please. Are you going to step on my neck now?"

"No, I want to make Caesar salad with you."

"I'll be your cucumber any time."

"You can be my hot tomato."

"Anything you wish."

"We are so lucky this has come to a happy ending."

"Tell me about it. You were nearly killed in a car crash. We were nearly annihilated by a drug crazed nut. What next?"

"Good things for a change."

"Let's hope so. I am so ready."

"Me too."

And the way it worked out, that evening, was that the two of them fell asleep on the rug, under a quilt, in each other's arms, fully dressed and happy as a pair of puppies in a litter. They had all the time in the world for love, without any limitation, and they knew it. Strangely, they each knew that this was the prelude to marriage and a happy life together. There was simply no rush about anything.

When dawn's gray light streaked in through the blinds, she rose and padded about. She peeled off her turban and dreaded looking into a mirror to see what had become of her hair. Richard lay on the rug, fast asleep with a sweet little smile on his face. She hoped he was as happy with her as she was with him. She padded into bathroom, stood on the balls of her feet, and brushed her teeth. Feeling minty, she grabbed her hair brush and wandered into the kitchen to start thinking about how many eggs a man like this might eat. Would he like them scrambled, sunnyside up, or poached? She remembered last night's battle in the parking lot with disbelief, but her aches affirmed that it had really happened. She had merely planned to have him take her to Papa's for a little pasta. It had worked out so much better. On the pragmatic side, as things got serious, would she move in with him in his Hartford house, or would he wander on down to spend more time with her in the house? She had a feeling that he had fallen in love with Emery. She could show him later today where the lawnmower was. Hearing him stirring in the living room, she poked her head in: "Sweetie, I am making us some eggs and pancakes. You can borrow my toothbrush so that you do not have severe parking lot mouth, okay, honey?"

"Mmphf," he said, stretching. He regarded her through slanty eyes like a slyly grinning cat, under mussy brown hair that she longed to comb—after brushing hers out for a good long while. She said: "Then maybe we can take a little walk down by the lake. Would you like that?" She opened and closed cabinet doors in the kitchen. Amazing how filled with happiness and sunshine the little house was, and its kitchen. "Can we walk by the lake? And will you put your arm around me?"

She turned, and saw the happiest man on earth leaning in the doorway, smiling, with eyes only for her. Looking handsome in his jeans, shirt, and barefoot, he nodded with manly authority and resourcefulness. She laughed. He could not keep his hands off her. They slow-danced to a little soft radio music while the kitchen began to smell of pancakes and coffee. Taking it slow, she thought. Slow boat. Slow goat. Slow dance.

"Can I hold you?" he asked.

"Please." She opened her arms to him.

He embraced her tenderly, tightly, and she surrendered to his strength and love.

"I don't ever want to let you go," he said.

She kissed his neck and nuzzled her cheek on his shoulder. Her fingers kneaded the strong, steady muscles there, and she closed her eyes to enjoy his rock-hard strength and firmness. "Please don't ever let me go."

He put his hand flat on her back and rubbed gently but firmly. "We could make big plans together, you and I."

"Really?" she bounced back, still in the secure ring of his arms. She pretended to be surprised, when her whole heart was fluttering toward him like a young, eager dove. "I might hold you to that, stranger."

He pressed a very self-assured, grinning smooch on her lips. "I'm no stranger to you, lady. I feel like we have known each other for a long time."

She laid her cheek back on his shoulder, feeling happier than she'd been in years. It was a fresh new happy, not a replay. It was her new life, finally, and here he was in her arms. "Yes. Last time I checked with my heart, you were holding it in your hands. I love you so."

He whispered in her ear, so she could feel the puffs of wind from his voice: "I love you forever, Marian the Librarian. You are mine, and I am yours. It's so simple and so wonderful, isn't it? Nothing complicated, unlike all the rest of life."

She nodded, too overcome to speak, but held him as tightly as she could. The best thing in life was as simple and enduring as it was powerful. This man was her life, her destiny, her joy. She would never let him go. She would make him a good wife, and he would be a good husband for her. Her heart told her so, and her heart was always truthful—true blue, all the way, always—two souls forever as one.